THE
FATHER OF
LIGHTS
Book II

CORINA ZURCHER

Nevermore Publications, LLC ®

www.nevermorepublications.com

Library of Congress Cataloging-in-Publication Data Available

Library of Congress Control Number: 2016946841

ISBN: 099117240X

ISBN-13: 978-0-9911724-0-5

Printed in the U.S.A.
Second American edition, July 2016

DEDICATION

To my champions, my beloved friends who have continued to encourage me and inspire me: Archana Patel, Erica Sims, Bethany Girolami and Maryann Beckman. Thank you for being so generous with your time and for adding your thoughts and suggestions — even the little ones — to help fine-tune this story. You are all angels! (No pun intended.)

And to my Maker, for setting my soul on fire over your love. May this story and all stories henceforth reach those whom you will, touch those whose hearts you desire, and do justice to your love and grace that you reap constantly over the world — as you do in mine.

NOTE TO THE READER:

Throughout this story, we will be jumping back and forth through time as this tale unravels. The following are references to the three periods we will be travelling through — along with their definitions:

THEN = Before the Fall from Heaven

NOT SO LONG AGO = After the Fall from Heaven leading up to present day

NOW = Present Day

"Every good gift and every perfect gift is from heaven and comes down from the Father of the heavenly lights, who does not change like the shifting of shadows. He chose to give us birth through the word of truth, that we might be a kind of first fruits of all He created."

- James 1: 17-18

INFERNO

Now...

"*F*ather...*why have you forsaken me?*"

Ash gently fell from the gray, smoke-filled sky. The colorless flakes swirled and danced all throughout the ebony domain, landing softly and gently on his scale-ridden face. He didn't even notice the brimstone powder as it collected on his deformed, reptilian visage. Like a magnet, his one reptilian eye and one cerulean eye were locked onto the malevolent waves of the Lake of Fire before him, watching as they rose and fell.

Up and down...up and down...

And with each roll of magma, he could hear the whispers of his fallen brothers summoning him; brothers whose existence ended the moment the lake opened its mouth to receive them in, swallowing them whole as they were hurled down from heaven by God's mighty hand.

He heard their last words, words spoken in a patterned framework like that of iambic pentameter — rhythmically, knowingly — they uttered a single name. And the closer he listened, the more he understood the tone as the name was spoken. It was a name that was once heralded across the

1

seven realms of heaven with the undertone of power and conviction. A name that no longer held the same meaning when it was sounded in the light. And as the whispers rose and fell, they continued their loathsome moaning as they spoke, "*Lucifer...Lucifer...*"

He winced slightly as if the sound of his own angelic name wounded him with every consonant, every vowel, as the beat of its echo thumped across his memory, pounding against his blackened heart. And even in the thrumming of his mind, he heard her voice, clear, strong and utterly right in all its utterance thundering over the beat, *"You should have listened to me. If you had, you would have never come to this place..."*

This place.

The prince of hell stared at the malevolent waves, unable to tear his eyes away from the rolling lava that poured forth the memories of yesterday, a millennia ago, and the moment just past. He played them over and over in his mind.

"You miss Him, don't you? You miss heaven, God, the light."

He tried to shut his eyes, but wide they remained as he swayed with the rhythm of the waves as his tail slithered within its coil. *The rhythm. The beat.* He felt the angst and the yearning rising; rising like the smallest of seeds that fought to emerge from beneath the hardened soil, grasping for the sunlight. A seed amongst the thorns.

"I sometimes miss...the light. But what I miss most...is the music, the music, the music...you know I do."

The melody. The song. The voice of his true heart.

"Lucifer...Lucifer..."

Hearing their mournful chant of stricken grief, he was locked in a place in time where the shout of his name once brought him joy, for the sound of it thundered throughout the heavens — a cacophony of echoes rumbling across the realms of the seven skies. The whispered melody brought forth the memories of the past, and he remembered it; standing on the throne in the kingdom of heaven, the entire Angelic Host calling his name over and over again.

Moving to the melody of whispered tongues, speaking the old language with voices he had long forgotten, he remembered how his name once sounded — triumphant, supreme — the chant of a victor. But the whispers he heard now all throughout perdition were the cries of a victim, invoking vengeance, justice, and wrath upon the one whose name they spoke, *"Lucifer...Lucifer..."*

He could not tear his eyes away from the phantoms in the waves, for the desire of his fallen brothers was strong. *"Destroy. Pay. Amend. Avenge...me."*

No matter how long he stared at the rolling magma, he could not will himself to turn away from their curses — especially after what the witch had told him.

These waves. This place. This lake. My destiny.

"Lucifer...Lucifer..."

Satan lifted his horned head to the ashen sky of the inferno, but instead of darkness, he saw the light. *Heaven.* A small sigh escaped his blackened mouth as he thought about his long forgotten home. He could see its incomparable beauty across all space and time — its own quantum dimension; the ever-changing sky of his home as the color of its canvas dissolved from blue to violet to green as the heavens moved across and within each other, rolling over one another like the waves before him now.

"Lucifer...Lucifer..."

Gone were the blackened mountains in Hell replaced by the ivory cliffs of the second realm of Heaven. Gone were the cries of human souls wailing throughout his brimstone kingdom. And as he longingly searched for the memory of his paradise lost, he heard it, the softest of sounds. His breath caught as he clung to the faint echo of melody. He clutched the memory, grasping for it, focusing all his will onto it so that it could not escape him like all the times before. *The rhythm. The beat.* Satan's horns bent to the sound of fire, frantically listening for the harmony that plucked at his heart — and then it was there. First softly, then gradually the pulse of its sound rose up. *Like the dawn. Like that of the Morning Star...*

The drumbeat. The rhythm.

A cold wind suddenly swirled all around him, viciously swiping at him, and cutting off his thought. It lashed out at him, whipping the words down upon him, *"Not worthy anymore..."*

He lost it, the melody; it was fading, fading, fading away.

Satan grasped hold of the pentagram in the middle of his chest, its once sharp design now eroded over time; he winced in pain at the wind's spiteful telling, and yet he refused to let it go. He grasped onto the sound with the full force of his will — until he heard it again. *The beat.* He grabbed hold of it in his mind, and the sound continued to rise, summoning the identity of one lost in the black hole of pain and rage and nothingness. *Rising and rising...*

The pain continued to move throughout his reptilian form, moving up through his veins, pulsing through his legs and stomach, up through his chest — *rising and rising again.* And as the wind whipped all around him, the beat took aim and hit its mark, stabbing the prince of hell directly in the center of his shrunken heart. But instead of recoiling to bend over in pain, Satan's massive chest extended, expanding as he lifted it to the midnight sky — the angst and yearning in his heart exploded and out poured *the music...the music...the music.* A symphony of a long forgotten dream filled his mind and echoed in his ears. *Strings. Winds. Brass. Percussion. Song.* Satan lifted his clawed hand, closed his eyes, and moved his hand over the waves as he conducted nothing and no one. The master musician from within conducted only a memory from his own mind from a time long forgotten.

And no matter how hard he tried to focus on the notes, he lost the vision of his dream with each stroke of his hand. Satan frantically attempted to resurrect the song, but it continued to fade, like all illusions — until it was no more. Only the sound of human cries answered the movement of his clawed hand, until the song softened into silence. Unwilling to open his eyes, his face contorted in agitation like a babe yearning for its milk. His eyes clenched in distorted fury; his scaled hands curled into massive fists; his rattle-snake tail slithered and writhed like the funnel of a tornado as it was about to strike down, for he had lost it — *the music...the music...the music...his song.*

It was gone — back into its black hole of nothingness. And in that moment, the Lord of Hell saw directly into his own heart, and all he could see was the rage. He looked down at his massive scale-ridden hands with his onyx-colored claws and shuddered at his own deformity. *The Father...He has done this to me!*

It was in the Garden of Eden when his body began to transform into the hideous beast he had now become. Thinking on that moment, he cringed in fury. It was the last time God had spoken to him, and it was a curse. A curse that left him crawling on his belly. He was vile. Loathsome. Not even the fallen angels desired to remain in his presence longer than they needed to. It was difficult for them to look upon him in this serpent-like form. And with that thought, the sharp pain pierced his heart once again. And it was then that the rage continued to rise until he could stand it no longer.

Gone! Gone! Gone!

Satan erupted like a dormant volcano. His eyes burst open as he roared to the brimstone clouds, his massive chest expanding as he breathed forth fire and smoke. He craned his enormous head in all directions of hell's grounds, expunging his rage across the cage he called Kingdom. The Black Mountains vibrated against his torment; the human cries ceased as he raged;

all went silent in the realm of perdition. All except the phantoms in the waves.

"Lucifer…Lucifer…"

Satan slowly turned his head back to the Lake of Fire. His face was marked with dread, the witch's words clearly written in the molten lava before him. As if on cue, he heard her cackle sounding from the Valley of Darkness. His jaw clenched at the sound of her laughter.

Satan's black, webbed wings expanded, his tail rattled viciously as he rose from hell's grounds. He soared across the inferno, past the Onyx Mountains, across the Circle of Judas, over the River of Acheron, beyond the Woods of the Suicides until landing at the river that divided the boundary between Heaven and Hell.

He breathed in long and deep. He took in the jagged rock before him until his eyes fell upon a set of footprints a few feet away. His breath stilled at their imprint. *Still here.* No matter how many times he tried to wipe them away, they remained; a reminder to him and all the rebel angels in hell, that God was still in control, and not even this house of pain was truly theirs to rule. The footprints were proof, for the markings etched in the sand were from *the Son…the Son…the Son of God…*

He remembered when the Son was crucified. He thought it was his greatest moment of triumph: showing God that the world he created, the mankind he loved, destroyed his son, and in so doing were saying to God, *"We don't want you here."* He was so certain that God would end the world at that moment, for it was the first time he ever heard the Father weep. The roar of agony swept through the grounds in Jerusalem as the temple was torn in two. He thought the rumble would roll across the earth, ripping and shifting its plates to split the world apart, but the rumble never came. And so Lucifer continued to wait.

It wasn't until he saw the Son of God walk through Hell's Gate that he knew there would be no more rumbling and that the world would not end. For *the Son...the Son...the Son of God* had done something unthinkable, unbelievable...he asked the Father to forgive the world, to forgive these...*kind of men.* And the Father did.

It was on the second day that he passed through the gate and entered hell's grounds. The Son walked through the City of Judas, past the Tower of Lucifer, through the Valley of Darkness, the swamps and the Woods of the Suicides, taking souls with him as he gathered them like sheep. *The Great Shepherd...* Not a single fallen angel dared move the entire time he was there. Even now, the sound of the Son's name struck fear in their hearts, for there was power in the name — conviction. Any time a mortal spoke the name when a fallen one was near, that angel was hurled into another dimension, across all time and space, and back into hell. And although the fallen ones were given seven years of time to do their most damage upon the mortal world with the help of the Lawless One, the antichrist, his footsteps...*they were still here...* which meant only one thing: *the prophecy was true.* And for Satan, there was only one way to change it. The witch had answered his question. He knew where to look for the key to his prison door.

Looking up at the flow of the River of Christ as it poured down from heaven and into his domain, the pathway was clear. There was only one thing left to do. He pondered the witch's words, *"Your ally of former days is the Keeper of the Key."*

"How do I get it?"

"Ask and you shall receive. Seek and you shall find. Knock and the door shall be open unto you."

His wings retracted as he slithered past the footprints. Grasping onto the sharpened rocks before him, the prince of hell began to climb. Using his massive tail as leverage, he vaulted from ledge to ledge moving up along the rocks like a spider. He stopped the moment he reached the portal. He slowly extended his clawed hand at the invisible boundary waiting to be struck down by the green lightning that sealed the two dimensions. But just as he was about to touch it, he changed his mind and removed his clawed hand, unwilling to put himself in harm's way. He looked up at the rising cliff, its opening leading up to the stairway to heaven. He stared at it — thinking. Closing his eyes, he took a deep breath, knowing there was only one way to do this; only one who would answer when he called. His face faded back into the angel he once was — that of the angel Lucifer. When his form was reverted, he opened his eyes and stared at the portal. It was then that he called…*her*…*name*…

THE DRAGON

Twenty-seven years ago...

"*Hic sunt dracones*....here be dragons."

Benjamin's large brown eyes grew even wider the moment his grandfather's deep baritone voice completed the translation. He was sucking on a straw, devouring his fruit punch while his grandfather uttered the words. All flavor from the fruity taste evaporated, and not even a loud gulp could distinguish the flood of emotions and fear that filled little Benjamin's mind. He was in the family library watching his grandfather as he bent over an old map translating its inscription through an even older magnifying glass, his weathered hand etched with the deep carved lines of age as it lay gently against the faded parchment.

Benjamin stared at the inked lettering, too young to understand Latin, yet old enough to understand that monsters existed. He had seen them quite often: in the shadows of his bedroom, hiding under his bed, crouched behind his closet doors — just waiting to get him. And he had not yet built up the courage to send the monsters away, for he knew he was outnumbered and had no means to fight. He was only six-years-old and the only shield he had been given was the blanket to cover his head to block out the view of the shadows and the dark every time he went to sleep.

"Did you know, my dear Benjamin, that there is but one dragon in the world?"

Benjamin shook his head, the rings of his dark curly hair swung back and forth like a bells on a bell tower. The look of wide-eyed innocence on his face gave a melody of utter sweetness to anyone who looked upon this beautiful boy.

Benjamin's grandfather sat back in his chair lowering the magnifying glass onto an ashen-colored desk. "El Draco…that's his name."

"Why is there only one, gwampa?"

"Because he's the worst of his kind; he destroyed all the others. He *wants* to be the only one. The most powerful, the most feared, the most adored. He exists without love, and without love, one cannot truly exist as one was meant to; one cannot be free, for there is no peace without love. Love is a power of its own kind, and El Draco chose to scorn its kind. Here, come sit and I'll show you some more."

Benjamin climbed on top of his favorite seat in the entire world: his grandfather's lap. His grandfather opened an old, red, leather-bound book with gold-trimmed pages and illustrations that looked like the stained glass windows he saw in the church his grandmother took him to on Sundays. He had always liked going to the church, for the pictures in the colored windows were like the pictures in his books telling a story without any words.

His grandfather opened the book to a page where a large man with golden-brown hair and amber-colored eyes stood over a large, ferocious dragon. The man's foot was embedded in the monster's back, pinning him to the ground. The man had wings like an eagle, and they were colored an emerald green. He held a sword covered in blue light in his right hand and a shield in his left. His sword was aimed right over the dragon's head as the reptilian beast hissed at him in fury, waiting for the impact of the deadly blow the large man was about to strike down upon him. Benjamin clearly noticed that the man had a shield stronger than a blanket.

Benjamin pointed to an inscription on the man's shield and asked, "What does that say?"

"Quis ut Deus, which means 'Who is like God'."

Benjamin looked at the man in the picture. He had come to learn to pay attention to the small things, the details, even with his small mind. His grandfather always made a point of showing him things he would have missed had he had no better teacher. He absorbed all these lessons like a sponge, for in every detail there was meaning, a story left unsaid. And there was no better storyteller than his grandfather.

"Now, I don't mean to scare you, but it is a piece of truth I want you to know. It's really quite important." He pointed to the dragon pinned under the large man's foot. "You see, Benjamin, this particular dragon used to live near ivory mountains where he had a cave filled with gold. The walls of rock inside his domain were adorned with rubies and diamonds and emeralds and sapphires. And dragons, you know, love their gold. They love their jewels."

"Where did the gold and jewels come from, gwampa?"

"Excellent question. They came from the Master of the Mountain. And just like there is only one dragon, there is only one master. And the Master loved his dragon. He loved giving him gifts of gold and jewels. He planted them in the rock until they were ready to be given to the dragon, for you see, there are some things that take time in order to grow. It's like a small seed that is planted in the ground. And over time, with the right amount of sun, and the right amount of water, in the right piece of soil, that seed will grow to rise up from the ground and live. Gold and diamonds and rubies need to do the same thing. They need time to grow deep inside the mountain and underneath the rock. And when they are ready to rise up and live, the Master would give them to the dragon as gifts for no other reason than the Master knew that the dragon loved them.

"One day, the dragon saw the Master giving gifts to other creatures on the other side of his domain. Creatures he had never seen before. And the dragon became enraged. He flew to the Master and roared his argument all throughout the mountains: *Those gifts are mine! They were created for me!*' But the Master pointed out to the dragon that the gifts he gave the other creatures were not the same. They were not gold, but silver and copper and platinum. They were not diamonds and rubies and sapphires, but quartz and amber and jasper. Different gifts with a different purpose all given by the Master.

"But the dragon roared even louder. He thought that gifts given to the other creatures meant that the Master didn't love him anymore, or maybe just a little bit less. The dragon, never having seen silver or copper or amber before, didn't understand their difference to his gold and jewels. So he feared what he did not understand and believed that the creatures' gifts were better than the ones the Master had given to him. And the dragon was sad and angry about it, but he refused to listen in all his pain. The Master told the dragon, 'I love you just the same — no more, no less.'

"And these words tore the dragon's heart in two. 'I deserve to be loved the best! These creatures don't love you as *I* do!' he said. '*I* do everything you ask, but these creatures have done nothing, yet you give them gifts all the same.'

"So the dragon spread his wings and soared over the kingdom and breathed fire down upon all the other creatures outside his domain. He destroyed their homes, smashed their amber and quartz and jasper. He melted their metal with his fire so that they could no longer use their gifts from the Master anymore. The next day he vowed to return to their domain and destroy the creatures themselves."

"What did the Master do?"

"Well, the Master went to El Draco's lair and called him to come outside. 'I understand your pain,' he said. 'I know why you've destroyed all the other gifts for all the other creatures outside your domain. But you were wrong to destroy what was not yours to give. You were wrong to bring pain to others who have never hurt you. You were wrong to think that such an act would go unnoticed and unaccounted for, El Draco. But I know you have goodness in your heart. I know you will turn this wrong into a right. Come, let us walk together amongst the mountains and begin again.'

"But the dragon did not come."

"How come?"

"Pride, my dear Benjamin. Pride."

"Huh?"

"Well, let me see here. How to explain…It's when you know the truth of what is in front of you, when you see the answer, but you refuse to accept it because you feel people will think less of you; that they won't respect you because, somehow, you've given up something or are about to give up something that you never really had. Understand?"

The rings around Benjamin's head swung back and forth fervently.

"Aw, well, it's something better explained when one encounters it. Anyway, moments passed where the only sound was the wind blowing gently through the valley. But the Master waited. He had hoped that El Draco would change his mind. He knew that the dragon's pride had been hurt, thinking that he alone was deserving of the Master's love and attention. But the Master loved all the creatures in his domain, for the Master loved to love — especially those he called family. So the Master stood outside the dragon's cave for three days. And when the dragon did not emerge at the dawn of the last day, the Master turned away from the dragon with a heavy heart. He had so wanted El Draco to change his mind."

"What did the dragon do?"

"Well, as soon as the Master turned, a large blaze of fire burst forth from inside El Draco's cave."

Benjamin gasped.

"He breathed fire down upon the Master when he thought he wasn't looking, but the Master turned quickly and lifted his hands, wrenching forth from underneath the earth, a large stream that ran beneath him. Like a geyser, the water rose up and squelched the blaze of fire before it reached the Master's skin. When all that was left was steam and moisture hanging in the air, the Master eyed the darkened cave. But still, El Draco would not emerge. The Master had had enough of the dragon's antics, and knew that the dragon would not turn from his ways.

"So the Master lifted his hand and threw the top of the mountain up into the sky. He swiped his hand from left to right, removing each and every rock, layer by layer as he dismantled the mountain. And finally, when the dragon's head emerged, finding no rooftop to hide his angry head, he screeched loudly and furiously across the land. He rose up with his webbed wings and horned head and finally faced the Master. He breathed his fire down upon the Master's head, but the Master used the wind to blow the fire away from him so he would not be scathed by El Draco's breath. He threw the wind at the dragon, forcing him to come down from the sky, for the dragon's wings could not fight against the force of the strong wind. And when the dragon was finally brought down, he lay at the Master's feet too tired to rise up, although he tried. And when the Master looked into El Draco's heart, all he saw was the dragon's hatred and fury. And the Master's heart grew sad, for he had loved his dragon.

14

"Then the Master lifted his eyes to El Draco's cave and flattened it with one swipe of his mighty hand. The dragon roared as he watched his home be flattened with all his gold and jewels buried inside for all time. He shifted his eye to the Master, rage darkening his snake-like eye as he looked upon him. 'You are banished from the realm, El Draco. You are banished for all time.' The Master took his hand and pointed to the ground. In reply, the ground shook violently and split right underneath El Draco.

"The dragon fell into the pit beneath his clawed feet to live underground, in the dark amongst the shadows, trapped for all time. The rock was sealed once again and El Draco was never seen in the Master's domain ever again."

"Is El Draco still alive?"

His grandfather's gray eyes seemed to glow, "*Always.* You must beware of the dragon. He is beneath your feet even now, blowing fire and smoke to blot out the light in which you live. He waits for you to crack. He waits for the ground to move upon which you stand that makes you waver. For you see, he still hates all the creatures that live outside his domain. He blames them for his punishment, for had they never existed, he would still live beside the Master. Even now he smashes his head against the ground once in a while trying to make you fall to the ground where he can snatch you in the crack of the rock and pull you down to where he lives. And he will always try to make you fall, especially when you least expect it — when you are footsteps from where your treasure lies, he will try to take it from you. He will try to steal your joy and destroy all your gifts from the Master."

"Why?"

"Because he doesn't think you deserve them."

Benjamin looked back at the picture lying on the desk. "Who is the man with the gween wings, gwampa?"

"He is a guardian, a warrior for the Master. And his job is to protect all creatures who shout his name when the dragon is near."

Benjamin took in the sight of the guardian's large muscles. "Is he stronger than the dragon?"

"He is the strongest guardian in the entire universe. And his strength comes from the Master. Because of that, the dragon hates this guardian."

"Why?"

"Because he knows the Master is on his side, and with the Master on your side, no one can defeat you, Benjamin. *No one.*"

Benjamin's doe-shaped eyes took in the glowing blue sword in the man's hand. "What's his name, gwampa?"

"His name…is Michael."

HE WHO IS LIKE GOD

Now...

Michael's eyes were on fire, burning in flames the color of emeralds. He heard it. He *knew* he heard it. And he had not dared move, waiting to hear it again. The prince of angels remained on bended knee, having had his prayer interrupted by an alien sound while kneeling on the sapphire steps of the kingdom. Michael sifted through the sounds rumbling throughout the seven realms, listening ever so closely for the one he had thought he heard. It was so soft — like a drumbeat. But he knew the rhythm had a melody to it, for Michael's ears were highly attuned to all the sounds of heaven, completely aware of the ones that were not of the realm.

Thump-thump-thump...thump-thump-thump...thump-thump-thump...

Michael's six emerald-colored wings immediately jutted forth from his back upon hearing the sound; he rocketed into the sky. He soared fast and furious through the third and fourth realms of heaven, listening for the source of the beat.

"Michael! What are you praying so hard about! You've been there for days..."

Michael faltered in the sky, taken off guard as the sound of Lucifer's voice burst forth from his mind.

"Leave him alone, Lucifer. Always so nosy. Why this? Why that?" And Gabriel — always at his side.

Like a tidal wave, more memories barreled forth, hammering down upon him. Michael tried to shut them out so he could focus on the thumping sound, but instead his mind was seized with the flashing memories of Beelzebub, Gokor, Nero, and Vitor. Memories of his brothers, his friends, as they once existed side by side in heaven. Like waves, the memories kept rolling forward as he flew through the fifth and sixth realms. And, for Michael, this was no ordinary circumstance. He flew faster.

The Wind of the Holy Spirit blew all around his shoulder-length hair, breathing forth more moments of the past, and all Michael could do was bend to the will of the Spirit and let them come. *What is it I'm supposed to remember? What is it I need to know?* With each domain he crossed, he kept listening, still listening...

He saw the Tree of Knowledge of Good and Evil rising up in the distance. He swooped toward the large tree, slamming onto the ground in front of it. Grabbing hold of its trunk, he placed his ear to its bark, listening...still listening. *Not here.*

Thump-thump-thump...thump-thump-thump...thump-thump-thump...

He lifted his head toward a location far off in the distance. A flash of lightning struck behind his amber eyes as he raced forth across the third realm of heaven. His emerald-colored wings expanded once again as the prince of angels rocketed into the sky.

"Michael, join me..."

His eyes narrowed as he attempted to block out Lucifer's voice from the past, focusing all his energy on the sound of the present.

"Where are your friends, Michael?"

Thump-thump-thump...thump-thump-thump...thump-thump-thump...

"You who were never worthy of the crown!"

Michael landed hard on his feet just outside the cave where the River of Christ flowed down from the Great Waterfall. He jumped onto the rock and pressed his ear to the mountain.

Here.

He did not dare breathe as he continued to make out the sound. The moment he deciphered its meaning, his jaw clenched into severe lines as the muscles along his jawbone tightened all along his face.

No, not a drumbeat — a voice.

It was the rhythm of syllables calling forth a name. And the source of the sound was the voice that carried a deep melody, a melody Michael was not used to hearing in heaven anymore. Every feather on Michael's wings stood on end as the melodious sound continued to call as Lucifer shouted from hell, *"Gabriel....Gabriel...Gabriel..."*

*   *   *

Gabriel's eyes snapped open. Lying in a field of grass in the second realm of heaven, surrounded by flowers and colors of imaginary illusions to those who dreamed them upon the earth, Gabriel did not move. She waited. The light of the Father shone down upon her, warming her as the Wind blew gently by. She shifted her ebony eyes to the Father's light and drank in every breath with a long inhale. Gabriel sighed deeply, more than willing to believe the voice she heard was either a memory or a forgotten dream.

Softly, the sound of the Angelic Host singing hymns from the throne filled the grounds of the kingdom, rising up and down with each note and melody like waves of a rolling ocean barely reaching shore. Beams of glittering stars softly fell all around her. The rays of light lessened as the sky shifted from apricot to gold. The light and the Wind moved on.

"GABRIEL!!!"

Gabriel quickly sat up. Raphael slammed down onto the field behind her and moved swiftly toward her; his sapphire-colored wings retracted into his body upon his approach. Gabriel immediately stood, seeing the serious look behind his glowing silver eyes.

"I've been calling you for ages!"

"Well, you didn't look very hard. Everyone knows I come here when I want to be alone. I'm surprised this wasn't the first place you looked."

"I did come here! It was the first place I flew over, but you were not by the waterfall where you usually are."

"I was dreaming in the field."

"*Dreaming?* Of what? I didn't even know you slept."

"I don't, but I still dream. And remember..."

Raphael looked at the large ivory tree several yards behind Gabriel. Even with its enormous size and ever-reaching branches, it emitted no shade, for heaven knows no shadow. He could see the faint remnants of flint marks in the center of the tree. His gray eyes locked onto its trunk.

"Raphael?"

Even though he heard her speaking, he could not tear his gaze away from the tree. He started walking toward it as if a tractor beam were pulling him in.

"What is it you said you wanted?"

He continued to move toward the tree, staring at it as if in a daze. "I didn't. Michael sent me to find you." Raphael finally blinked; he turned to face her. "He sounded the horn."

The horn. Gabriel was alarmed, for the only time Michael vowed to ever sound the horn again was if there was an enemy in heaven, or if it was time to descend to the earth for the Final Battle. "What! But I didn't even hear it!"

"Like you said — you were dreaming." He turned back toward the tree, staring at it once more, hypnotized by it.

"Raphael! Why did Michael sound it?"

Raphael did not hear her; he continued staring at the trunk and began to sway before the tree — *back and forth* — to a rhythm, a beat. "Not sure…"

The trunk made an odd sound, as if it were breaking apart somewhere inside its base. She watched as the branches dipped low and lifted up as the they gained moment. With each dip and lift, Raphael swayed with the branches — back and forth.

Gabriel's eyes locked onto the tree. Looking up at its branches, they suddenly looked skeletal to her, like the long fingers of the Ferry Man collecting his toll at the River Styx. Watching them dip and lift, she was suddenly seized with a feeling of dread. *There is no portal here.*

Raphael continued to stand right in front of it, swaying back and forth with the rhythm of the branches. She ripped her sword from her sheath. "Raphael…get away from that tree."

He did not hear her as he continued to sway to the rhythm and the beat. The branches dipped low and stopped mere inches above the ground. It was then that she saw it: *shadow.*

Gabriel's eyes grew wide. *"RAPHAEL!!! GET AWAY FROM THE TREE!!!"* She raced toward him.

Raphael turned his head to look back at her when the branches suddenly lifted back up. The trunk twisted open, and two black horns emerged from the archway plunging straight through Raphael's chest. Gabriel roared as Satan emerged from the portal.

Raphael screamed in agony as Satan lifted his body off the ground and hurled it violently across the field. Raphael slammed into another tree. Gabriel could hear the cracking of bones as he smashed into it before collapsing to the ground. A dark liquid spouted forth from Raphael's wounds. He choked on the liquid, looking helplessly at Gabriel. *"Gabriel…"*

The moment Satan saw Gabriel racing toward him with sword in hand, a cruel smile formed on the corner of his blackened mouth. *"Beloved. I have come for it. I know it's here."*

He dipped his head like a bull and charged straight for her. Gabriel aimed the tip of her sword at Satan's heart. They raced toward one another and were about to collide...

"GABRIEL!!!"

Gabriel's eyes snapped open. She was lying in the field. She immediately started swinging, throwing her fists viciously at the being kneeling over her; it was Raphael. He grabbed her by the wrists and wrestled her down, pinning her hands to the ground. "Peace, Gabriel. You were dreaming."

Gabriel's heart was hammering inside her chest; she was breathing rapidly as if she had just finished running the fastest race of her life.

"Breathe, Gabriel."

She breathed in deeply, attempting to collect herself, gathering her wits about her as she took in her surroundings. She was completely drenched in sweat.

Raphael released her, moving a strand of hair from her eyes. "You had a vision."

She sat up and grabbed hold of him, checking his body for wounds. He grabbed her wrists and held them tight. "Stop. *Stop!*"

Gabriel locked eyes with him. "You're all right." A deep breath escaped her before she lifted her arms and wrapped them around Raphael, burying her head in his chest as she held him tight. "You're all right."

Raphael kissed the top of her head and held her close. "I'm all right, Gabriel. I promise. What is it that you saw?"

Gabriel slowly lifted her head and looked at the ivory tree. "I saw him...I saw him, Raphael..."

Raphael looked at the tree. "Who?"

"Satan. He was coming through a portal."

Raphael's brow furrowed at her words. "Peace, Gabriel. It was only a dream. Satan can never step foot inside the kingdom again."

She closed her eyes. "Ah, my friend…" Her head collapsed against Raphael's lean, muscular chest.

"You make it sound as if your dream revealed the death of me."

The moment he said these words, Gabriel's body tensed and her eyes snapped open. She immediately stood and moved toward the tree. Her ebony eyes scanned every root and every leaf, examining the trunk for any sign of movement — twisting or otherwise. All was still.

"What did you see?" Raphael was right behind her.

Gabriel extended her hand and touched the bark. "An impossibility, and yet…it was so real. Tell me I'm not mad for envisioning the devil making his way back into heaven." She stepped back from the trunk and walked all around it, looking it up and down.

"You're not mad, Gabriel. But…"

"What?"

"Michael sent me to find you."

"What for?"

Raphael hesitated.

"What for, Raphael?"

"He's been calling your name."

Gabriel shook her head in disagreement. There was never a time when she did not hear Michael's call — not ever. "I didn't hear him."

"No one heard him — no one except Michael."

Her eyes narrowed in confusion. Gabriel dropped her hand and looked into his silver eyes. "What do you mean? I thought you said Michael was calling for me."

Raphael stood there, staring at her in her forlorn state. He hated being the bearer of bad news. "Ah beloved, not Michael. *Lucifer.*"

Gabriel did not utter a single word. She continued to stare at Raphael for what seemed like an eternity. She thought back on her dream and the vision it revealed, attempting to recollect anything of importance. "How?"

"He's been shouting it across the portals."

She almost cringed the moment he said it. *A portal.* Remembering the final words Satan spoke as he came through the portal in her dream, she shook her head. "That's not all of it. What more have you not said?"

Raphael's jaw clenched. He swallowed hard before speaking the next few words, "He has conjured the witch."

Not a flicker of emotion touched Gabriel's face. Raphael watched her reaction, but Gabriel's face was one of a stone. Over the billions of years that he had known her, Raphael had learned one thing about Gabriel that he never dared share with anyone else: that the more emotional she was about something, the less emotion she revealed.

Several moments passed before she spoke. "The Witch of Endor."

Raphael nodded. Gabriel was not one to share her thoughts, but her silence spoke volumes nonetheless. He knew she was thinking rapidly about what this could possibly mean. She suddenly looked back at the tree and did not speak another word.

"You were the only one he ever confided in, Gabriel. After all this time, it seems he still thinks that you are his friend."

She looked up at the ever-changing sky of heaven. "No, not his friend, Raphael. Not his friend. I am God's messenger. Lucifer only calls my name when he wishes to tell me something or ask me something about what the future holds. Even when I was in the inferno with him last, he only desired to know one thing: God's final command. Lucifer must be anxious to know when it will be given now that seven years have passed. There's something he has to say, and more importantly, wants me to deliver."

"Gabriel, what else did you see in your dream? You should go to Jeremiel. He will know how to interpret it for you."

Gabriel did not turn. He slowly approached her. "Gabriel…"

He moved in front of her, but she vainly attempted to avoid his eyes.

"Gabriel…look at me."

She covered her eyes with her forearm like a little child and tried to move away from him. He continued to follow her when he suddenly stopped dead in his tracks. "Wait. You didn't refute my last comment about your vision and seeing my death. Tell me.'"

She dropped her arm and looked at him. The look on her face was so filled with sadness that Raphael was suddenly filled with grief for no other reason than seeing her own. His silver eyes bored into hers. *"Tell me."*

"He almost killed you. For a moment, I thought he had."

Raphael smiled faintly. "I'm an immortal, remember? I cannot die."

"But you can feel pain. And I don't ever want to see you in that kind of pain, Raphael. Not ever."

Raphael grabbed her hand and held it tight, "Evil never stops, does it, Gabriel?"

She smiled faintly and shook her head.

"What was it like?"

"What?"

"Hell."

The smile faded from her lips; her face paled until her skin was the color of ash. Her voice was barely a whisper, *"Raphael…don't."*

"You've never spoken of it. Neither you nor Michael. I've always wanted to know — not because I'm curious about dark things, but because I want to know what I'm up against if I'm ever tempted to walk in the shadow — by force or command. And now that you've had a dream of my demise, I'd like you to share it with me."

Gabriel touched his strong face. "I pray that you will never see such a place as the inferno. One such as you must always be kept from so grim and ugly a dimension. I never want to see that light that burns behind your eyes grow dim. They cannot be like mine."

There was always an intrigue when it came to evil things — an attraction to the dark. And Raphael pondered that notion often as to why that was — even for him. He had been thinking on it more than usual since having learned about the witch. Knowing that Armageddon would soon be coming, he had been thinking of hell and facing his fallen brethren. No other angels besides Gabriel and Michael had ever been to the inferno. And the closer it came to the Darkest Night on the Earth, the more he wanted to know what Hell was really like.

"Please."

Images of the Cold Ones filled her mind. The stench of the marsh consumed her senses as she wiped the tears away, leaving her face unreadable. "Listen to me, and listen very closely. Hell is an unimaginable place of pain and horror — a never-ending nightmare of woe." Images of intertwining bodies of Hell's Gate flooded her thoughts. "To be the target of the devil's wrath...you must never be touched by it, my friend. Not ever." The mortal bodies rooted to ground in the Woods of the Suicides, continually bleeding as their fingers reach up to the onyx-colored sky pour across her memory.

"Satan...he..."

She remembered the moment Satan impaled his horns into her back; her body tensed at the thought. "He ripped me to shreds, Raphael, while I heard the cries of men and women all around me." She heard his laughter as he slithered toward her. "Hell's Bells sounded in triumph every second a mortal was carried through the gate. Fire is its only light — and it burns brightly amongst the blackened sky." She could see Felix cascading down the mountain and into the Lake of Fire. "You can barely breathe, let alone see. I could not bear it if…"

She looked down, trying to collect herself, but the tears continued to stream down her face. Raphael was stunned, never having witnessed such sorrow in Gabriel before.

"Gabriel, don't cry. Please don't cry."

She wiped the tears from her cheeks. "We can't always have perfect moments and perfect days, can we, my friend?" Gabriel looked into Raphael's silver eyes; he had not blinked once the entire time she had spoken. "Sometimes we're dragged into the horrors of other people's choices, a piece in a plan of someone else's sin-laden design — and it was my day to be dragged; it was my moment to shift the design — even if it meant I'd never make it home. I only made it through because I was reminded of the Son. I was reminded of his journey into darkness and that he rose into the light. It gave me strength, even amongst my fear."

Though I walk through the valley of the shadow of death…

Gabriel remembered the moment when she crawled to the rock, quivering in pain before crying out to God to help her in her greatest time of need. "I cannot stand the inferno. Only the Son ever conquered it, Raphael. As only He could. And only He knows how. The rest of us are not so lucky. When it comes to us, hell takes it much more personal."

Raphael took in Gabriel's words. And for some reason, although he could hear her loud and clear, his mind refused to truly listen. Almost as if there was a fog on his brain that was bouncing her words all throughout his mind, disallowing the idea that he should comprehend them and absorb them, anchoring them into his heart as a shield of knowledge to use. Then again, he thought, maybe he was just refusing to listen because he didn't truly believe that hell was so impossible a place to fear and loathe. For Gabriel and Michael had survived it. They were here and they were whole.

The fallen angels lived there. Couldn't he, another archangel, survive it too?

Gabriel saw the look on his face. "Raphael, think not on the dark and the pain, think on the light and zero in on it. There are too many shadows lately. It's so very easy to fall into them." She touched his face with her hand.

"Ah, Gabriel. Do not fear for me. You forget, there is the heart of a lion in this archangel's body."

She smiled faintly. "Who said I was afraid?"

He laid his giant hand over hers. "I can see it in your eyes."

The vision of Satan coming towards her flashed across her mind. His tail as it slithered within its coil, rattling as he made his way over to her as she crawled toward a rock to escape.

"You will never leave this place...your screams will bring me joy..."

"Gabriel."

Gabriel snapped out of her horror-filled memory. She looked up at him and saw the light dancing behind his silver eyes. "Joy be to thee always, my friend." He rested his forehead against hers. "I *am* sorry that I asked about the inferno if it has brought forth unbearable pain, but thank you for telling me anyway."

"You're not welcome."

Raphael smiled at her response, yet neither archangel moved from their pose. Michael landed a few feet away. Seeing them standing there, he was reminded of Gabriel and Lucifer from the days of old. And for a moment, Michael almost wished that such witnessed moments never ceased — even for him.

"When I give you a command of urgency, Raphael, I expect it to be *urgent.*" Michael moved toward them. Upon his approach, both Gabriel and Raphael stood at attention and pounded their fists into their chests.

"Michael. I, uh, found her." Raphael whispered to Gabriel. "I forgot to tell you, you were supposed to meet him at the cave."

"Some time ago."

"In his defense, Raphael did tell me about the witch."

"*And* Lucifer calling your name at the portal." Raphael nudged her ribs. "Don't forget that."

She locked eyes with Michael. "What do you need me to do?"

Michael could see the slightest shaking within Gabriel's body as she waited in anticipation for his answer. "Nothing."

Raphael did a double take. *"Huh?!?"*

Michael did not turn his head, but continued to look at Gabriel. "I just wanted you to know." He could see the slightest bit of relief behind Gabriel's eyes. He looked to Raphael, "We have been commanded to remain in heaven these seven years. There has been no other command to do otherwise. Not yet, anyway."

"Then why did you sound the horn?"

Michael looked back at Gabriel, his eyes narrowing. "I didn't."

Gabriel looked confused. Raphael leaned in and whispered, "That must have been in your dream."

Michael watched the exchange between Gabriel and Raphael. "You were dreaming? Then, you had a vision."

Gabriel still had a confused look on her face as she attempted to sort out her dream versus the reality she now faced. She offered Michael no other answer to his question. "So you *don't* want me to find out why Lucifer summoned the witch or why he is calling my name across the portal into heaven."

"No."

Raphael looked back and forth between Gabriel and Michael. "Well, *I* want to know."

Uriel suddenly slammed down onto the ground beside Michael. His orange fiery sword was ablaze; he pounded his chest upon seeing his commander. "The portals are secure."

"Good."

The moment Uriel looked toward Gabriel and Raphael, his violet-colored eyes noticed the ivory tree several yards away. The look on his face was severe. He shifted his eyes to Gabriel; a look passed between them as the slightest of tears filled Uriel's eyes upon seeing the faint marks etched in the wood of the tree. "Why are you here? You were not at the waterfall."

Raphael crossed his arms over his lean chest and nodded his head. "Ah-ha! See? I wasn't the only one who couldn't find you."

Gabriel did not answer. Instead she looked at Michael. "If you don't need me, there's something I need to do."

Michael nodded. "Go."

She nodded and pounded her fist into her chest. Her six phoenix-like wings jutted forth from her back. She rocketed into the sky. Michael watched her flight, while Uriel looked back at the tree. "She never comes here, Michael."

He continued watching her soar across the peach-colored sky. "None of us do." He lowered his eyes to the roots of the tree. He could still see the blood stains on the bark even though they were not there. It had been a long time since Gabriel had a dream. The fact she did not share it with him, gave him pause; knowing that she shared it with Raphael reminded him of what had changed between Gabriel and him the moment he followed her to this tree.

Thump-thump-thump…thump-thump-thump…thump-thump-thump…

"What is that?" Finally hearing it, Uriel and Raphael looked all around for the source of the sound — all except Michael. "Is that him?"

Michael nodded; he crossed his massive arms over his muscular chest.

Raphael moved toward the other archangels. "How long do you think

Lucifer will keep it up?"

"Until she comes."

Uriel looked at his commander. "I thought you were meeting Gabriel by the cave so you could send her across the portal into hell."

Raphael was taken off-guard at the news. "You were going to send her to hell?"

Michael continued to stare at the tree.

Thump-thump-thump…thump-thump-thump…thump-thump-thump…

"I was." He dropped his arms to his sides and looked at Uriel and Raphael. "I changed my mind. I have a feeling that Lucifer will find a way to tell Gabriel what he wants the moment she crosses any portal — no matter how long it takes before she does."

"*The portal*...Gabriel's dream was of a portal." Raphael thought for a moment. Michael noticed the deep furrow in the middle of his brow.

"What is it?"

"Lucifer won't have to tell her." Raphael ran his and Gabriel's conversation rapidly through his mind — her vision, what she said — *and what she didn't say*. He looked up meeting his commander's eyes. "I think she already knows."

* * *

Gabriel soared over an emerald forest and past turquoise lakes and streams, gliding over the White Mountains until the kingdom of heaven came into view. The sky of heaven continued to shift in color — from peach to violet to turquoise to green — as the archangel flew from realm to realm. As she approached the kingdom, she slowed her flight as throngs of angels hovered in the air and moved along the ground all around the kingdom.

The city was one massive square with twelve gates: three on the North, three on the South, three on the East and three on the West. The wall of the city had twelve foundations. The walls were made of jasper and decorated with every kind of precious stone known to man: sapphire, emerald, topaz and amethyst. Each of the twelve gates was made of pearl. As Gabriel approached the throne, seven lamp stands made of gold lit the road to the kingdom while tabernacles draped with curtains and veils made of purple linen flapped in the distance.

The streets to the kingdom were made of pure gold and weaved toward the sapphire blue steps that led directly to the throne of God. Before the throne was a sea of glass as clear as crystal. Thousands upon thousands of angels were gathered there, all in robes of white, belts of gold and wings of doves. Some spun and danced in the air; others swayed and sang with arms raised while standing on the ground below; some were prostrate, while others were on bended knee.

Gabriel slammed down onto the sapphire steps near the throne. She continued to move forward, never breaking stride as she beelined toward the left side of the steps where a massive instrument resided; it was a grand organ of monstrous size. The instrument itself was molded into the marble wall that rose up from the steps. The brass pipes reached up to the heavens; trumpets extended from each of its ends. Gabriel looked at the vacant seat of the organ's pedestal where Lucifer once sat. Her eyes zeroed in on the base of the organ's legs.

"Beloved. I have come for it. I know it's here."

A look of determination settled behind her ebony eyes. *"There is a prophecy of old and it will play through as it was mean to..."*

The Wind's gentle breeze blew through her raven hair. She closed her eyes to it, breathing in the essence of the Spirit. *He knows it's here, but he doesn't know where.*

Thump-thump-thump...thump-thump-thump...thump-thump-thump.

Gabriel opened her eyes the moment she heard the sound. Her eyes rested on the instrument before her, thinking on the days of old and long forgotten. Even now, she could hear Lucifer's magnificent voice as he sang to the Father — words of love and praise thundering amongst the music he composed for the orchestra of silver trumpets, violins and drums — while the voices of the angelic host accompanied each and every song as they sang the colossal hymns.

She stood there, paralyzed in the remembrance, hearing it, seeing it. The Wind funneled down over her, swirling around her as her thoughts drifted to the beginning.

Thump-thump-thump...thump-thump-thump...thump-thump-thump.

Gabriel could see him — the master musician — sitting there on his pedestal just beside the throne singing and playing, his face lit up, full of love for their Father, overcome with emotion and passion as he and the entire Host sang to their Maker. She could see the Father's light cascading down all around Lucifer — *like a lily in the field.* And it was in her memory that she heard it — the rhythm, the beat — until the past and the present merged as one.

ANTI-MYTH

Not so long ago...

"*A*ngels, *our Father has done the unthinkable. He has experimented with the great divide and made what was immortal — mortal...he has created a kind of man....it is to the players we go!*"

Like birds in V-formation the fallen angels soared higher and higher into hell's sky. They glided silently toward the portal from which they were cast and on towards Hell's Gate. They stopped, hovering in midair just before it, taking in its design. Lucifer's eyes scanned the gate, taking in the masterpiece of craftsmanship and sheer horror. It was a labyrinth of arms, hands and wings of fallen angels woven together to form its base. The gate itself continued to grow higher and higher as the bodies of fallen angels piled up one on top of the other. Seeing their brothers' faces gazing up at them in agony and woe, the rebel angels looked to their leader to see what they should do. Lucifer flew forward without uttering a single word; the others silently followed as they passed through the gate, barely glancing down or back at their former friends.

The moment they reached the other side, the gate closed. The angels whirled around at its sudden movement, ripping their swords from their sheaths as they scanned the grounds in search of the unseen force.

Nothing.

Beelzebub and Gokor looked at one another, their massive chests rising and falling rapidly as dread marked their faces, for they knew who it must have been.

Father.

Beelzebub shifted his burnt eyes to Lucifer. He watched as the chief seraph took in the ominous script carved on the gate's adamantine metal just under its base. Beelzebub's face paled the moment he saw the inscription. Lucifer read it silently; his face was set while Beelzebub read aloud, his voice was barely a whisper, *"Through me is the way into the doleful city, through me the way into eternal pain; through me the way among the lost. Justice moved my High Maker. Divine Power made one, Wisdom Supreme, and Primal Love. Leave all hope…ye that enter."*

A mighty Wind blew past Lucifer. He whirled around, gripping his sword tight, following the Wind's path as it blew toward the portal that led from Heaven's Gate and into Hell. The Wind swirled like a tornado, horizontal in length, lighting afire in green flame, sealing the portal to heaven.

Lucifer looked ahead and saw only darkness; he nodded to Nero. Nero's burnt wings extended; he rose up toward the doorway home. A large green flame ignited the moment Nero reached the portal. He screamed in pain as he was rocketed back down toward the ground.

Lucifer did not even blink as he continued to stare at the doorway to heaven. "So be it."

He turned toward the pathway to Earth. Lucifer commanded Azriel, "Go."

Azriel did not move. "I…"

Lucifer whirled around at him; his blue eyes were ablaze in fury. *"Go."*

Azriel nodded and slowly crept forth. He moved toward the shadows of the tunnel, readying himself for the green flame. He stepped slowly forward, inch-by-inch. He tensed, flinching in the expectation, but it never came. He continued on into the darkness.

Gokor stepped closer to Lucifer, "It is open. God is allowing us to pass through."

"That he is."

Azriel's voice shouted from the darkness, "I can't see how far it goes!"

Lucifer lowered his head like a bull, his eyes glowing in determination. "Brothers, *we fly.*"

He walked forward and extended his six seraphim wings as he vaulted into the sky.

The fallen angels followed Lucifer through the darkness. Blind on all sides, the flapping of their wings was the only sound that could be heard amongst the shadow land. They flew for what seemed like an eternity. And the longer they did, the faster they seemed to go — almost as if the black hole they were flying through was a force of its own, pulling them toward the other end by some unseen hook that had latched onto them. It was then that Lucifer saw it: a white light at the end of their blackened tunnel.

Gokor shouted, "I see it!"

The fallen angels flew faster toward a small marker of light they could see glowing faintly up ahead — a sight no bigger than the end of a pin. The tunnel in which they passed through was like a wormhole, an avenue to another dimension that bent time and space, linking the inferno to the world of man.

The light grew brighter the closer they got to the end of the portal that led to Earth. They flew straight through and found themselves inside a large cave. Lucifer landed first beside a small pool of water, followed by Beelzebub, Gokor, Nero, Asmodeus and Azriel. The sound of a small waterfall thundered in their ears. They took in the cavern of rock before them, examining every crack and crevice.

It was Azriel who spoke first, "Are you sure this is Earth? It looks just like one of the waterfalls in heaven, although the water remains one color."

He turned and found his fellow brothers staring down at the pool of water in utter silence. But instead of admiring the turquoise blue liquid, it was seeing their reflections laid bare that held their attention.

Asmodeus touched the burnt skin on his face, while Nero looked at his discolored flesh covered by the brimstone dust in hell. Beelzebub examined his eyes. Instead of the golden brown color they once held, they were a deep, dark red — dry and irritated from the heat of hell. Gokor looked at his profile, taking in his massive form and scarred body. He examined his battle wounds, seeing the large stump extending from his back that once held his two cherub wings. And Lucifer...the only image that anchored his stare to the water below was his faded pentagram; the brand that represented the name his father had given him — that of the Morning Star. Taking in their battle scars — both physical and mental — the angels were paralyzed — the perfect mirrors of their father's face no more.

Lucifer turned away from the angels and took in the sight of the cave with its intricate markings and slopes. His mind was on overdrive; thousands of thoughts flood his mind as he recognized the similarities to heaven all around the cave. He remembered his father's words and the excitement that filled his father's voice as he shared them with Lucifer, *"My Morning Star, I have created a place of paradise..."*

And there he was standing in a cave, bearing witness to mere words. Dueling emotions snapped at Lucifer from inside as he absorbed this new environment. On one hand, the desire to run through the cave to see what else lay before him seized him with excitement. But on the other hand, he was reminded that this place, this very world, was why he was in hell. The excitement quickly dwindled until the chains of resentment anchored his feet to where he stood. He was frozen; his eyes remained unblinking as he looked out at the doorway that led to the unknown world beyond. *You told him he was wrong. You told him it was folly.* He began walking forward — step by step — pulled by a tractor beam of curiosity maimed by pride to prove what he believed, yet fearful that he could possibly be wrong. *You told him they were an abomination.* Seeing him move forward, the other angels followed.

The moment Lucifer stepped forth from the cave, a blinding light from above radiated down upon the angels. Lucifer's eyes grew wide in fear. Gokor cried out, *"It's God!!!"*

The angels frantically dove for cover under the surrounding trees and shrubs. They gripped their weapons tight. They waited. They listened. For what seemed like an eternity, they remained in position, but nothing happened. Lucifer's cerulean eyes scanned the ground watching the movement of the light as it passed over them. Lucifer finally dared to look up. It was then he saw that the light had shape — *almost like a round ball. Not God. God has no shape, but is all light at all times.* It was then that he looked down and saw something more: *shadow.* Lucifer quickly looked up to the light once again. He suddenly understood. He swiftly rose, looking down at his own shadow. He moved forward with powerful strides and disappeared into the garden in silence.

Beelzebub cried out after him, *"LUCIFER!!!"*

Beelzebub and the other angels remained immobile until Beelzebub himself saw the shadow amongst the trees. His eyes narrowed as he deciphered what he was seeing. *"Shadow..."* He pointed to it.

Asmodeus was in disbelief. "How can this be?"

Beelzebub was gazing up at the light. He raised his hand up to it, looking at the ground, watching his shadow move across it with every gesture he made. "It is a false light." He lowered his hand. "Lucifer was right...God is not here."

Gokor grumbled, "What do you mean?"

"The light is not God at all, but a reason for light itself for this earth." He motioned toward the plants all around him as they bent toward the direction of the light's rays. The angels were bewildered.

They moved away from their crowded positions in the garden taking in their surroundings, examining the ground, the trees, the leaves, the flowers. Azriel gently rubbed a petal between his burnt fingertips, "So much like heaven, yet so very different."

Beelzebub noticed Asmodeus looking out toward the east. His back was stiff and rigid; his knuckles were bone white as he gripped the hilt of his sword. Beelzebub moved slowly toward him. "What is it?"

Asmodeus was frozen to the spot — listening. "I heard a voice. And it wasn't Lucifer's." He nodded in the direction of the sound.

The angels stopped all examination and froze, looking off in the direction Asmodeus was facing. Not a single one of them could breathe as they waited. The sound of gentle laughter echoed forth among the garden. They immediately reached for their weapons. Beelzebub spoke softly, "Whatever lay beyond these trees, be on guard. Follow me."

*   *   *

Lucifer walked through the trees to the West. The thoughts that swirled through his mind were that of a man who had been fighting for a cause and realized the cause he was fighting for, wasn't what he once thought. What a man did with that moment defined the kind of man he was — or wanted to be. But for a fallen angel who knew what he was and had warred over the idea of what he wanted to be, what the garden meant to such a being meant a redefinition of an unknown objective.

His argument had always been over the idea that creation had to have a

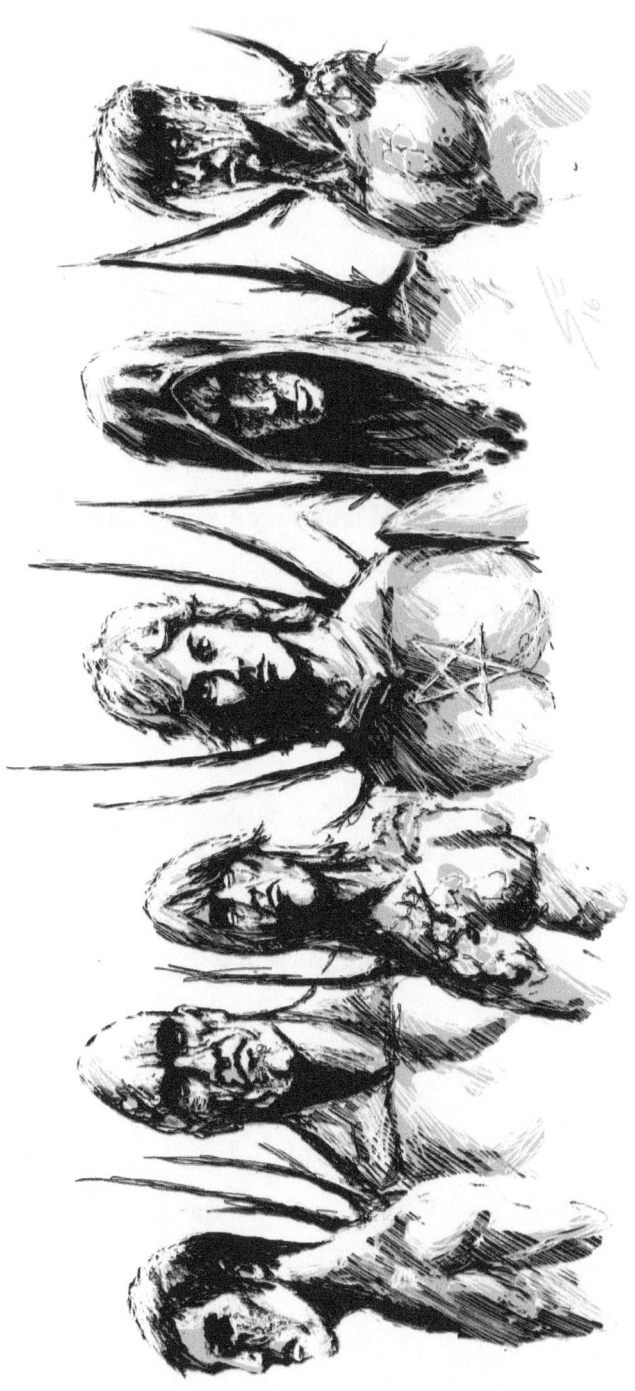

41

purpose or all would be in chaos. This created world should be in chaos. But as he took in the garden, he saw beneath it...*a pattern*. He noticed the division between sky and water as he moved along the riverbank; he peered into the water world and saw creatures swimming beneath it, some of which emerged from the water and hopped along the ground. As he followed their footsteps, he watched as small land creatures squatted on the ground pecking and snapping their mouths at the hopping creatures. He scanned the foliage, taking in the variation, height, and movement of the landscape all around as the creatures embraced existence as comfortably as if it were...*home*.

Lucifer pondered how everything around him was different in nature but linked all the same. *There is purpose here* — and it was still growing, it was still changing. Even the light above his head was shifting direction over the land the longer he walked through the garden. And just like the angels reaching their hands and extending their bodies to God's light in heaven, so these leaves, branches, and petals bent. *Yes, there was purpose behind it, indeed.* A purpose that baffled him, for he realized he had no idea what God was capable of. And with all his reason to reiterate his cause as he looked at the design, he couldn't. What he saw before him was the *lack* of chaos. It was beauty. Its results weren't as harmful as he presumed it to be. It was like...*home*.

The very thought made his face tighten into a sharp grimace. Clenching his teeth, he attempted to ignore the stabbing pain in his chest. And he knew what the pain was. He felt it now and again — even in heaven. He knew it was his own fault — even Gabriel had reminded him of it and called him out on in it when the pain would throb from deep within. He called it stubbornness, she called it pride. And the pang stabbed at him in the moments where he found that he could possibly be...*No! Do not think it.* To acknowledge the thought was a sign of defeat that where he now found himself to be was just. He wouldn't say it. He refused to believe it. *It cannot be so. There had to be more to this place that proves my point and will absolve me.*

But the more he saw of the lush green grass, bright colors of red, orange, blue, and yellow radiating from the flowers, the stabbing pain sharpened. *I can't be...*Lucifer clenched his jaw, holding it in, swallowing it down; the thought itself tasted like acid in his mouth. He turned the thought from himself and onto his Maker. He gripped the trunks of the trees as he stood between them, trying to control the emotions storming in his mind; the bark crunched beneath his grasp as his grip continued to tighten. His chest seized as his emotions took over; he could barely contain himself as he looked to the sky, vomiting out the words, "Creator God. You have falsified yourself to me. This paradise is a painting that colors the canvas of your desire to enslave me. I shall never be chained to any desire of your making. I shall make my own masterpiece and show you your horror. *From hell's heart I will stab at thee...*"

He waited.

Lucifer continued gripping the trees. Looking at the sky, all he could see was the vivid color of blue; the color of his eyes. All he heard was the strange sound of chirping from the branches overhead. He didn't know what he expected at his challenge, but he knew it wasn't silence. Perhaps, God would strike lightning down? Maybe the thunder would roll across the sky? But nothing happened.

A gentle breeze blew through the garden instead, brushing past his golden hair. And it was through the quiet that he heard the soft sound of laughter from amongst the trees. He slowly released his hold on the bark knowing that the laughter was from his unknown enemy. The moment he stood, the trees toppled over behind him. Clenching his jaw tightly, his teeth began to grind. He shifted his eyes to the sound of laughter. *Enemy mine...*

He extended his six opaque-colored wings and attempted to rise. His body did not move. He tried again, focusing his mind.

Rise.

Not even a single lift from under his feet occurred. He willed himself to move.

Rise!

He was anchored to the spot.

What is going on here…

Retracting his wings, he saw a few leaves falling to the ground beside him. His eyes narrowed.

A law to fall.

Before Lucifer could continue to think his way through this new law of nature where he found himself bound to the ground, he heard the faint sound of laughter once again. He shifted his eyes to the distant landscape, abandoning the idea of flight, and moved swiftly forward, thrashing amongst the trees and brush with the sudden realization that he was weighted down to mere footsteps. The burning flames of a new type of grudge took root deep within his heart. Not a single chirp answered him as he raged throughout the garden.

Lucifer turned east, following the lovely sound of happiness. He moved past a magnificent waterfall that poured and separated into four rivers that flowed into and out from the garden. He found Beelzebub, Gokor, Nero, Asmodeus, and Azriel hiding amongst the trees looking out at a scene before them, spellbound by what they saw. He slowed his feverish movements and came up silently behind them. He moved toward Beelzebub, his heart hammering inside his chest. *It is them…it is them…it is them.* He looked out over the brush and saw one man and one woman — and they were beautiful.

Mirrors.

His body trembled as he tried to contain the hurricane of emotions storming within his body. Beelzebub whispered to him, "They look exactly like us, Lucifer, but smaller and without wings."

No…not like us.

He couldn't even speak his thoughts aloud as he stared at the woman before him, a woman of such beauty, that any being would bow down to see the magnificent smile that was currently fixed on her face. Gokor was gazing intently at the woman. The man beside her was perfectly sculpted, outlined and carved with muscles of the most proficient athlete. Looking upon the man, Lucifer could not help but think of Michael. *But is he a warrior?* The man was playing with the woman's raven hair as she wove a crown of flowers for it. *No, not a warrior.*

The man called the woman *Eve.* Lucifer contemplated her name: *life giving.*

Gokor's eyes twinkled. "*Eve*…she is magnificent; the most beautiful creature I've ever laid eyes on. God has outdone himself."

Lucifer could clearly see Gokor's mouth moving, but none of the words resonated in his ears. *She's perfect.* Lucifer focused all of his attention on Eve as she abandoned her crown and moved away from the man to pick some fruit from one of the trees. Eve walked past the largest tree in the garden. It was the Tree of Life that once existed in the courtyard to the kingdom of heaven. Lucifer immediately recognized it; his eyes grew wide in horror, "Pieces of heaven…*here!*"

He caught himself, quieting himself, hearing only the slightest chirp from the birds in the trees above. He noticed the quiet as he and the fallen angels stirred in the shrubs — and yet, the man and woman did not notice. He thought of the birds. *How can mankind have not heard?*

Beelzebub tilted his pale head toward Lucifer, "Lo, Lucifer…this *is* heaven."

Azriel whispered, "I feel as if my eyes deceive me. Like this is some dream I'm walking through, for this man and his Eve look like us but then not, and the garden resembles heaven, yet it's so very different. These are the players and this paradise is the battleground for war — this is not what I expected. They are merely children — innocent."

Beelzebub's voice was low, "So were we once." Azriel looked at him, having heard the faintest hint of sorrow in the tone.

Eve walked toward the second largest tree in the garden and was about to reach for a piece of the most delicious-looking fruit, when the man stopped her and said, "Eve, you know what God said."

Lucifer's eyes narrowed the moment the man said the words. *God...speaks...to them?* Remembering his position in heaven, he being the chief Seraph, trickling the communication down from God to the rest of the Angelic Host...to hear such words spoken by a lesser being immediately caused his chest to constrict until he could barely breathe. *He holds them so close. Which means...God is here...* Lucifer's eyes slowly scanned around the garden.

The man continued, "We may eat the fruit of any tree in Eden, except the tree that gives knowledge of what is good and what is bad. If we eat it, we will die."

Die?

Gokor clutched the twigs of the bush he was crouched behind; they snapped in two. A look of panic formed on his face. "She must not eat it! Not the beautiful one! She will die! She must be warned!"

Nero placed his hand on Gokor's shoulder, calming him. Azriel turned to Lucifer, "Lucifer! How can this be? You said God breathed his spirit into them, giving them souls. How can she die with God's spirit residing inside her?"

All the angels looked to their leader — the Enlightened One. His eyes were fixed on the mortals in the garden. He knew the answer. The father had told him. "Their bodies are mere dust and bone; the soul is within the body. Should the body die, the soul will be released from its fleshly casing."

Gokor looked back at Eve as she continued to eye the tree. "And where will she go when she dies?"

Lucifer slowly turned toward the mighty cherub. "Don't you know? If she defies God, she is against God. And as we have clearly seen, when one is against God, there is only one place *to* go."

"Hell?"

"It would seem the only logical solution. Would you not agree?"

Gokor looked back at Eve. "Then it will not be long."

"No, I don't believe it will be. Then our theory will become fact if I am correct." He narrowed his eyes at Eve.

"But aren't you curious, Adam? Don't you wonder what will really happen if we were to eat it? What does it mean? To die?"

Adam. He named him Adam. First man. Lucifer smiled wryly at the irony. *God, you are clever, indeed.* Lucifer caught himself; the habits of talking to his father at all times made him flinch in the knowing that the habit would be no longer. He heard Adam laughing.

"Curious? About causing myself harm? No, I have no desire, Eve, for self-inflicted pain."

"That's not what I meant. I meant that perhaps…" Eve continued to gaze at the tree.

"What?"

"Perhaps…not everything is as it seems."

Lucifer's stance suddenly shifted at her words. The seizing in his chest lessened just a bit.

The rhythm. The beat.

He felt a pair of eyes on him and turned to see Beelzebub staring at him. "She's right, you know. Not everything or every*one* is as they seem. And the man is right as well. Why choose pain? Should the souls of mankind come

47

to hell, then God is giving them to us. He is filling our unwanted lair with more pain. Do you really want them there, knowing that they are the beings you so desperately wanted to be rid of? Or do you not think it wise to warn them against us…and our hell?"

Beelzebub and Lucifer stared at one another for what seemed like an eternity. Looking at the powerful cherub with the long, pale hair, Lucifer remembered what Beelzebub was like when he resided in heaven. They were never friends or enemies. They floated in different circles. Beelzebub adored Michael. He emulated him in all ways, speaking from strength, honoring truth, loyal to God, and willing to fight when there was a cause worthy of championing, defending.

Staring at this battle-weary being before him, Lucifer could clearly hear the accusing tone in his voice. And he remembered that moment before the Lake of Fire when he saw Beelzebub charging toward him with his sword with no other intent but to destroy him. Looking at him now, he knew he was treading on thin ice with the powerful cherub. He knew Beelzebub walked on a tightrope of choosing to follow Vitor's path toward grace or continuing on to lead hell's army back home; he had seen Beelzebub's face as he absorbed Vitor's argument. Either way, Lucifer knew Beelzebub would be taking other angels with him whichever path he chose. And as much as he despised the idea of needing anyone, he knew he needed Beelzebub. He needed him to command the rebel army, to keep them in line, to remind them of loyalty based on a cause they could all champion — ultimate freedom. Supreme independence would lead them home. Patriots of a mighty purpose.

Beelzebub continued on. "Truth is all around them, Lucifer. Even the man knows curiosity of the great demise is one footstep toward death. Why tempt it and lose all this? Temptations are rewards merely overrated. There is no test to examine truth here, Lucifer. It is something else." He looked back at Adam and Eve. "That tree is a moral compass over an argument that was laid at our feet. A symbol of what is innately rooted deep within their souls — as it was in ours. You know it and I know it, though you have not said it while standing here in this garden." He slowly turned his enflamed eyes back onto Lucifer. "They have free will. Just…like…us."

Asmodeus whispered, "Masters unto themselves."

Adam leaned back against the tree. "If you continue on this way, you may die and you will leave me. Is that what you want? To find a way to bring me pain?"

A look of fear formed on Eve's face. *"No!"* She buried her head in his chest. Adam kissed the top of her head, running his fingers through her silky, midnight-colored hair. "That's enough talk of death. Come." He stood up while the angels watched as Adam and Eve walked hand in hand toward the waterfall.

Lucifer continued his stare-down with Beelzebub. He could see the challenge behind Beelzebub's eyes; he could see Beelzebub studying him, listening to each word he spoke, never once lifting his voice to join the others. "Whatever you're thinking, *say it.*"

Beelzebub's eyes darkened, "There will come a time when I'll look into your eyes and have the answer that I seek."

Lucifer knew what Beelzebub truly wanted, but he would never get it. Instead, Lucifer offered him a confession rather than an admission, "I'm willing to concede to the idea that mankind is not worth the attention or grievance I find it to be."

Beelzebub smiled faintly, shaking his head. "That was not the question." He pulled his sword from his sheath and offered it to Lucifer.

"What am I supposed to do with this?"

"Kill them."

All the angels turned toward Beelzebub and Lucifer.

"You said that your kind of truth would set us free. We are here to watch and understand so that we may call God's attention to us. Behold, the great experiment is before us. *Experiment.* Kill them and see what happens. See if the theory becomes fact. See if God will come down here to protect them. See if Michael and Gabriel come down to fight. Kill them."

Lucifer considered his next move, knowing it would determine which way their relationship would go. Yes, this wasn't just thin ice, but quicksand, and Lucifer knew he had to fix this fast. His face softened into a gentle smile. "I can't." Beelzebub's eyes narrowed. "In case you haven't noticed, we can't even be seen or heard, let alone wield a sword to destroy the flesh of God's creatures. I can't even fly." He looked up at the trees surrounding them. "Although the creatures in this garden can see us and hear us; they've been silent this whole time."

"What do you mean?"

Lucifer picked up a stone and hurled it at a nearby tree. A flood of birds screeched and stormed into the air. The angels were bewildered. Gokor cried out, "They have wings!"

Panic rapidly formed on the angels' faces. Asmodeus immediately extended his own wings — nothing happened. "I can't fly!"

Azriel retorted, "What do you mean?" He extended his wings and willed *himself* to fly. Again — nothing happened.

Gokor growled, "What's going on here?" He slammed his fist into a nearby tree. Dozens of birds screeched and vaulted into the sky. Only then did Adam and Eve take notice as they watched the birds. Lucifer looked at Adam and Eve. "They *are* the great experiment, Beelzebub, but this world...this world was not meant for us. We are bound by its laws and rules, but just as the woman has pointed out, Earth allows an opportunity for certain rules to be bent."

Lucifer stepped out from behind the bushes and followed closely behind

Adam and Eve. Azriel cried out, "Lucifer! They will see you!"

Lucifer turned and smiled at Azriel. He then ran in front of Adam and Eve. The angels cringed anticipated what would happen next, but nothing did. Adam and Eve didn't even notice. Lucifer ran back toward the garden and moved toward the tree in the middle of it. He whispered to himself, *"Be the trees, dangle the fruit."* He looked up at the branches. *A standard. Good. Evil. Two opposing sides. A moral argument in the design — and these creatures know it. Beelzebub is right.* He suddenly decided to pluck a piece of fruit from its branches. He bit into it, swallowing it in three bites. He turned back toward his brethren. "It's good." He plucked more fruit and tossed them to each of the angels.

Azriel shook his head, "But why would God allow something so beautiful to be something so lethal?"

"There would be no reason for the tempting if it were not so. There must be a prize to obedience. Do you not see, my brothers? Our Father has done an ironic thing. He's making them earn their place in the kingdom of our heaven. And we are left to witness their actions for the reward alone, but not to kill them. We are bound by the laws of this world; rules we have yet to know or understand."

The angels stared at him in silence.

"It's all a test." He looked up at the trees. "I can hear His voice in the midst of the garden saying, 'This day I call Heaven and Earth as witnesses against you that I have set before you life and death, blessings and curses. Now choose life, so that you may live, that you may love the Lord your God, listen to his voice, and hold fast to him; for the Lord is your life." He touched the trunk. "The Tree of Knowledge of Good and Evil." He looked back at the angels. "I feel we have inspired this in our father, but I am not yet ready to engage. Nor do I believe we should. Not yet."

He watched the birds soar off in the distance, seeing that more land lay beyond the garden. *I have underestimated the Father. There is more to this world than this one place. There is more than this man and this woman. To understand how to achieve the goal, one must understand the game.*

Beelzebub was looking down at the piece of fruit in his hand when he uttered, "I don't think she'll eat it." All eyes turned toward him. "Just because one is tempted, doesn't mean one will choose the temptation." He dropped the fruit and put his sword back in his sheath. "There'd have to be more forces at work in the tempting; she has too much to lose." He leveled his eyes at Lucifer. "There's no other force at work here but her own reasoning. Even in heaven there was a force at work in the temptation — and we all chose when we didn't even know what the punishment would be. She does." He shook his head. "No, she will not risk losing her man or this paradise."

"Oh, but she will. She has already taken a step toward her loss. Eve is already thinking too much about this tree. She's thinking on what she wants and what it will do to her. She is not thinking about her Adam, her soul…or her God. She doesn't really think that it can be…all…that…bad. Besides, *she knows*. The man has told her she will die. God has told her she will die." His blue eyes seemed to glow in the revelation, "But she does not believe death has significance in her life, for she does not believe that disobedience to the father's will is truly disobedience at all."

Nero finally decided to speak; his voice was low, "Lo, the woman is beautiful, no doubt, but I agree with Lucifer. She is a fool. Did you see how freely she walked to the tree? A tree that bears fruit she knows will be the death of her. And yet she danced toward it like it were a game to see if something so desirable could truly destroy her. And the man…he is no man! He is a weak creature bending to the will of the woman so long as she smiles bewitchingly at him. They are both fools! No wonder God willed that the hierarchy stand at their side to help them. They need all the help they can get!"

Asmodeus chimed in, "I still say we should simply burn the garden down."

Nero shook his head, "God would not stand for it. He wouldn't let us get away with it."

Gokor was thinking. "He'd come down from heaven to try and stop us."

"Maybe. Maybe not."

Azriel came closer, "Do you think there are more men and women out there?"

"I don't know. If there are, why are these two — this Adam and his Eve — so special to the Father that he created a mirror of our home for them to reside in; a place where he continues to speak to them, but then not show his face at all times? It would seem that these creatures are not truly free then, if the father watches them so closely."

The angels turned to Adam and Eve swimming in the pool near the waterfall. Gokor spoke, "Are you saying that we should leave them alone?"

"For now. I still don't know what we are dealing with." He moved past the angels and looked off at the land that lay beyond the four rivers. He looked all around the garden, finally reaching for a flower in the brush. "I'm going to explore this created world to understand its principles. Already, I'm intrigued. It is only then that I think we can truly understand what it is we need to do to get what it is that we want."

Beelzebub answered, "We'll split up. It will be faster if each of us takes a different direction. Which way are you going?"

"East."

"Then I will go west. We shall report to one another all that we find."

Nero and Gokor nodded in agreement, "We'll take the south."

Azriel and Asmodeus stood together. "And we shall go north."

Lucifer took in each of the angels' faces. *Hope.* They actually had hope.

And something more — peace. He didn't quite expect it. He had not seen that look on their faces since before the rebellion. This place hinted at excitement, discovery. He could feel the angst in his heart rising over the calmness of their emotion. He wanted them to hate this place. He wanted them to be aghast not intrigued. But they had to find their resolve toward his argument on their own. He had to squelch the threatening feeling he held inside.

"Agreed."

He saw Beelzebub's body flinch at his response, as if the response alone were not meant to be trusted. "We shall travel to all ends of this earth and come back here to reveal all that we have seen and have come to learn about this place."

Azriel pointed to the ground. "Look at that!"

A creature suddenly slithered past Lucifer's foot, startling him. Intrigued, Lucifer crouched down to it and picked it up by its neck. "And apparently its creatures."

He studied it closer, holding the snake so that its face was turned toward his. The snake suddenly snapped its head and buried its teeth deep into Lucifer's hand. Lucifer cried out in pain and shock. Enraged, he took the snake and bashed its head against a tree until its body went limp. Lucifer was clutching his wrist when the other angels huddled around the serpent. Asmodeus grabbed a fallen branch and nudged the snake with the stick. *No movement.* Azriel was bewildered, "Lucifer, what did you do to him? It's not moving."

Lucifer looked down at the immobile form. Asmodeus spoke, "Is this possible? It no longer lives."

Beelzebub's eyes dimmed. "Of course it's possible. We once witnessed the possibility."

Asmodeus understood his meaning, "You mean when Lucifer attacked

Gabri…"

Nero placed his massive hand over Asmodeus' chest, silencing him. Gokor shoved Asmodeus out of the way and grabbed the snake. He shook it, attempting to throttle life back into it. It fell limply from side to side. He dropped it and stared at it. With wide eyes, he looked at Lucifer. "Are they as fragile as this?"

They all looked back at Adam and Eve. "Like us, but not like us…"

Beelzebub was crouched to the ground, staring at the snake. "Apparently you *can* kill creatures in this world." He examined the snake's fangs. "I wonder how." His eyes slowly shifted to Lucifer's hand; he was still gripping his wrist tight. "I wonder how the creatures know we are here." Beelzebub noticed Lucifer's skin had started to turn a shade of gray.

Lucifer looked down at his wrist and saw the veins turning black. His eyes grew wide. Lucifer's breath quickened as sweat drops rapidly multiplied all across his forehead. He looked up and saw Beelzebub staring at him. *"Go."*

Beelzebub nodded and commanded the angels, "Scour this Earth and engage with its elements. See what goes noticed and what is left unnoticed. Come back when you have reached the end of your side of the world. Wait for the rest of us to return."

The fallen angels nodded in obedience to their commander. Azriel extended his wings, willing himself to fly. He quickly retracted them, remembering that he could not rise. The angels walked on, disappearing beyond the rivers and the trees. Only Beelzebub and Lucifer remained. Beelzebub looked at Lucifer's hand; the nails had turned black. Lucifer looked up at him. "I said go."

Beelzebub turned toward the west, walking unnoticed past Adam and Eve swimming in the pool of water at the base of the waterfall. Lucifer closed his eyes in pain. He wiped his brow; it was now completely drenched in sweat. He opened his eyes and looked down at the carcass on the ground.

"What have you done to me?" He looked up at the sky as his body began to shake. "I promise you, I will right this wrong — if it's the last thing I do."

He noticed a few birds in the sky flying overhead. He watched their wings as they moved up and down. He slowly extended his six ivory wings and moved them in similar fashion. It was then that the fallen angel rose. He flapped his wings harder and rose above the trees. He shifted direction and soared East of Eden.

From the garden, a slight breeze began to blow all around the Tree of Life. Its branches began to sway; the sound of shifting wood could be heard grinding within its trunk. The branches dipped and lifted, swaying from left to right as they gained momentum. They dipped even lower and lifted even higher until the trunk itself twisted from left to right with each sway of the branches. With one final dip and lift, the trunk suddenly split open, creating an opening in the middle of the tree — a portal — and out stepped Michael.

The warrior scanned the garden's grounds, rapidly searching for the fallen angels. Uriel and Raphael emerged from the portal behind him, their swords were drawn and lit afire, ready to battle it out with their fallen foe.

"Look to Adam and Eve."

Uriel and Raphael pounded their fists into their chests and headed toward the waterfall. Michael moved through the landscape looking for any sign of disturbance, any feeling of angst or despair; and like a magnet, he felt it, he felt the mark of coldness — the mark of death. It was then that he moved through the trees and found the snake's carcass. He crouched down and picked it up, feeling the slight onset of rigor mortis amongst the cold body lying limp in his massive hand.

Feeling the broken body in his palm, taking in the smashed skull, Michael needed no further investigation to discover the cause of this creature's death. The angels had heard the cry of rage pulsing forth from the earth.

They had felt the shift of time the moment the fallen angels passed through the portal. They knew the day would come when Lucifer would come to the earth, but what they had not realized was that it would be so soon.

Gabriel warned him of it; she had just returned from hell having heard the argument amongst the other angels. Michael did not even know she had gone, for none of them had ever ventured into the inferno before. She had relayed to him all that she had seen and all that she had heard — that is when he felt the shift.

Looking down at the snake's body lying in his hand, Michael knew this was a sign of the times.

"Michael, there's no sign of them anywhere."

Michael turned his amber eyes to Sariel, another archangel under his command. He looked out at the land beyond the Four Rivers. "They're here, Sariel. They've walked through the door...and brought hell with them."

*   *   *

Lucifer followed one of the main rivers east of Eden. As he stepped out of the garden and into the world beyond, his body temperature continued to rise. His ten foot frame ached deep within his joints; every step was an effort in and of itself as he forced his body to put one foot in front of the other.

What's happening to me?

It was then that he realized that he had been gripping his other hand, clasping it tightly this entire time. From his fingertips to his elbow, the skin had turned a sickening shade of gray. Black lines were drawn across his limb polluting his veins with the serpent's venom. Lucifer's teeth began to chatter as the fever set in, but still he willed himself on. Step by step he moved through the landscape until it seemed that time itself had slowed all around him.

The garden evaporated with every step he took away from it, until Lucifer found himself amidst barren land, sporadic foliage, and a dry heat lingering in the air. He was breathing rapidly as his body racked in pain. And the deeper he tried to inhale, the shorter his breath became. As he limped along the road less travelled, his body continued to sweat — more from the pain than the heat — for no place was as hot as hell. Lucifer knew he wasn't well.

He took one more step when his knee buckled. He fell headfirst into the hard, sandy ground, weak from the venom; he could not move as he fought to continue breathing.

In...out...in...out...

His eyes focused on a piece of dried brush a few inches away.

In...out...

He watched as a strange creature emerged from a hole in the ground; it was barely two inches long as it crawled across the sand toward Lucifer until it began its climb along his clammy hand, up his arm toward his broad shoulder, until it settled in the nook between Lucifer's collar bone and his neck.

In...out...

Lucifer laid there, too exhausted to move. And as his gaze began to blur, he caught sight of something white, half buried beneath the sand. His eyes focused as he tried to decipher what it was. The white object was dome-shaped with two holes etched side by side between a protruding triangular hole. Taking in the teeth, the image became clear. It looked like the shape of a face.

In...

Lucifer's breath caught as Adam's words thundered in his ears, *"We will die."*

Out…

"What does it mean to die?"

In…

"I have made a creature in my image…one of dust and…bone."

It was a skull.

A small smile curled faintly on the corner of Lucifer's pale lips. He closed his eyes.

In…

With the last of his energy, he took his hand and smacked the small creature against the nook of his neck. Its insides exploded against his clammy skin. Lucifer breathed deeper; a calm washing over him as he whispered the words, *"Death…lives…here."*

Out…

"No, not like us…" He fell into a deep sleep as the dust swirled all across his face.

In…

And as he slept, he dreamt of the past, *"And not like heaven….heaven…heaven…"*

Out…

THE REALM

Then...

"**M**ichael! *Eat!* You've been fasting to the point of exhaustion!"

Michael remained on the sapphire steps, kneeling before the throne, praying silently as manna collected in his hair. He continued to pray with his head bowed low, while Lucifer tried to distract him by throwing more manna at him.

Gabriel hit Lucifer in the arm. "Leave him alone, Lucifer. He's communing with our Father."

Lucifer was sitting beside Gabriel catching the manna in his mouth — communion-like — as it fell from the sky. The rest of the Angelic Host did the same, flying through the air trying to catch it with their hands, arms, and mouths. They made a game out of it, a dance, a reflection of their joy to God for giving them all that they needed.

Lucifer shook his head. "But he's been fasting longer than usual. He is a rock, I tell you." Lucifer's eyes narrowed. "I wonder what he's praying so hard about."

"Always so nosy. 'Why this? Why that?' Why are you so curious about what he's praying about, anyway? What does his prayer have to do with you?"

Lucifer laughed. "You see, my love, I'm rubbing off on you. Now you're the one asking all the questions."

"Touché, my friend. However, the difference is you demand answers but tell nothing of your own."

He leaned back on his elbows still staring at Michael's motionless form. Gabriel studied him. "Oh, I see... you're trying to figure him out. Wondering what it is about our Michael that makes him such an outstanding warrior. You are sorting through your memories and thoughts, putting the pieces together on how it is that he beat you when you challenged him last. How could he possibly defeat me, the Thinker, when he is all brawn?" She nodded her head in agreement at her own answer. "Yes, that's it. You're still sore about losing. Ego is a very hard road — especially for you."

Lucifer eyed her. "Has anyone ever told you that you talk too much?"

She smiled. "Just you. But I know you love the sound of my voice, so I oblige your desire... *often*."

"It's not your voice but your laughter that brings me to my knees."

Lucifer lay on his back, draping an arm over his eyes. "I never should have told you about our duel."

Gabriel continued eating without looking at him. "You never should have challenged him."

"Enough, Gabriel."

"I told you, you would lose."

"I said *enough!*"

Gabriel smiled and continued to goad him. She rolled over onto her elbows. "Don't worry. I have kept your secret. No one but Michael, you and me knows of your loss. But you still haven't answered my question."

Lucifer ignored her. Gabriel lifted the arm he had draped over his eyes. "Why did you challenge him? You're not one to grapple."

He pulled his arm away and covered his eyes again.

Gabriel sang his name, *"Oh, Lucifer...."*

No response.

She played with his lip. He smacked her hand away in annoyance.

"To quote your favorite word, *Why?*"

Lucifer rolled over onto his stomach and stared at Michael. His eyes narrowed in determination. "Because I wanted to see if I could beat him."

"So you think in winning, you would have truly been deemed the greatest angel in all of heaven: the wisest, most creative, noblest and strongest." Gabriel rolled her eyes. "How annoying."

He shifted his eyes to Gabriel. "I didn't just want to see if I could win, Gabriel. I wanted to see if I could *defeat* him."

Gabriel pondered his answer. Lucifer picked a piece of manna from her hair. A laugh escaped him as he watched the wheels in her head turning.

"What?"

"Gabriel, you act as if there was something wrong with wanting to be the best. To test my limits."

"No, I don't."

"Then you agree that you must challenge the best in order to become the best."

"Yes, but you never thought you would lose. So what do you do now to test those very limits in order to become the best of the best?"

Lucifer smiled at her wryly. "Such questions, Gabriel. Why, you try again and again to push past them by figuring out how your opponent thinks. If you think like him you can always anticipate his next move. And in so doing, you will be one step ahead and you will defeat him. Then the road ahead will be... *limitless.*"

Gabriel looked at Michael. "But you cannot figure out our Michael, can you? Hence, no second challenge." She turned back to Lucifer.

"Not yet."

She sat up, leaning back on her hands. Lucifer quickly pushed her elbow back, making her arm collapse as she fell to her side. Lucifer jumped up quickly, laughing, and attempted to run. Gabriel recovered and grabbed at his foot as he tried to sprint past her, tripping him. They both scrambled to get up. Lucifer pushed Gabriel's face into the ground; she swung her arms wildly, trying to grab at any available limb so that he could not escape. Lucifer quickly rose and sprinted through the courtyard. Gabriel was right behind him as they ran past various angels, past the Tree of Life, and through a field that led toward an aqua-colored lake amongst burgundy hills.

On the hilltop two more angels sat under a tree eating manna. Along the shoreline, they watched as Gabriel chased Lucifer. "Well, Raphael, who do you think will win this time?"

"Not really a fair question, is it, Vitor? She never beats him, but I do think she will surprise us one day. She's faster than she thinks she is."

The light-haired angel with the emerald-colored eyes continued to watch unfazed, "Perhaps."

Lucifer spread his two white wings to launch into the sky, but Gabriel jumped onto his back before he could rise. They both fell backward into the lake. Raphael erupted in laughter.

Lucifer and Gabriel continued to wrestle in the water. Vitor merely shook his head. "She has no idea how to fight. So sad."

Lucifer continued to dunk Gabriel's head underwater as she wailed her arms about.

"You're right. It is sad." Raphael shouted from the hilltop, "C'mon, Gabriel! You can take him!"

Lucifer laughed. "Don't encourage her, Raphael! This is much more fun!"

Gabriel swung her arm and landed it in Lucifer's abdomen. He keeled over in pain and sunk back into the water.

Raphael flinched. "*Ooo*...nice shot."

Gabriel was standing in the water with her hair stuck to her face. She looked all around for Lucifer but could not find him anywhere. She looked up at Raphael and Vitor, "Where did he go?"

Before anyone could answer, Lucifer rocketed out of the lake, soaring into the sky, disappearing from view. Gabriel grunted in frustration. "I hate it when he does that." Gabriel walked onto shore soaked from head to toe. "Always running away..." She continued to search the sky for any sign of Lucifer.

Raphael called out to her again, "Gabriel! Why do you let him whip you so?"

Gabriel turned to look at him. She placed her hands on her hips and was about to reply when a pile of manna fell from the sky landing directly on top of her. She gasped as the manna stuck to her drenched body like a man tarred and feathered. Raphael roared with laughter while Vitor allowed himself a mere chuckle. Their laughter was joined by Lucifer's as he hovered directly above her. His laughter was cut short the moment Gabriel launched out of the lake after him. The smile vanished from Lucifer's face as she rocketed straight for him; he quickly fled.

"They're utterly ridiculous."

"What's even more ridiculous is your theory on 'alien beings.' I thought I was the comedian around here."

"Do not mock me, Raphael."

"I'm not mocking you. But, Vitor, other intelligent beings existing outside of the heavens doesn't make any sense. What would be the point? Why would God create beings that existed away from Him? Away from heaven?"

Vitor rested his head against the trunk of the tree; he was deep in thought. "Because God is constantly expanding, always creating. I haven't seen anything new in quite some time. So I ask myself, What if He was doing it elsewhere? What if He has expanded and created a domain we have yet to see by using his energy someplace different? What would this realm be like and what would God have created there?"

Raphael shook his head. "That would not be, my friend. It could not be. Life without God is death…and death does not exist. It is simply an idea."

Vitor shrugged. "True. But perhaps God has perfected His design and created a being and a place where our Father need not be directly near them for them *to* exist."

Raphael laughed. "And I'm an angel without wings!" The smile slowly faded from his lips as he continued pondering Vitor's argument. "Lo, there is only one place I know of that exists beyond the heavens, and it is not a place I wish to see."

Vitor's eyes dimmed. "You speak of hell; I thought *that* was a myth."

Raphael's face was grim. "It seems to me that you have already drawn your conclusion. If you had not, you would not be so grave."

Vitor sighed deeply. "There is a feeling deep within me that claws at my spirit. It's a feeling I have never known. I've been praying on it for quite some time."

Raphael took in the tone of his dear friend's voice. "Vitor, if God has created other beings beyond the heavens, they would not be as we are. They neither see the Father, nor the Father's light. His wisdom would not be theirs, for they are not in His kingdom. They would be weaker and less intelligent than we by design and logic. There would be nothing to fear from these beings."

"It is not these beings that I fear, Raphael…but our reaction to them."

Vitor studied Raphael. "Why do you not think it possible?"

Raphael tried to find the words, "I…look, say God has done such a thing without our knowledge, and all our knowledge comes from Him. Ask yourself this, What would be the point of those other beings and their existence if they are not aware of God and do not reside in His kingdom?"

Vitor looked him deep in the eyes. "To find God. And get to the Kingdom."

Raphael had no answer. "I don't know about you sometimes, my friend. All I know is that I'm still hungry. I'll race you to the throne."

A smile slowly formed on Vitor's face. "You're on."

Both angels extended their wings and rocketed into the sky. From behind the tree, Lucifer emerged. He had heard the entire conversation between Vitor and Raphael — and he did not like it.

Another being. Another world. But there'd be no need for it.

He silently and slowly walked forward, daze-like, thinking on all that he had heard.

Raphael is right.

He tried to dismiss the argument, but a feeling of dread slowly settled in his stomach until a knot anchored itself in the pit of it. He walked down the hill taking in the surroundings of his home, his heart and mind weighted down by worry.

No, God would not want imperfection in the realm.

As he passed a grove of trees, still sorting through his thoughts, Gabriel pounced down from one of the branches, knocking Lucifer to the ground; he landed face-first in the grass.

"Ha! Got you!"

As he pushed himself up from the ground, his voice was low and lethal, "Gabriel…if I were you, *I would fly!*"

She squealed in laughter as he rose; she launched into the ever-changing sky, zooming all across it as Lucifer chased after her — all thoughts of alien beings vanishing from his mind — *for now.*

BENJAMIN

Now...

Benjamin hated being hung over. And worse than that particular state of being, he hated anyone *knowing* he was hung over. Staring at the old Turkish man sitting across from him in the small, stuffy room, seeing the look of disdain etched into the lines of his weathered face; he knew the man was on to him.

"Dr. Jacobsen, you don't look well."

Yep, he was totally on to him.

Benjamin sat back in the hard, wooden chair and attempted to feign a professional demeanor as he looked all around the four, blank walls that surrounded him on all sides. *Not...a good...idea...*Sadly, even that small movement caused his head to spin. He leaned forward, resting his elbows on the table. He clasped his hands together and closed his eyes.

Breathe, Benjamin.

The old man turned to the bodyguard standing in the corner behind him and said something to him in Turkish. The guard looked back at Benjamin in disgust and left the room.

Great, now they were both *on to him.*

But instead of trying to regain some kind of composure to collect himself to

68

exude any lasting effort worthy of respect, all Benjamin kept thinking was, Why couldn't I have been a better actor? Why had I not inherited my grandfather's poker face? Or *anyone's* poker face, for that matter? Life was so unfair.

He did not mean to drink half a bottle of Fireball Whiskey the night before, but it was one of those nights where he knew without it, there would be no other way to sleep. And he needed to sleep — he was absolutely exhausted.

All because of Rachel.

The bodyguard returned and placed a glass of water down in front of Benjamin. He opened his eyes. One look at the glass of water, and Benjamin suddenly turned green. He looked at the bodyguard and forced out the words, "No, thank you."

He could have sworn the guard snorted at him in reply, but with the pounding going on inside his head, he was unsure. Benjamin shifted his lid-heavy gaze to the old man. "I've been travelling for over three years to find you and this place. I don't want to waste any more time. May I see it?"

The old Turk sat in silence. Moments passed before he finally whispered, "Blood has been spilt over the ages to possess that which you hunt."

Benjamin suddenly smiled. Never before had be been called a "hunter" in reference to the field of archaeology. It reminded him of when he was a child and had seen *Raiders of the Lost Ark*. He wanted to be the next Indiana Jones, travelling across the world on adventures to seek lost treasure, battling it out with corrupt men whose goal in life was obtaining legendary relics that were once believed to be the keys to rule the world. But the moment he signed up for his first lab course his freshman year at the university, he realized very quickly that whips, guns and swordfights would be replaced with a different set of tools: brushes, shovels and magnifying glasses. To most, archaeology was a forgotten field left to paleontologists, anthropologists and evolutionists. It was far too expensive to fund. And as Benjamin was often told by the many women in his life: much. Too. Boring. Only Rachel Julia Devereaux found it exciting enough to keep the conversation going. Then again, her father was an archaeologist —

as well as his former boss. Perhaps she was biased.

Nah.

His head pounded harder at the sudden thought of her.

"Blood has been spilt over many things in the name of religion."

He thought he heard the guard snort again. The old Turk tilted his head to the side. "All for the greater good."

Benjamin held his gaze, "No, not all."

The old man laid his gnarled, discolored hands on the table. Benjamin could see one of the old man's thumbs missing where the discoloration was most noticeable — the mark of a bomber. Looking up at the bodyguard in the corner, Benjamin thought he just might fulfill his childhood wish. Seeing the menacing look behind the bodyguard's dark eyes, he suddenly wished he was Indiana Jones. But Harrison Ford would never have walked into a situation like this without some type of weapon. However, a whip did not seem appropriate for the tiny space where barely three people, a table and two chairs fit. Too bad his grandmother never let him play with guns or he would have been more fond of them to realize that even guns have a purpose worth using.

Breathe, Benjamin. His head was pounding.

The old man asked, "How did you know it was here?"

"It's what I do." He sat back in his chair. "Then again, I don't know that it really is here. There have been many false claims over the years."

The bodyguard hissed at him.

"Why does he keep doing that? Hissing and snorting?"

The old man spoke to the guard in Turkish. The guard turned and left the room.

"Forgive my nephew. He only despises men he knows do not honor Allah and insult the remnants of his power."

"He thinks me an infidel."

"No, he thinks you have no self-respect. And without respect of oneself, one dishonors Allah for that which he has been given."

70

Benjamin tried not to lash out at the old man, but it took the last of his energy to refrain from what he truly wanted to say. "My having too much to drink the night before is not a reflection of my self-worth — even in my own eyes. Even Noah drank a little too much, if I remember correctly."

"Noah was a great man. A patriarch to the people."

"Noah was made up. Now, where is it?"

He saw the old man's gnarled hands curl into tight fists; he waited for the hiss, but all he got was a sharp pain behind his right eye as his headache escalated to the beginnings of a migraine.

Get it and get out of here.

He hated dealing with people who claimed to be religious — the piousness, the judgment, the ignorance. He had grown up with all the dogma and doctrine he could stomach over the years, and he had vowed that he would always remain objective when it came to his work — even in this acquisition. But something about the missing thumb on the old man's hand staring him in the face, along with the earlier comment about blood being spilt for the greater good, combined with his pounding headache, shifted Benjamin's perspective — and objectivity seemed unworthy of so subjective a moment.

"Look, I'm not here to debate with you about who I am or what I stand for — especially in the name of a god or religion. I only want the spear. I don't care what it stands for or where it came from. I don't believe in God or a man who claims to have been the son of a being who does not exist. Religion to me is a poison, a myth — and God is a delusion. It always has been. We live. We die. And that's it. End of story."

The old man's skin tightened around his eyes.

"The offer was given to you before I arrived. Take it or leave it, but know that you will never get this kind of offer again. After the Deadly Plagues from seven years ago, the world changed. People changed. They turned to their gods and have no tolerance for the holy terrors you call war. They have no tolerance for fundamental justification that does not bring peace. No one will fund you. So you have a choice — a small one, but a choice. They will hunt you down off of my benefactor's recommendation, and they will find you if you do not give me that spear. They will take it from you and you will not get this kind of money again to fund your weapons, your travel, or your plans to bring about the kind of death that dishonors your god. I'm going to give you one minute to gather that spear before I walk out this door. And if I don't get the chance to walk out of here alive, my benefactor will make that call to the U.W.F. He is waiting to hear from me, and all he wants to hear is that I have it. Now, what's it going to be?"

The old Turk pounded his fists into the table and shouted for his nephew. The guard walked in carrying a solid wooden box. He laid it down on the table between Benjamin and the old man. Benjamin looked at him with his deep blue eyes and said, "I know you want to hiss at me. Open the box."

The old man waved his nephew away and opened the box himself. He pulled out a small metal object and handed it to Benjamin. Benjamin took it and examined it. The moment he touched it, the room suddenly shifted and the temperature felt as if it was rising. Perhaps, it was his head spinning again, but the shift was external and the warm air was not making it harder to breathe — but easier. Benjamin took a deep breath — the first one since he arrived in this hovel of a room. He let his eyes slowly roam, looking around at the four walls surrounding him to see where the warm air was coming from.

No windows.

He looked past the old man's bodyguard and saw the door shut behind him. Holding the metal in his hand, he suddenly felt a vibration in his hand. It felt — *powerful.* He looked up quickly at the old Turk and the bodyguard and found the old man smiling at him. "Dr. Jacobsen, you look worse than you did before. Something wrong?"

And then he felt it. Someone else was inside the tiny room. He could feel their eyes on him — that gnawing feeling of someone watching from behind the shadows in the corners of the room but not really being there, and yet feeling that they were there all the same. He looked behind him but saw nothing there. His eyes scaled the ceiling and corners, looking for any sign of technical device. Nothing. The pounding in his head beat harder.

Benjamin pulled out a cell phone from his pant pocket and dialed a number. Someone picked up on the other end of the line, "It's me. I have it." He listened for the response. "It's the last of the three that claim to be authentic. This is the one." He listened again. "Send the helicopter and wire the funds."

He clicked off his cell and looked at the old Turk. "The money is being wired to your account now." In the distance, the sound of a helicopter approached. Benjamin replaced the spear inside the wooden box.

"Who is your benefactor?"

Benjamin ignored him and stood, grabbed the wooden box, and moved toward the door.

"Dr. Jacobsen!"

He stopped but did not turn to look back at the old man.

"You may not believe in the power of what you hold in your arms, but the man who wants it does. You know what it represents. And whether you want to be or not, *you* are responsible for what happens to it the moment you leave this room. Religion may be a poison to you, but mankind is a poison in and of himself. It takes much faith to be an atheist, and to be a man who walks in life without realizing there is meaning to his own as well as others, is the most dangerous kind of man — for he injects his nothingness into others seeing there is no value in their worth or their purpose. God exists, doctor — whether or not you see His face. He sees yours."

Benjamin stared straight ahead, "Then if God exists, I dare him to stop me from delivering this into the wrong hands if it will cause others so much pain. If it means the beginning of something or the end of something, let him show his face to me." He turned his head slightly, "But you know, he won't. Not because I don't believe he exists, but because he has never stopped all the bad things like this from happening before. And if you are God, why wouldn't you? And if you're God, you should."

Benjamin opened the door and headed outside where the loud sound of a helicopter awaited. The bodyguard pulled a cell phone from his waist. He looked at the text message that had just arrived. "The money has been transferred."

The old Turk looked down at his gnarled hands and thought about what just occurred. Whomever this benefactor was, he wanted that spear and he wanted it for nothing good.

Just like the dictator...

The old man lifted his eyes to the opposite end of the room. He had felt it. He had heard it. He knew. He could feel the being's eyes on him — watching silently — they were staring at him from the darkness in the corner of the room.

"What is it?"

"The young doctor has challenged Allah. And his test to our master has not been taken lightly."

And with that, a warm breeze blew violently past the old man and the bodyguard, zooming through the open door. *BAM!* The door suddenly slammed shut.

The bodyguard's eyes grew wide, "What was that?"

"The doctor's guardian. And he is angry."

PURPOSE

Then...

Michael felt the shift. He winced as if the movement were merely the sound of a small pin dropping, yet he heard it all the same. He could not quite place it or name it, but he knew the shift was rooted in a feeling he had never sensed before. He focused harder on his prayer, for the mighty warrior was fierce in his intentions, filling his spirit up in the strength he received from praying to his Father.

Lord, who may dwell in your presence? Who may worship on your sacred hill?

While he prayed, Lucifer leaned against a tree that resided high up on the hill that overlooked the steps to the kingdom below. He crossed his muscular arms over his lean chest as he took in the motionless figure of Michael down below. Michael continued to pray silently to God, his adamantine sword resting gently against his side. A few other male angels had joined him on the lower steps assuming his same position of quiet communication to the Father. Music played in the background while angels sang softly to God. A throng of angels inspired by Michael's example, knelt down all around him and silently prayed.

He who obeys God in everything and does what is right...

Gabriel passed through the courtyard and on toward the Tree of Life. Various angels were seen caring for its leaves, wiping them and draining them of its healing oil. She headed toward the sapphire steps of the kingdom. Lucifer spotted Gabriel moving toward the throne. He watched her movements as she climbed the steps until she reached the last one; his eyes narrowed as he attempted to decipher the sad, yet hopeful look on her face. He had never seen this look on Gabriel's face before and was suddenly alarmed by it. A feeling of deep concern filled his heart, prompting him to action. He dropped his arms and was about to fly down toward her when she suddenly knelt down beside Michael.

Whose words are true and sincere, and who does not slander others...

The Wind of the Spirit blew past the angels, while the light from the throne blazed forth with renewed force.

Who always does what he promises no matter how much it may cost.

Lucifer watched the throng of angels praying down below and wondered about Michael's prayer and even more — about Gabriel's. He looked to the light blazing from the throne.

He who does these things...

Lucifer emitted his own prayer just as Michael finished his.

Will never be shaken.

"Father, what is it that I am not seeing? What is it that I do not know? The angels here gather in silent prayer for what seems to be an intention rather than praise. Why? What is it for? What is it that they seek that they have not been given? I don't understand it." He looked all around at the ever-changing sky. "You have given us everything there is to give, and yet you leave it to us to discover if there is something more." He looked down at Gabriel and Michael. "Action speaks louder than words." He looked out at the blazing light. "And you are beside me in all I do. Then why does this moment and this sight gnaw at my spirit so?"

The Wind gently blew through Lucifer's wavy, golden hair. He closed his eyes to breathe in its peace just as Michael opened his. A calm serenity covered Michael's face; his soulful, amber-colored eyes reflected a peacefulness deep within, while on the hilltop above, Lucifer's face was filled with a temporal calm. It was then that Michael felt the shift again. He tilted his head, listening for it just as Lucifer extended his opaque-colored wings and soared into the sky. The feeling was gone as soon as it came, leaving Michael with the feeling of the sudden passing of woe. He looked down beside him suddenly realizing that Gabriel was kneeling to his right, her head bowed in prayer.

Gabriel slowly raised her head to God's light and opened her eyes; Michael saw the tears of longing behind them and was disturbed by the sadness he saw. *Was the feeling coming from her?* She turned her head toward Michael and smiled.

"Hello, Michael."

"Gabriel. I didn't realize you were beside me. How long have you been here?"

She looked up at the light. "Not as long as I should have been."

"Are you all right?"

"Yes, I am. I always am after I speak with Him."

"Amen, Gabriel."

They rose at the same time and bowed their heads to God before turning and walking down the steps, side by side, in silence. When they reached the Tree of Life, she finally spoke, "Michael, may I ask what you were praying so long about?"

He answered simply, "Strength."

Gabriel laughed.

"Why do you laugh?"

She nodded toward his chiseled arms. "Because you already have it."

He smiled faintly, "I'm not talking about the physical kind."

Gabriel raised an eyebrow. "What other kind do *you* need?"

"The strength of God within me. I want it to burn as the light of God burns here in the kingdom."

Gabriel took in his words. "That's a good prayer."

They continued walking side by side. "Michael...why do you desire that strength? Is it something you have always sought or recently been compelled to seek?"

"Both. The desire has always been there, but now my very being thirsts for it like no other. For it will serve a greater purpose; a reason to my existence."

"Your purpose..."

Michael paused and studied her. "You know that of which I speak."

Without looking at him, a small smile formed on the corner of her mouth. "You see more than you tell, Michael."

"I find that action speaks at the heart of every angel."

"Attempt great things for God..."

Michael finished her thought, "Expect great things from God. We understand each other well, Gabriel." He grinned at her.

Gabriel smiled but it soon faded. "Michael, I've been feeling the same way. And this feeling...it came upon me so suddenly that I'm not even sure if it was always there or placed on my heart at this very moment for a specific reason."

"What do you mean?"

She looked up at him and faced him, "My purpose. Every day I revel in what lies before me, yet ever so suddenly, I've been wondering if there is something more — more for me to do, more for me to discover, more for me...to become."

"And why do you think that is?"

"I don't know. It's almost as if there were…a shift…within me. And I'm excited about what I don't know, yet I long to know it now — almost to the point that I find myself in a frenzy of anticipation of an unknown pathway on a road I've always been on that will lead me someplace new."

"You feel angst."

"Yes, I do."

"But there is no need for it. God will reveal it to you when it is the right time for you to come upon the path."

"I know He will, but I feel as if I am to prepare for the pathway in some manner now, yet every moment of my life lately has led to nothing new that does not repeat something of the same. And I don't like it."

Michael's amber eyes softened as he listened to Gabriel. "So you have been praying for the knowledge of what it is you are supposed to do in this moment until the next one comes."

Tears filled her eyes, "Yes!"

Michael smiled faintly, "And yet, you have no answer."

Her shoulders slumped as she shook her head.

"You know what I think?"

It was now Gabriel who smiled faintly, "No one knows what you think, Michael."

"I think you are exactly where you are supposed to be. Doing exactly what you are supposed to do. It is this moment of seeking the truth and reason for your future existence that defines you in this moment. The answer will come, Gabriel, for not even I know the reason *why* I seek the strength within me. I just know…I simply do."

"You wonder too?"

"I revel, Gabriel. God gave me a gift and I have no idea what it is for, yet I thank Him every moment I can for whatever purpose it is to serve —

even if the purpose is just to know that I have it."

Gabriel lowered her head. "But that's the problem, Michael."

"What?"

She looked up at him as tears streamed down her face. "I have no gift."

Michael was taken aback by such an admission. "Gabriel, that's not…"

She put up her hand and stopped him, shutting her eyes as she attempted to shut out the comforting words she thought Michael felt compelled to give. She smiled in appreciation, "I don't."

Michael stood there helpless in the revelation that he had not helped Gabriel fix her situation or brought her words of comfort that could possibly bring her peace. The look on his face was one of deep concern. The sight of such a glimpse into Gabriel's mind made Michael pause, for throughout all of history, this was the first time she opened a doorway into the confines of her mind that did not include sharing it with Lucifer alone.

"I want to know why I was created." She continued. "I want to know why I'm here. What was it that I was created to do?"

Gabriel looked into his amber eyes. "Because I know I'm not doing it." She paused. "I see you, and you know what it is that God has equipped you with. You're strong. You're noble. The other angels want to be like you as you walk with strength alongside our Father. Your confidence is like a light all its own, Michael. I see it. And watching you gives me peace and a knowingness that there is a reason for it. Vitor has the gift of deep philosophical thought and discovery; Raphael makes everyone laugh; and then, of course, there's Lucifer who can do everything — but beat you."

Tears stung her eyes as she attempted to laugh through her tears. Michael waited for her to continue, hearing the pain in her voice. "I have no gift and I know it. I have no talent. There are things that I like, sure, many things I enjoy…but nothing I can *do*. Doing makes a difference, Michael. It's tangible. It's its own driving force with a sense of purpose. And I have none."

She swallowed hard, embarrassed. "My prayer continues to be a selfish one. I'm always asking God if he could just let me know…what the point of me is…I have so much yearning and longing, but I don't know for what. It's this insatiable thirst. And nothing fills it, not even my prayers."

"What do you need, Gabriel?"

She shook her head, "Nothing."

He repeated his question, "What do you need *from me?*"

Gabriel looked up at him with the eyes of a hopeful child. "Your prayers, Michael. Pray for me, that whatever it is God has put in my heart to do, that he reveals it to me — soon. And if He is not going to reveal it for some time, to take this frenzied anxiety from my mind. I asked Him already, you know, but I often find that a legion of prayer warriors make louder noise when it comes to laying petitions at God's door. There's no way He can avoid such an army."

Michael took her hand. "You shall add me to your legion, Gabriel."

She tilted her head to the side and looked at him, "Thank you, Michael."

From the sky above, Beelzebub slammed down onto the ground beside them. He slapped Michael on the back in greeting. "Michael."

Gokor slammed down on the other side of Gabriel. He wedged her out of the way and cut in front of her path so that he was on the other side of Michael. He put his massive arm across Michael's shoulder and pulled him in. "We have an idea."

Michael looked at Gabriel and nodded.

Gabriel smiled knowingly and moved away from the male angels. She watched as the angels headed over the hill. She took in their massive forms, the strength of their gait, the power of their movements. She looked down at her own hands and body. A low sigh escaped her. "It's impossible…"

"Why haven't you asked me to pray for you?"

She slowly turned and saw Lucifer approaching. She rolled her eyes and shook her head in annoyance that he was around at so private a moment. "Because you *wouldn't* pray for me, Lucifer, you'd merely try to fix the problem."

"I didn't realize you were a problem that needed to be fixed."

She eyed him. "I'm not. But you don't always need to know everything. Besides, the moments when I've desperately tried to tell you something, you aren't really listening."

"Hm? What?"

Gabriel hit him. Lucifer laughed.

"You're impossible." She walked on. Lucifer's face went from one of humor to one of concern as she moved away from him.

"So stubborn." He begrudgingly followed her. "Gabriel, wait."

She continued moving forward. He ran after her. "Gabriel...stop." He grabbed her arm and turned her to face him. "I'm listening now. I hate it when you don't ask me for my help." He searched her eyes. *"Ask me."*

He could see the struggle behind her eyes as she was thinking. Why this was so difficult for her, he could not understand. What could be so important and so personal that she would not simply share it with him? Gabriel looked him dead in the eye. "What do you think I'm good at?"

This is not the question he was expecting. He laughed nervously, stumbling over the words, "Well...I think...you..."

Gabriel scoffed. "Forget it!" She moved forward.

"Gabriel!"

Her two wings jutted forth from her back. She launched into the air. Lucifer shouted after her, "You're good at flying!!!"

She did not even bother to turn around. As she flew off, he whispered aloud, "I know what you're good at, Gabriel." Lucifer watched her in flight. "You're good at keeping secrets."

THE PORTAL

Now...

*T*hump-thump-thump...*thump-thump-thump*...*thump-thump-thump*...

Gabriel continued to stare at Lucifer's instrument of old. She contemplated her next move, keeping her eyes fixed on its base.

He isn't here. He doesn't know. Leave it where it is.

Her hands rested on her hips as she continued to think.

Thump-thump-thump...thump-thump-thump...thump-thump-thump...

She tilted her head listening for the sound. She launched into the sky and out toward the Great Waterfall, following the River of Christ down toward the cave that led out of Heaven and into Hell. She landed just outside its entrance.

Thump-thump-thump...thump-thump-thump...thump-thump-thump...

Gabriel moved slowly towards the rock, pressing her ear to the cold granite base. She looked all around her and, finding no one there, moved inside the cave and climbed down toward the portal.

The dull thumping became clear as she made out the syllables over the sound of the river's force. Lucifer continued to shout her name, how long he had been doing so, she could not tell. Only the raspy sound of his spent voice was any indication that he had been shouting for a very long time. The water moved past her, and the closer she got toward the inferno, the hotter the cave became as steam from the river rose.

There was a time when she would have done anything for him. A time when the same could be said of him about her. There were very few moments when she truly shared what was on her mind with her friend of old, for only God knew what lay deep within her heart. But there were moments when Lucifer seemed to know it anyway — as those who are constantly around you often do. And even though he was never willing to admit it, Lucifer knew that Gabriel understood him better than any other angel; there was nothing he could hide from her no matter how hard he tried.

I know you of old…

Gabriel slipped on a rock; it dislodged, ricocheting off the hardened walls as it bounced further down the cave. She froze the moment Lucifer's shouting stopped.

"Beloved…"

It almost sounded like a sigh. He knew she would eventually come. But instead of moving forward, Gabriel did not move. She leaned against the rock debating whether or not to turn back. *There is only one reason he could possibly want it. Only one purpose for which it could serve him. There's only one way to know.* It was then that she heard him, the softest of sounds as he suddenly started singing to her. His deep, musical voice rose up from the depths of hell — a song she heard only once as he sang it for her in heaven. She closed her eyes as she listened to his melodious voice.

"Sing to me, Lucifer…"

Then…

Gabriel's head was resting in Lucifer's lap as he sat against a large bronze-colored tree. "Sing to me. *Please.*"

He pulled a bunch of leaves from her hair. "When will *you* sing to *me?*"

"I can't sing."

"Yes, you can. I've heard you."

"There are many things I can do, Lucifer, but singing is not one of them."

"So you won't sing for me?"

"No."

"Never?"

He pulled at a twig tangled in her hair.

"*Ow!*"

"How do you get all of these stuck in your hair? What have you been doing? Rolling around in trees?"

She closed her eyes and smiled. "Nope."

Lucifer studied her face. "You're keeping something from me. What is it?"

Without opening her eyes, she shook her head; a smile was still planted on her face. "Nope."

"You know you want to tell me."

"Nope."

He looked at the twig he pulled from her hair and examined it closer. "This twig is from the second realm. I recognize its color."

Her eyes slowly opened.

"It is from a large ivory tree planted somewhere near the Great Waterfall."

She grabbed for the twig, but he moved his hand away, keeping it out of reach. "Give it to me."

"Nope."

She grabbed for it again. "Give it to me, Lucifer."

"Nope."

He continued to dodge all her efforts from obtaining the twig. "Tell me what you've been doing."

She sat up and grabbed for it. He rolled over and clasped the twig to his chest, guarding it with his body. Gabriel grunted in frustration.

"You know you can't keep all your secrets from me. I'm bound to find out sooner or later."

Gabriel sat a few feet away from him braiding her hair. "Then it'll be later rather than sooner."

Lucifer watched her as she continued to ignore him. "It'll be sooner." His two wings jutted forth from his body as he launched into the sky.

"Lucifer!"

Gabriel rocketed into the sky after him. Lucifer soared through the seven realms until he entered the second one. He flew over the Great Waterfall and out toward a hidden piece of landscape where he saw the large ivory tree. He landed down beside it. Gabriel slammed down immediately behind him. "How did you know this was here?"

"I've seen you fly to it."

"Spying on me?"

"You leave me no choice. You keep too many things from me."

She snatched the twig from his hand and glared at him. "All right, if I tell you, you have to promise me you won't laugh at me."

He lifted his right hand. "I promise."

"I mean it!"

"So do I! I said I promise." He tried not to smile.

Gabriel dropped the twig and started climbing the tree. Lucifer watched as she made her way to the very top. He could barely make out her form amongst all the leaves. The moment she landed back on the ground, Lucifer could see not only a few more twigs in her hair but a bundle beneath her arm.

She huffed as she clutched the bundle gently in her hands. She finally looked up at him. The look on her face was one he could not quite decipher. There was a twinkle in her eye, but also one of fear and sadness all rolled into a hidden joy that exuded from some place deep within her spirit. Lucifer was taken aback as he memorized this look. He touched her arm understanding that whatever lay grasped beneath her arm was one she was not quite ready to share. And for a moment, a bit of sadness touched Lucifer's heart as he realized that Gabriel — his very best friend — did not entirely trust him. And with that realization, Lucifer could not help but feel hurt.

"God…has answered my prayer."

Lucifer watched as she took the bundle from beneath her arm and unwrapped the cloth surrounding it. She held it up to him. He looked down at her hands and saw an object. He looked up at her recognizing what it was. She tried to hide her smile. "Breathtaking, isn't it?"

"It's magnificent, Gabriel. May I?"

She allowed him to take the bundle from her; he moved the rest of the cloth away to reveal a golden trumpet. The light of heaven reflected off of it and into Lucifer's eyes, setting them aglow. He was stunned by its beauty, captivated by its craftsmanship. It was perfectly molded with its flowing form, rounded out at the end like a ram's horn. He had never seen anything like it before.

"And this is *yours?*"

She snatched it back. "Yes, it's mine. God gave it to me."

"What kind of a prayer was this? If you wanted to learn how to play the trumpet, my love, all you had to do was ask me."

Gabriel scoffed at him. "That was not my prayer."

"So what was it?"

Gabriel hesitated.

"I'm not going to laugh. For God to give you this, I would not laugh."

Gabriel looked at her trumpet, her voice was barely a whisper, "I wanted...I wanted to sing to Him."

Lucifer looked at her blankly.

"What."

"That's *all?*"

"What do you mean, *'that's all?'*"

"Well, I thought it was something...*deeper.* A prayer of greater importance. You even recruited Michael to pray for you."

"That was a *different* prayer. Besides, it *is* important! *To me!*"

Her wings jutted from her back; she rose into the air to leave. Lucifer quickly grabbed at the tip of her wing and pulled her back down.

"Peace, Gabriel. I cannot bear to see you in such angst. I didn't mean to offend you. You didn't exactly share with me your thoughts on the matter, so how can I be guilty of not understanding their importance? I cannot read your mind, you know."

She slowly retracted her wings. "You're right. I'm not being completely fair."

Lucifer shook his head. "It's just...you *can* sing."

"No, I can't. Not like you, Lucifer, who has the most magnificent voice ever sounded. I can't even sing like the rest of the angelic host either. I'm awful."

"I see." He looked at her trumpet. "So God has answered your prayer by fashioning you a voice from which you can sing. The impossible made possible."

Gabriel nodded her head in silence, looking lovingly at her trumpet. "He fashioned for me the most perfect gift, Lucifer. A gift just for me."

"But why a trumpet? Why not a guitar? Violin? Piano even."

"God knows I can already play the piano."

"Gabriel, you *pound* on the piano."

She merely shrugged in reply. "Perhaps it's the only instrument suitable to echo how loud my voice can be." Gabriel could barely look at Lucifer. "I know you think me a fool. I knew you would. That's why I couldn't tell you."

She leaned against the tree, clutching the trumpet to her breast. There was a look of such longing on her face that it pierced Lucifer's heart.

"Lucifer, you have no idea what it's like to be amidst the entire angelic host singing to God, and knowing that if you open your mouth to join in, you will utterly destroy the melodious beauty of that musical prayer. And I yearn, beyond words, to sing like that — almost like a tugging on my spirit to express my love for God in such a way that I can barely breathe."

Lucifer smiled in the understanding. "He alone knew how to make you sing."

She nodded.

Lucifer moved toward her and snatched her trumpet. "Then one must teach you to play and therefore sing."

With the swiftest of movements, Gabriel snatched the trumpet back. "You have your own trumpet. I'll play on mine as you play on yours. And if you won't teach me, I'll just ask the Spirit." Gabriel blew into the trumpet; a loud horrific sound followed. Lucifer cringed.

"I would not wish you upon the Spirit. He has been too good to me."

Lucifer took the trumpet from Gabriel's hands.

"Hey!"

He played a tune on the trumpet and started to dance. Gabriel shook her head. "Just because you happen to be a musician..."

"*Master* musician." He smiled at her and blew the instrument loudly.

Gabriel tried not to smile but failed as a large grin spread across her face. He handed the trumpet back.

"And my friend."

Lucifer offered his arm to her. Manna fell from the sky, giving the angels their daily fill. Gabriel looked up and caught the manna as it fell upon her. Lucifer watched her in silence as they walked side by side. She caught him looking at her; her eyes narrowed.

"What?"

His voice fell into a whisper, "I love you more than you know. I just wish you knew you could trust me."

"I do trust you, Lucifer. But sometimes I can't find the words to say what is stirring in my heart. All that comes out is pure emotion, and I don't always want to be emotional. So it's not that I'm always keeping something from you, but that I don't always know how to articulate what I'm feeling or mean to say — and I don't want to be misunderstood."

She laid her hand over his arm as they continued to walk across the field. "I'll try to be better about it, but I'm still not giving you my trumpet."

Lucifer roared in laughter.

Gabriel tried to hide her smile. She rested her head against his shoulder. "Now, teach me to sing."

He kissed the top of her head. "Anything for you, beloved."

"You know, Lucifer, I think this is a beginning for me. I think God has a purpose and a plan for me greater than I could ever imagine."

"You know, Gabriel, I believe the same holds true for *me*."

COSMOS

Not so long ago...

Lucifer opened his eyes and found himself lying face down in the sand. He blinked slowly, taking in his surroundings, wondering where it was he found himself to be.

And then he remembered.

He slowly pushed himself up from the ground and saw that the land all around him had grown dark. Not quite understanding how that could be, he raised his head to the sky and saw something he could not quite comprehend: the sky itself had changed. And unlike the sky in hell, this sky was...beautiful.

Thousands of stars illuminated the darkness, cascading their dying glow upon the fallen angel like the twinkling lights he always saw in heaven. Night was like no other experience Lucifer had ever known, for it mirrored the beauty of the day and unearthed even more creatures who relished in the shaded ambiance of another world whose light was yet another orb.

And as he looked to the celestial heavens, the words came pouring forth from Lucifer's mind, *Remember your Creator in the days of your youth, before the dismal days come when you will say, 'I do not enjoy life...when the light of the sun, the moon and the stars will grow dark, and the rain clouds never pass away, when the house trembles, and the strong men stoop. Remember him, before the silver chain is snapped, and the golden lamp will fall and break, and your bodies return to the dust of the earth and the breath of life goes back to God who gave it.*

He listened to the sounds of an awakened world that had arisen in the darkness of the night. Feeling the cooling temperature all around his skin, he could not take his eyes from the stars. They looked like clusters of distant balls of fire that had exploded, and all that was left amongst it were the remnants of distant embers flickering at varying paces from one main burst.

A bang.

"And God said, 'Let there be light,' and unto the light we angels were born. So was this sky. And so was this place." It was at the same time that God created what he loved and what he was going to love. He had created something out of nothing — *or so it seemed.*

Lucifer's eyes narrowed as he digested the thought.

How? Why? Who was my father's Father?

But he knew there was no other father. And even with that knowledge, he pondered it still. He had never asked God how heaven had been created or where the myth of hell had even come from. He had no need to. Truth was before him in all his realities and it was only now, on a place called Earth, that he began the journey of seeking a different kind of truth.

Why create me? Why allow me to fall and cause chaos in the beauty of my perfect home? Why not stop me? Even now, why have you not...destroyed me?

And before he could stop the swelling rupture of pain, rage and anguish from his heart as he looked up at the beautiful galaxy above, he cried out to the universe, *"WHY?!?!?"*

His hands were clutched in tight balls of fury as his bloated head listened for a response to his cry. All Lucifer could hear was silence, for even the night creatures had grown quiet at the sound of his plea. For all the pain Lucifer had brought upon himself, the one factor he simply could not bear was his father's silence. But he knew what he had done. He knew he had brought his father unbearable pain — and he was glad. But the fact he could not see that pain on his father's face, the fact he could not hear it, tormented him — for one often brings pain to another for no other reason than to level the playing field.

There was a comfort in seeing another's pain when one finds that they were in a house filled with it, for it often eases one's own. But here, amongst the beauty of the stars and the strangeness of this world, Lucifer was ripped of the comfort and the ease — reminded of the fact that the world goes on with or without your pain. He felt the need to cling harder still to his goal of inflicting pain, and pull stronger against the tide of forward momentum so that he would not be left behind or forgotten as he looked at the cosmos above.

He's still growing…

And if God was still moving forward, so could he. Lucifer finally stood, knowing what it was he needed to do as his body continued to rack in pain.

Level the playing field.

The once-noble seraphim angel looked up at the magnificence of the stars above and clenched his fists tight. He could feel the elongated nails that had grown almost overnight; they were like the claws from one of the scale-ridden creatures he had seen moving about the desert earlier in the day. He shifted his eyes to the ground and saw a large piece of dead skin lying in the sand where he was lying unconscious. He shuddered upon seeing the grotesque remnants of his infected self. His body tensed in frustration as he felt the venom burning within his veins.

He stretched his wings from his back, and dozens of feathers fell from his wings as they rapidly molted, revealing the skeletal frame of their making, but the emergence of a new webbed skin filled the void between their frame. A sharp pain shot forth from his infected wrist and down his spine with such lightning speed and knife-piercing force, that Lucifer keeled over in mind-bending pain; his body dropped, and like that of a small child, he curled into a fetal position. He writhed and screamed with each shooting pain as it ripped through him over and over again from the top of his skull to the end of his spine.

He howled and whined, growling like a rabid dog. And with a sound that echoed across the sandy dunes, he shouted and roared as his tailbone began to elongate further still. It pushed beyond its fleshly casing until the shooting pain suddenly stopped as soon as it began. Lucifer was lying on the ground, panting, sweating, barely moving. He reached behind him where he felt the needle-stabbing pain near his tailbone. It was then that Lucifer felt an extension of the bone. It writhed upon touch. Lucifer shuddered the moment he realized what it was — *a tail.*

* * *

Michael soared over the garden grounds but could find no sign of Lucifer or the fallen angels lurking in the darkness. He drifted over the crisscrossing rivers that led out to all four corners of the earth, hovering amongst the starry sky when...*BAM!* He saw it.

Michael plunged down from the sky like a falcon in the dive, slamming down onto the ground between two toppled trees. He looked at their upended roots as they lay opposite one another.

Pushed over.

Michael stepped closer to examine one of their trunks. Fingernail marks scarred the bark of the tree. He moved over to the other one and saw the same mark carved into the middle of the wood. He looked back at the garden lit in moonlight.

Adam and Eve had not seen the fallen ones. They had not heard them. Why not?

Michael's eyes narrowed in determination in his attempt to decipher this mystery.

"By the look on your face, Michael, I can see you're thinking the same thing that I am."

Michael turned and saw Gabriel examining the nail marks on the tree opposite him.

"How did they not see? How had they not heard?"

Michael moved toward the tree beside her. "The only answer I can come up with is that God has not allowed it."

Gabriel nodded, "Yet, Lucifer and the others can move and mark these trees. That has been allowed." She moved her fingertips over the wood.

"Hmm...He's done more than scar trees." He nodded to the garden beyond. "Lucifer killed a creature near here — a snake."

Gabriel locked eyes with her commander, "How?"

"I don't know."

Gabriel's face was fierce, "Can he touch the man and the woman?"

"I don't think so. I have a theory on what our fallen brethren will and will not be allowed to do, and I believe it will hold true for what our purpose will be amongst this world and mankind as well." He looked out toward the garden. "Adam and Eve's guardians have come down, as have all the rest for the people beyond these borders."

He turned back to Gabriel. "Our Father said they are to remain unseen behind the veil. It is the only way to allow freedom of the will by not revealing that their guardian is beside them — never influencing man or woman in any way to protect them."

But Gabriel was not listening; Michael could see the look on her face and that she was rapidly thinking of a means to influence what was to be left alone. "Gabriel…"

She was lost in the confines of her mind with a look of sheer determination.

"Gabriel."

She snapped out of her private thought and looked at her commander.

"Don't."

Gabriel gritted her teeth, begrudging the thought that he knew what she was thinking and that he was not going to allow her to do it. "Why not?"

"God is allowing Lucifer the opportunity to see the world — without influence. You are not to follow him or interfere in any way."

Gabriel moved away from the tree and looked out toward the garden. She stood with her hands on her hips, not liking the situation that had presented itself. "It won't matter what he sees, Michael. He's coming into this world with an agenda. And it will not be changed. It cannot be influenced. It will only be anchored in the root of time by rotting iron of what he has always felt. To topple a tree was a mere knee jerk, to smash a snake was a reflex. What do you think he will do when he has the time to stop and think about how he can crush an entire forest with a single blow or smash a pit of snakes under a single footstep?" She looked up at the branches of the trees. "He will be a vine of anarchy cultivating in the world. He is out there trying to find where best to plant his seed and grow his root."

"He cannot do what God will not allow."

Gabriel looked back at Michael, her face softening under the understanding. "I cannot bear it, Michael. You know what he was capable of in heaven…"

"I know, Gabriel. But to think Lucifer can accomplish what he sets out to do means that you agree he can do it. Have faith in the men and women here. They, too, have a choice on what will and will not be allowed to influence their life with forces for or against them."

She nodded in understanding. "Then you know where he will go."

"He will return here. Mankind is the seed, the world is the soil, and Lucifer is the weed that will thrive amongst the garden if allowed, Gabriel. Anarchy and chaos he may be, but he will only thrive where he knows there are thorns."

"Adam and Eve are hardly thorns."

"They are roses, Gabriel. And the closer he gets to them, their thorns will pierce his side. He will choose to lie amongst the roses, you know he will."

She shook her head. "That's too hard a victory. It would be better to go for the dandelions beyond this place — there are many tribes beyond these borders."

Michael lowered his head and leveled his eyes at her, "Don't you know?"

"What?"

"That's where the other rebels have gone. That is where their victory lies. But not for Lucifer. Lucifer only wants the roses. You said it yourself, Gabriel. Think of what he was capable of in heaven. Who did he go after to build his army? Who did he lie to in an attempt to win his war?"

Gabriel's face grew pale in the understanding of his meaning.

"The harder the task, the greater the victory."

Gabriel lowered her head and rested her hand on the hilt of her sword. "Victory lies in those who know God and seek his company. You are right, Michael." She looked out at the garden. "He will go after Adam and the lady Eve."

He nodded. "And he will continue what he started in heaven."

Gabriel was horrified. "You think he will bring the Seven here?"

Michael's amber eyes lit afire. "Yes, Gabriel, he will bring the Deadly Seven here."

REMEMBERING RACHEL

Now...

I miss her. Like a dream that has stirred me to awakening and then forgotten, I long for the clarity of the visions that so shook me. I long for the moment when I walked away from a moment in life, a path, that I should have travelled upon — and didn't. But like so many other moments that haunt me, I only ever said the words, Later. Next time. Soon. Before I realized, those were the moments that were not meant for standing still. They were the moments of now, today, never again.

Benjamin was sitting in a helicopter on the way to the airport, not thinking about the artifact resting in his lap, but of a woman who had risen from the dead, only to live again in the confines of his mind.

Rachel.

He closed his eyes and rested his head against the seat inside the chopper. It had been a long time since Benjamin allowed himself to think about her, but she had forced her way back into his life anyway, every time he fell asleep. And he longed for his dreams. He yearned for them, for every time he saw her face, it was filled with light — and she was happy, happier than he had ever known her to be. And he wanted to share in that happiness, for it was infectious, the kind of emotion he had never really known but often felt the rousing of whenever she was near. It was one of the many reasons he had loved her.

And I let her go.

His body flinched as if this private confession of walking away from such a gift were an insult to the gifting of mercy. It felt like a whipping of its own kind knowing that he had what he had always wanted, but chose to let it go, thinking that such a moment, such a person, such a feeling would come again.

And it never did.

The moment he realized he was ready to let the fear go — the fear of fully committing, the fear from allowing himself to have what he truly wanted, the fear of giving his heart to another no matter what the cost — he was too late.

It was her birthday. He had flown to England with a plan. He was going to pour his heart out to her and tell her all the things he always felt but never said. He was going to tell her she was the one — the one who by a single look could bring him to his knees, the one whom he trusted, the one who understood his pain and gave him a glimpse into a life that did not have to be filled with it. And so he called her — almost seven years ago — hoping that his plan would work. Hoping that she was willing to give him a second chance, that she would listen to all the things he had to say, but he never heard from her again.

He had gone to her flat and did not find her there. He had gone to the university and seen her office ripped to shreds by the sudden storm of hail and fire that pulverized a third of the world. And then he got a phone call — her father Jonathan, his boss, was found dead somewhere in Rome. And then another call came through. And then another. And another. His grandfather was dead. His grandmother was dead. One by one, the ones who loved him were gone. Just like that. No good-byes or let-me-tell-you-how-I-feel moments. Simply...*gone.*

And then he got the final call a few days later.

Rachel.

Rachel was dead; her body was found on a beach — and that was it. No second chances. No moment to take that risk you torment yourself about until you finally do it. Nothing. None. End of story. His head began to throb once again.

But then something happened a few weeks ago. He got a second chance. He saw Rachel once again.

But only in my dreams.

He could not wait to get back to his hotel room, the desire for alcohol and sleep consuming all his thoughts — all except the ones of Rachel. Those thoughts were the ones he prized.

"Benjamin, there is something you need to do. It's about the..."

That's how his dreams always began — she was trying to tell him something — always the same thing — but the moment she began to speak the rest of the sentence, he would suddenly wake up, feeling a pressure on his chest — almost as if someone were sitting on it, trying to make it hard for him to breathe. He would wake up, night after night, always at the same moment in his dream. And every time he awoke, he had this gnawing feeling that someone was in the room with him. And not just one person...but two. It was the same kind of feeling he had when he was a child, thinking there was a monster under his bed or staring at him from behind his closet doors. But he was a man now and monsters did not exist unless they were named "man" or "woman" and their purpose was to torture, maim or kill.

He would always try to fall back asleep, not to hear the rest of her sentence, but just to see her one more time. And the more he tried to fall asleep, the less success he had with it, so alcohol became the means to help him slumber. But with a drunken mind comes a sluggish heart, and Rachel did not seem to care much for it. She never seemed to return to him until he had fallen asleep by natural means, but Benjamin drank anyway; he needed to sleep and do things his own way — just like he had always done. This circumstance was no different and he was the type of man who did not like to be told what to do or how to do it — a stubbornness and survival skill that helped his career thrive.

Hearing the sound of the chopper as they soared over the mountains, Benjamin slowly opened his eyes. He thought back to the feeling he had while sitting inside the small room. It was that same feeling he had every time he woke from his dreams — that feeling someone was watching him. He looked down at the wooden box in his lap thinking about what it held inside.

"You are responsible…"

It was just a piece of metal.

"I dare him to stop me…"

A piece of metal that supposedly pierced one man's side.

"Benjamin, there is something you need to do."

A piece of metal that an emperor used to march into battle and was granted a victory that changed the Roman Empire. He closed his eyes to shut out the thoughts once again.

"You must beware of the dragon…"

His grandfather's voice suddenly thundered in his ears. Benjamin's eyes snapped open.

"You all right, Dr. Jacobsen?"

Benjamin looked at the pilot and nodded. "It's been a long week."

"We'll have you back in Jerusalem in no time."

Benjamin tried to breathe in deep but his diaphragm refused to fully expand.

"He will always try to make you fall....when you are footsteps from where your treasure lies, he will try to take it from you. He will try to steal your joy..."

He thought about his grandfather's words and answered back in his own thoughts. *"He already has. And it was no dragon that stole my joy. His name was not El Draco. His name...was God."*

He closed his eyes and tried to sleep.

EVOLUTION

Then...

Lucifer and Gabriel were sitting on a hill that overlooked the Great Waterfall in heaven. Both angels were playing their trumpets completely in sync. When they finished their melodies, Lucifer lowered his instrument from his lips and looked at Gabriel with pride. "You pick things up all too quickly."

"Well, I do have an excellent teacher." She lowered her trumpet. "Thank you...for doing this for me, Lucifer."

"Think nothing of it. You are my favorite angel in all the realms. I would do anything for you, Gabriel. All you need do is call upon me and issue your command."

"Really? You sure you want to offer that to me? The limits of my imagination know no bounds. You, a slave to my commands...what I could do, what I could say."

"You have a command already. I can tell. What is it?"

"Write a song about me."

"That's it? That's your great command? Write a song?" He could not help but laugh in reply, "Do you know how easy that is for me to do?"

"Yet, you've never done it."

She brought the trumpet to her lips.

"All right, Gabriel, if that's what you want." He shook his head in disbelief.

Gabriel began playing her trumpet once again. The light of the Almighty beamed down upon Lucifer. He looked up at it and reveled in its embrace. He breathed in the Father's light. "I shall return soon. Keep playing! I want you to be able to play all seven tunes on your own upon my return."

"Is that a command?"

"I mean it."

"I shall play them better than you. I'll give them a purpose."

Lucifer grinned in amusement and flew toward the kingdom. Gabriel continued practicing her trumpet when debris from the cliff above landed on her head.

"Hey!"

Annoyed, she looked up just as more dust and rock fell on top of her. She coughed and dusted herself off. She stood up and decided to climb the cliff in order to see what was going on.

Just as her head reached the top of the ledge, two angels' fists almost knocked into her face. Gabriel quickly dodged out of the way before she was struck. The fists disappeared from view amongst the sound of grunting from a fierce struggle above. She pulled herself up and looked over the ledge where she saw Beelzebub and Michael wrestling and rolling all over the ground. The moment they rolled away, Gabriel jumped up onto the ledge and ran over to a nearby tree to get a better look at all the action.

A large group of male angels surrounded Beelzebub and Michael. Among them were Uriel, Sariel, Jeremiel, Nero, Azriel, Felix and Gokor. Gabriel slowly crept amongst the trees unseen, while the crowd cheered on their chosen champion. She continued to watch the match as she continued to creep.

"*Ow!*"

She bumped into a solid object. Gabriel looked up and saw Raphael.

"Hello, Gabriel."

"Raphael. I didn't see you standing there."

"That's because you were creeping amongst the trees."

She frowned. "I wanted to see what was going on…what are all of you doing?"

"*Fighting!*"

He pulled her toward the action.

Michael and Beelzebub were in a clinch, pummeling each other, each attempting to gain the better ground. Michael saw his opening. He grabbed the back of Beelzebub's neck and smashed Beelzebub's face down upon his knee. Beelzebub dropped as angels jeered and roared. Before Beelzebub could regain his clarity and focus, Michael was on him, gathering him into a guillotine chokehold that he could not escape.

"*DO YOU YIELD???!!!???*"

Beelzebub, gurgling, tapped out. Michael released him. The angels cheered even louder for the victor, his name a battle cry. The angels surrounded their champion chanting his name, *"MICHAEL! MICHAEL! MICHAEL!"*

Gokor and the other angels congratulated Michael. He turned his attention back towards Beelzebub and extended his hand to help him up. "Good match, my friend."

Beelzebub rubbed his neck and took Michael's hand. "Every time you win…every time."

Michael draped his arm around Beelzebub's shoulder — like an older brother to a younger. They walked toward the crowd.

"You gave me a good run."

Beelzebub attempted a laugh. "No, I didn't. But I will beat you one day."

"No, you won't."

"*WHERE ARE ALL THE FEMALE FIGHTERS?*"

Silence.

All heads turned toward the voice; it was Gabriel's. Hands on her hips, she stood amongst the male angels with her trumpet in her hand. Beelzebub and a few of the other angels chuckled in reply. Michael moved toward her, "Back to your exercises."

The angels moved in unison, pairing off with their sparring partners to begin a series of drills. Gabriel was fascinated by what she saw; their movements captivating her as their strength was amplified through their sport.

"Well, hello, Gabriel."

"Michael."

"How long have you been watching us?"

"Long enough to see there are no females out here."

"I have never seen you at one of our matches before."

"No, but I've heard of them."

He dropped his head and nodded, smiling to himself. "So, Lucifer told you." He looked up at her. "I was surprised to see you weren't there. You two are never far from each other's side."

"I was not prepared to see my friend receive a beating, although at times he does deserve one. That's why I didn't try very hard to sway him against it."

Michael laughed. "Remind me never to cross you, Gabriel."

She moved along the camp watching all the angels practice their drills. "How did you all learn to do this? Where does this knowledge come from? *You?*"

He nodded. "It was what I was created for."

"*Fighting?* No wonder you pray for strength."

"*Defending*, Gabriel. Protecting — the weaker being, the one who cannot fight for himself. Only the strongest and the bravest are fit for this. It's not an easy thing to learn, and it is to be taken very seriously. I believe it will one day serve a greater purpose."

"Hmmm…So where *are* the females, Michael? Or are only *males* the strongest and the bravest?"

"When you say it like that, Gabriel, you make it sound worse than its meaning."

"By whose standard was this criteria designed?"

He coughed nervously. "Do not be angry, Gabriel. Your smile better suits you. Besides, God told me of your marvelous gift."

He motioned toward her trumpet.

"Nice change of subject." She allowed him this opening as she lifted it up to him for examination. "Isn't it the grandest trumpet you've ever seen?"

He nodded in admiration. "It's even more beautiful than Lucifer's. I'm surprised he hasn't tried to swap you."

"He has, but the Father has a deeper meaning behind giving me this that He has yet to reveal."

Michael thought about what she said. "You see deeper than I know, Gabriel." He looked at her trumpet. "You shouldn't carry it around like that."

He jogged over to a spot nearby and picked up a satchel.

"Here. I made this for something and now I know the purpose." He gave it to Gabriel, placing the leather strap over her shoulder and adjusting it against her back.

"Perfect fit."

"Thank you, Michael."

"Come back later and watch another match."

He walked back toward the training camp. She yelled after him, "JUST WATCH?!?"

Michael turned around and grinned at her. Gabriel looked at the camp, taking it all in as quickly as she could — memorizing the moves, the exercises. A determined look came upon her face. She saw Azriel and Asmodeus clumsily attempting to perform the drills, their lack of coordination insulting to the female eye.

"Only the strongest and the bravest...*please.*"

Sariel caught her attention; he was an archer. She watched his movements intently as he took his shot, the arrow landing in the center of the target. Gabriel watched his movements, his stance, his aim. She took in the size of the weapons and the substance from which they were made. Feeling her eyes on him, Sariel lowered his bow and turned toward her. Embarrassed, she smiled nervously and launched into the sky.

∗   ∗   ∗

Lucifer was seated at his monstrous organ, playing a melody he had composed for his Father. And this angel loved his Father more than he could say; only song could speak the words he longed to utter. And as the Angelic Host accompanied him singing *"Holy, Holy, Holy,"* Lucifer's voice rose above the rest and poured forth through all the realms of the kingdom as his body lit afire, singing with everything within him in praise of his Maker.

As Lucifer's song traveled throughout the seven skies, Gabriel heard it echoing forth in the second realm of heaven. She fired an arrow at an old, ivory tree, a perfect shot as it landed in the center of her target. She had gone back to the camp a few days after the match between Michael and

Beelzebub in order to study more of their exercises and drills. Sariel had approached her and offered his bow and a handful of arrows. He showed her the movements; he told her what to do to perfect her technique; and so she practiced alone with no other teacher. Never before had Gabriel felt so much peace. Firing her arrows one after the other, practicing the same exercises as the other angels, over and over again with the various weapons they used, she had never felt so much in her element.

Finding her target once again, Gabriel breathed in the music as she fired arrow after arrow, until they split upon themselves as she continued firing in rapid succession. Her movements were fast and swift as she reached behind her back for more. She had converted the satchel that Michael had given her to hold her trumpet into a quiver for arrows. She was alone in her place of solitude — just the way she liked it. She dreaded the day anyone discovered this place, for she reveled in her privacy. On her last arrow, she fired and lowered her bow closing her eyes, listening to the symphony from the throne.

There was nothing like hearing Lucifer sing, for the lyrics were the voice of his heart, and when one emoted the feeling of the words in complete understanding of their meaning, no other prayer was more powerful when that kind of song was sung — at least, for Gabriel it wasn't.

As she heard his powerful voice rising and falling in harmony with the celestial choir, Gabriel placed her hand over her heart, feeling the need to weep as if the words Lucifer sung were the ones she yearned to speak, for they were her thoughts, her words, her emotions — and yet — they were his. All the same, Gabriel claimed them as her own while Lucifer sang on; her spirit tugging and lifting upon each note she heard, feeling the wave of emotion. There was something in Lucifer's melody that always seemed to leave her feeling spellbound — it was the rhythm, the beat.

This is why he is my friend. He knows. *He loves the Father so.*

As Gabriel stood there breathing in the music, the Wind of the Spirit blew through the trees, circling around her. She opened her eyes as the Wind swirled around her, setting her eyes aglow.

At the bottom of the cliff, Raphael was lying on top of a leviathan, taking in the warmth of God's light and the melody and song as he floated down the River of Christ at the base of the Great Waterfall. The Wind moved from Gabriel and down toward Raphael, swirling all around him. The moment the Wind moved across his face, his eyes lit afire. At the same time, a large glow began to emanate from behind the waterfall. As the light churned brighter and brighter, Raphael slowly sat up; his eyes zeroed in on the glow. Even the leviathan halted in the water and reared its serpentine head toward the light as the sky began to rumble and thunder.

Gabriel heard the thunder and turned toward the edge of the cliff where she could see the glow rising up from beneath her. Her eyes mirrored the fire burning behind the waterfall. This was no ordinary glow, nor was this an ordinary circumstance. All light was born from the Father, but this fire growing within the water was something quite different. This was something…spectacular.

Michael paused in the middle of a fencing match with Beelzebub. He put his hand up to stop Beelzebub from advancing; he tilted his head and listened for the sound he thought he heard.

Another shift.

It was then that he, Uriel, Sariel, Gokor, Beelzebub, Jeremiel and Nero saw the light rising up from the second realm. They stopped their drills and exercises as they looked to the continuous flood of light. Michael's wings jutted forth from his back; he immediately leapt into the sky. Followed by the rest of the angels, they headed toward the throne.

Lucifer stopped singing the moment he saw the light rising up over the hills. He slowly stood as he and the rest of the other angels looked to the glow.

The thunder continued to roar across the seven realms of heaven. Back in the second realm, the rumbling was loudest. Gabriel covered her ears as the sound cracked and rolled across the sky. That was when the lightning hit the waterfall. The moment it struck down, the leviathan plunged into the river out of sheer terror, taking Raphael with him. Raphael rapidly swam to the surface as the lightning continued to snap at the center of the waterfall.

Gabriel was on her knees, watching the lightning electrify what lay behind it, almost as if the lightning itself were the energy needed to bring forth whatever lay beyond.

Raphael could barely see as the glare from the fire and lightning collided against one another, hurting his eyes more than the fire glowing within them. The Wind of the Spirit whipped past him and dove directly into the cave behind the waterfall.

A great roar of lions answered the Wind from within the cave. Its ferocious call rolled across the realm. Michael and the angels faltered in the sky at the sound of the unknown cry. Lucifer and the angelic host flinched at the roar of the unknown creature, while Gabriel and Raphael continued to watch from a distance.

With one final blast of lightning, four massive beasts burst forth from behind the waterfall. The moment she saw their gigantic form, Gabriel backed away from the edge of the cliff, falling backward onto her hands as the first beast emerged. Raphael swam backward as fast as he could until he saw the beast rise above him and into the celestial sky.

The beast's body was that of a lion; on it were wings of an eagle. The second beast followed and resembled a gigantic bear. It, too, had wings of an eagle. The third beast was in the form of a leopard, and on its back were four wings like those of a raven. It had four heads; all of which were cat-like, bearing the heads of a panther, a tiger, a lynx and a cheetah. The fourth beast — the most terrifying, frightening, and powerful of them all — emerged from the waterfall. Its body was pure scarlet. Its mouth was filled with large iron teeth; ten horns protruded from his head and down its spine. As Raphael watched them fly overhead, he took in their massive frames. They were five times the height of the tallest angel. Michael himself was the tallest, reaching ten feet tall.

All four beasts soared across the realms and on toward the kingdom. Gabriel and Raphael simultaneously launched into the sky directly behind them, flying side by side in utter silence, for there were no words they knew of that could describe the scene before them.

Gabriel could not even think as she followed the four beasts. Taking in their wing span and the force which each of their wings exuded, she found she was having a hard time flying behind them, pushed back by the strength of their force. Even Raphael flapped harder, making both angels even more determined to follow the beasts to their ultimate destination.

Raphael shouted to Gabriel, "They're headed toward the throne!"

They flew faster.

Lucifer stared wide-eyed up at the sky as he saw the four unknown creatures heading straight for them. The angels clustered together in both terror and awe. As the beasts approached the throne, they roared loudly announcing to God their arrival, causing the steps of the kingdom to thunder and quake underneath Lucifer and the rest of the host. Michael dropped down from the sky and landed next to Lucifer.

All the angels followed Michael's lead and gripped their weapons tight. Michael whispered to Lucifer, "Are they what I think they are?"

As if they heard the mighty angel's question, the beasts roared in reply. Lucifer watched them fly overhead, taking in each of the beasts' forms.

His voice was low, "Yes. The Ancients. We are witness to a myth that gives birth to truth. Why they have been awakened to emerge this day and for what purpose has never been foretold, Michael. I don't know if this is something good."

"From the look on your face, I can tell you don't think it is."

The beasts slammed down on the top step of the throne; lightning exploded behind them upon their landing. The beasts faced God and knelt on all fours, their heads bowed low. The thunder of God answered the beasts in reply. Michael, Lucifer and the other angels were utterly speechless as they took in the sight before them.

A look passed between Michael and Lucifer. "It looks like God was expecting them." He put his sword back into his sheath. Beelzebub and Nero were hesitant to do the same, but the moment Michael nodded for them to follow, they reluctantly did. Gabriel and Raphael finally arrived, landing silently behind Lucifer. Vitor moved toward Raphael.

"Vitor, what are they?"

"Another myth made real, my friend. I believe they are the Ancients."

Raphael stared at Vitor, unsure of what this could possibly mean. "I don't remember this myth. Who are they and what are they supposed to do? Eat us?"

Vitor turned his emerald eyes to his friend with a look of annoyance, "You need to pay attention better. The Ancients are creatures of old."

"Figured that. Just wondering what they were created for. From the size of them and the number of heads, I'm thinking they did some pretty serious damage once and could easily do it again."

Raphael waited for Vitor's answer.

"Well?"

Vitor blushed in embarrassment. "I don't remember either."

Raphael bit his bottom lip in nervousness as he took in the scarlet beast's iron teeth. "Yep. He's gonna eat us."

The beasts rose up and stood at their full height and turned to face the angelic host, roaring even louder. Gabriel grabbed hold of Lucifer's hand. They both held each other's hands tight. "The Ancients. What does this mean, Lucifer?"

Raphael heard Gabriel's question. "Quick, Vitor, Lucifer has the answer." They moved closer to hear his reply.

Lucifer took in the size of the beasts, "We shall soon be enlightened, my love."

Raphael lowered his head and shook it in disappointment. He nudged Vitor, whispering to him words of comfort, "Well, now we don't have to feel bad. If Lucifer doesn't know, none of us would."

None of the angels dared move as the beasts stood before them. An eerie silence followed as the beasts stood immobile. It was then that Michael saw the beasts' gaze shift in unison — and their eyes zoomed in on Lucifer. Michael's eyes grew wide as the Wind suddenly exploded from God's light and dove straight into Lucifer's chest. He gasped at the force of the impact.

Gabriel's hand was ripped from Lucifer's as he was immediately pulled into the air. Gabriel was knocked backward and onto the ground. Michael moved and immediately reached down to help her up, but she could not move as she stared up above, *"Lucifer..."*

Michael followed her gaze as Lucifer's body was pulled toward God's light on the Wind of the Spirit. His wings expanded the closer he got to the light, but his movements were not his own; he was at the mercy of the Wind. His body turned to face the Host; his eyes were lit afire in white flames. Lucifer opened his mouth to speak, and out poured the message from their Creator, "*ANGELS!* I HAVE SUMMONED THE FOUR BEASTS TO MY KINGDOM THAT YOU MAY BEAR WITNESS TO MY CREATION — TO THE THINGS THAT ARE SEEN AND TO THE THINGS THAT ARE UNSEEN. I LOVE ALL OF YOU, DEEPER AND MORE INTIMATELY THAN YOU COULD EVER

KNOW. I CAN COUNT THE FEATHERS ON YOUR WINGS AND THE QUESTIONS OF YOUR HEARTS. ALL OF YOU HAVE BEEN ASKING THE SAME QUESTIONS, SILENT ABOUT THEM IN YOUR PRAYERS, ASKING FOR THE ANSWERS. AND THE QUESTIONS… *WHY?*"

The angels were motionless.

"WHY WERE WE CREATED? WHY AM I HERE? WHAT IS MY PURPOSE?"

Gabriel's eyes filled with tears. Michael gripped the hilt of his sword in his sheath, while Vitor bowed his head.

"I CREATED THE BEAUTY OF THE HEAVENS THAT YOU, MY CHILDREN, WOULD BE ABLE TO RUN FREE, LOVE OPENLY, AND ENJOY THE FRUITS OF ALL I HAVE TO GIVE. I LOVED YOU BEFORE I CREATED YOU AND I CREATED YOU BECAUSE I WANTED YOU. YOU WERE MADE IN MY LIKENESS AND IMAGE, WITH VARYING GIFTS THAT IN ALL YOUR LIKENESS, MAKE YOU EACH UNIQUE. I HAVE WATCHED OVER YOU TO SEE HOW YOU HAVE USED YOUR GIFTS UPON DISCOVERY, HOW YOU HAVE MOLDED THEM. I HAVE WAITED A LONG WHILE FOR THIS RITE OF INITIATION. YOU HAVE BEEN GIVEN FREE WILL HERE IN HEAVEN. I AM PLEASED BY YOUR CHOICES AS I LIFT YOU UP TO THE HIGHER PURPOSE I CREATED YOU FOR: MY CELESTIAL HIERARCHY."

Upon these words, the beasts roared and reared on their hind legs. Lucifer, still prophesying, was illuminated by the light of God that filled him.

A bolt of lightning shot out from the center of the throne and struck Lucifer in the middle of his chest. His entire body caught fire but he did not burn. The color of the flames turned a shade of blue. He gasped as he arched his back —and four more wings emerged.

The First Beast branded him, *"Seraphim."*

The angels stared in awe as Lucifer's body was transformed before their very eyes. Before any of them could breathe or speak a single word, a huge burst of lightning exploded from Lucifer's chest and struck down upon thousands of angels including Michael, Gabriel, Raphael, Uriel, Raguel, Sariel and Jeremiel. All of them were lifted up at once, powerless to the force that bound them. Their heads were raised as one toward God, their arms were outstretched as if waiting to be filled with the fire and light that rained down from up above; their bodies slowly began to spin as the Wind moved all around them. As they turned, their wings were split and divided, until their two wings became six.

Beelzebub, Nero, Vitor and Gokor watched in awe as the newly formed seraphim slowed their spinning as their bodies continued to hover in the air above them. And all at once, just like Lucifer's moments ago, their bodies were consumed in blue flame. As one body of angels, the seraphim were pulled closer to God's light. And the closer they got, the other angels in the host watched as the seraphim's two top wings covered their faces, their middle wings flapped as they fly, and their two bottom wings covered their feet.

Vitor was overcome as he whispered to himself, "So close to God are they, they burn the hottest."

Another burst of lightning struck down from God and onto thousands more angels including Gokor, Beelzebub and Lilith — another female angel; their bodies were lit afire in orange flames. They, too, were lifted into the air, their arms raised to the Father, but instead of lining up alongside the seraphim, they were placed behind the first group.

The Second Beast heralded them, *"Cherubim."*

The Wind knocked a multitude of angels down to the ground, rolling their bodies over, lighting them afire. Their bodies wrapped around themselves until they took the form of a wheel of fire, continually turning upon themselves as they burned the color of brimstone. The angels rolled onto the steps of the kingdom, past the four beasts, lining up side by side — a burning wall guarding the holy throne of God.

The Third Beast roared, *"Thrones."*

Lightning struck even more angels in the host who had been standing with their heads bowed, hands in the form of prayer, dressed in robes of white. Their robes turned from ivory to black. These angels lifted their heads in unison; their faces were stoic. Simultaneously struck were the other angels, whose heads of hair were changed into that of pure silver; their eyes blackened and shiny — like that of pure onyx.

The Fourth Beast growled, *"Dominions and Principalities."*

More angels were struck by lightning, and as they rose from the ground, they stretched out their arms and hands in front of their bodies. Lightning answered their gesture as thunderbolts erupted from their hands.

The Fourth Beast pounded his paw, *"Powers."*

Next were the angels gathered around the Tree of Life in the courtyard. Lightning struck down on them separately. Upon impact, each of the angels transformed into different creatures: behemoths, hayoths, cockerels, and then back again. They had now become shape-shifters.

The Second Beast almost sighed as he said, *"Virtues."*

Lightning struck down upon all remaining angels in heaven. The moment they were hit, breastplates of gold adorned their chests.

The First Beast spoke, *"Angels — the guardians."*

The four beasts roared in unison at the work of the Father. And God himself looked at the angels and saw that it was good. In reply, the choir of angels sang in praise to the Father with everything they had to give. And if the beasts thought they were the loudest sound heaven had ever heard, they changed their minds the moment they heard the angels sing. The beasts bowed low to the ground once again. One seraph, the one hovering closest to God, rose above the rest. He turned away from the light and his wings unfolded — it was Lucifer. The Wind continued to blow all around him until a single flame of fire etched a symbol in the middle of Lucifer's armor; it was a pentagram.

Lucifer's eyes were still lit afire in white flames as he spoke to the Host, "MY KNOWLEDGE WILL COME TO ALL OF YOU — ITS ORIGIN BEGINNING WITH LUCIFER AND CONTINUING DOWN THROUGH THE HIERARCHY AT THE DAWN OF EACH NEW DAY."

The four beasts answered in unison without lifting their massive heads, *"Morning Star."*

"LISTEN TO HIM, FOR HIS WORDS FOR YOU ARE MY WORDS TO YOU. THAT YOU MAY FEAR NOTHING; THAT YOU LOVE ONE ANOTHER MORE STRONGLY; AND THAT YOU FIND AND FULFILL THE PURPOSE OF YOUR MAKING IN ACCORDANCE WITH MY WILL."

The Enlightened One.

The Wind left Lucifer and flowed out onto the Host. Each angel was knocked to the ground as the Spirit passed over them, while the four beasts continued to roar amidst the symphony and song. And it was on this day, the celestial hierarchy was thus created by the hand of the Almighty God.

THE ANSWER

Now...

Gabriel opened her eyes, pushing her body off of the rock wall, continuing her descent as Lucifer sang his song. The moment she came into view, the sound of his voice slowly faded. He watched in silence as she descended, until the only thing that separated them was the portal's boundary dividing Heaven and Hell. Gabriel took in Lucifer's spent form as he lay drenched and exhausted. He was draped over a large rock that barely rested on the edge of the cliff's ledge, clinging to it. The water poured over him, threatening to force his grip loose.

"I didn't think you'd come." His voice was hoarse. He closed his eyes and breathed forth the words as if the very act were an effort in and of itself.

"You knew I'd come. So long as there was a boundary between us, you knew I would." She watched him swallow, clearly seeing that it hurt him severely to do so. "I haven't heard that song in a long time. I didn't know you still remembered it."

"It was the last song I ever sang. It was also the last one I ever heard you play."

Her eyes narrowed at his response. "How would you know?"

He swallowed hard once again, feeling the rawness of his vocal chords. "I come here sometimes." His tired eyes roamed up along the rock walls of the cave. "And I can hear the Host singing from time to time when the river grows quiet. You'd be surprised at the sounds this cave carries." He met her eyes.

"What do you want?"

"I think you know. It was you who reminded me of its existence the last time you were here. It never occurred to me that when I gave it to you, that what I was handing over was the key to my prison door. All I want to know is if you have it still."

She searched his eyes, reading them for any hint or clue. "What does it matter?"

Lucifer closed his eyes and breathed in deeply finding the strength to speak once again. "Because I don't want to waste my time searching for it in Hell if it is still in Heaven."

"Or, you mean if I hid it somewhere on the earth — like...my...trumpet."

He opened his eyes and met her stare. She smiled challengingly. "And there it is. I can see the wheels in your head turning, trying to figure out what is the truth and what it possibly means if it were buried in either realm."

"I didn't ask you to tell me the meaning, Gabriel. I only asked if you still had it."

She paused. "No, I don't." She could see the slightest tightening of his knuckles around the rock.

"But you know where it is."

"Didn't the Witch of Endor tell you?"

Lucifer was taken off guard by her question and the knowledge to which she commanded. "You first."

They continued to hold each other's stare. She knew that he was tired, for she could only imagine the kind of energy it took for him to carry off the illusion of his former angelic self. Looking at him as he clasped onto the ledge, she knew he was utterly exhausted.

"I guess neither of us will get the answer we want." She turned and began her climb back to heaven.

"Gabriel, wait!"

She stopped and turned her head. Lucifer lowered his head against the rock breathing in long and deep as he struggled with the decision he was about to make. When he lifted his weary head, his eyes were filled with tears. "I don't want to be chained, Gabriel." His voice was barely a whisper; the look on his face was one mixed with pleading and dread. Gabriel slowly climbed off the rock and turned back toward Lucifer. She crouched down in front of the portal.

"Tell me."

He swallowed hard once again. "I conjured the witch. I asked her to repeat the Prophecy of the Darkest Night when the Son of Man returns."

Gabriel did not move but waited for him to continue. Lucifer could still see the witch's face rising up from the murky pool filled with blood. He could still see the worms wriggling all around her head, surrounding her like a crown.

"She said…I would be forever bound to hell — chained to the Lake of Fire to burn for a thousand years." He dropped his head against the rock, gripping it even tighter. *"I've* been *chained, Gabriel!"* He lifted his head so that his eyes met hers. *"I've* been *punished!"* He swallowed once again; it was painful for Gabriel to watch as he tried to find his voice.

It was then that Gabriel understood. "Adamantine." Lucifer remained silent. "You will be bound by adamantine chains."

His eyes bored into hers. "Tell me where it is. *Please.*"

She stood and looked down at the prince of hell holding onto the rock with the last of his strength. She turned and started her climb back up to heaven.

"GABRIEL!!!" His voice was completely hoarse.

She stopped but did not turn her head. "It's not on the earth."

Lucifer closed his eyes and breathed in deeply; he had his answer. Gabriel climbed back up the cave while Lucifer released his hold on the rocks and let the river's tide carry him back into hell.

Not so long ago...

Gabriel had watched the earth for years, waiting for the moment when the fallen angels would return from their quest around the world and back into the garden. Michael had told her they would return the moment she stopped looking, and for all she knew, the irony of such a thought was probably true. But she couldn't help it. It was a moment she hated for she knew it meant nothing good. And so, she continued to wait.

And as she did, even she had ventured across the earth at one point, taking in all the changes that continued to shape this world — for she noticed the changes each and every day. Nature itself was a mystery to her, for it had a way of surviving the harshest of elements and somehow ended up creating something new all on its own. Only the weakest of creatures and insects and foliage seemed to perish over time — even to the point of extinction.

And as much as she despised Lucifer, she wondered what he thought about the world. She wondered what he thought about the different landscapes, the various races of mankind, and the creation that the men and women of the earth found to survive in a world such as this. For Gabriel, she knew that as much as he would choose to hate it, he would begrudgingly respect it. She knew that he would never be able to fathom the slightest changes over time that this world evolved from, nor the massive changes that occurred all at once without any link to connect the measurement of change in so rapid a pace. She knew he would be able to see the intelligence in the design. How could any angel or being not ponder and wonder at it? How could they not see?

So many questions and thoughts surrounded each change as Gabriel bore witness to the forces of nature.

God, how did you do this?

Even as she soared over territories with forms of earlier man yet to experience the dawn of consciousness, Gabriel continued to marvel at the instinct of each creature to survive. Fossils and bones and markings were the remnants of former days and former eras that Gabriel hoped God would allow her to one day see. What was the earth like before this moment? What existed here before this particular day? And she knew if she was thinking about all these things, so was Lucifer.

Waiting on the earth, Gabriel recognized that the angels could be seen when God allowed them to be. And it was always when there was a message to be taken from heaven or to heaven. God had created portals for the angels to pass through, but He also bent time and space, merging the dimensions for them to pass instantly as they moved across time. He had also created a stairway to heaven. So many ways in, so many doors and passageways — she wondered when mankind would find the way.

"The hour has not yet come."

The hour did not matter so much to Gabriel as whether or not the fallen angels would find the doors. She hated the day they would find the keys. But Gabriel had a feeling the doors were not so much on the mind's of her fallen brethren as much as what the world had to offer — a lesser paradise, but a paradise all the same — and Eden was the cause.

Had he tried to engage? Had he found a means to do it?

Even if he had, Gabriel knew the answer was exactly as Michael predicted, *"Only if God allows it."*

And that was the greatest marvel of all. What would God allow and why would he allow it for some and not for others? But then, all Gabriel had to do was think of what happened before the War in Heaven, and the same questions could have been asked then. The only difference was that there were no angels for the angels; only free will to choose. That is what made Gabriel pause the most, for angels not only had free will — they could reason. And as Gabriel scoured the earth, she knew this one thing: only Adam and Eve could reason. Only Adam and Eve understood choice. Only Adam and Eve were the freest of all, for they held dominion over their environment and existed equally as partners, side by side in the garden. Even as God engaged with the world and with mankind, they were still free just as the angels were. And only Adam and Eve had the spiritual intellect to know God was there, for He spoke directly to them — and *only* them.

They are the beginning of God's perfect design.

Some might think there was slavery in an ever-watchful father, but God never truly interfered to impose His will, for God understood that no one wanted forced acceptance or imposition — not even the angels. And even with that thought, there were times when she wished God would intervene, for He allowed many things she wished had been stopped long before they became what they were, for Gabriel knew He would allow so much more. But although she did not know the reasons for which He did and did not do something, she trusted her Father. He was her protector, and now she was to be a protector of his other children. And as she watched Adam and Eve, she wondered if mankind would have the privilege of knowing and understanding the Father's will. Or would the reasons be hidden from them in order for them to trust and depend on the Father without that knowledge? And even if it were each other's choices that shifted their world and environment in the attempt to impose one's own will over the other, would these men and women hold each other accountable? Would they trust one another?

Even in heaven, the angels held each other accountable, and she hoped that it would be the same for mankind. But seeing the nature of this world, and the tribes of men and women outside of the garden, she knew that this same nature was in the heart of men — a fight to survive. And for some, Gabriel had seen: by any means necessary. Having just thought that last thought, she paused in the revelation. *That is what Lucifer will do: whatever he needs to by any means necessary.*

A cold chill ran down her spine.

It was hard to know what was meant for this world and the people in it, for the earth was so young and this destiny was new to all of them, but Gabriel could see that life here would be hard enough; to live in the world that thrived on survival would definitely be hard enough; to live in a world where each man's choice affected another man's outcome — even without the fallen angels to add to the order and disorder of the world would be hard to bear.

That was why she waited for the fallen angels to emerge. She did not want them in this world. She did not want them near mankind. And with that thought, God had revealed her purpose: to intervene when God felt it necessary to shift the order of the world onto a different plane, a path, a herald, so to speak.

"You will be my messenger."

Clutching her trumpet to her chest as she waited, she felt like a sleeping lioness, waiting for the moment the first herald would bring. Gabriel hoped it would be a warning to Adam and Eve that fallen angels were in their midst and meant to separate them from God. Whether or not that meant their destruction, Gabriel did not know, for she still did not understand the nature of this world and how an angel was to reside within it. And she knew if that were true for her, it was also true for Lucifer.

The Tree of Life began to sway and Gabriel knew it would soon dip and the portal would open. Her watch over the garden was over, for God had granted her the time she asked for to wait upon the earth. And with a heavy heart, Gabriel moved toward the tree as the branches dipped and swayed, twisting within the trunk until the portal opened, and the archangel stepped through. The trunk twisted again and, upon the branches' final sway, the doorway to heaven closed.

From the shadows in the trees, Beelzebub and the rest of the fallen angels emerged and stepped into the garden.

ARMY OF GOD

Now...

Benjamin awoke screaming in fear as the vision of his dreams drove him to terror; it was a nightmare. Drenched in sweat, heart pounding ferociously in his chest, he thought it would burst as it thumped rapidly against his ribcage.

Breathe, Benjamin.

He breathed in deeply but could barely get any air to fill his lungs. He sat up and turned on the light in his hotel room, attempting to calm his mind.

Breathe.

He was in the back seat of his parents' car strapped into his car seat. His mom and dad had just picked him up from his grandparents' house; they were on their way home. He couldn't wait to get there; his mom had promised to order pizza for dinner and watch his favorite animated DVD.

Benjamin never remembered the crash. He never saw the car that sped through the red light as his father was making a left-hand turn at the yield. All he remembered was the sound. That awful crunching sound that followed his mother's gasp — and then all went silent. For ten days, while little Benjamin was in a coma, all he dreamt about were the sounds and the headlights; they glowed like the eyes of the dragon. When he finally awoke and found himself in a room called ICU, the nightmares continued. Night after night, he saw the glowing eyes and heard the crunch of metal — over and over again — devouring the lives of his mom and dad as it destroyed them — just as his grandpa said the dragon would do. It was that same sound that thundered in his ears now, haunting him, taunting him — his only memories of the crash.

He alone had survived. He had not had that dream in years, but every time he did, it shook Benjamin to the core.

Breathe, Benjamin.

He could still hear his mother gasp.

Breathe.

Benjamin looked at the time: 4:30 a.m. He needed to talk to someone, but it was too early to make a call. But even if it were later, there was no one worth the effort. He thought about jumping on the internet to check emails, read the headlines or log into one of his five social media accounts, but even that was only a distraction to kill time — and it never filled his void.

The ones he wanted to call would prefer a text.

The ones who would listen were dead.

The one who would console him was gone.

The ones whom he worked for, he had no connection.

And so the thoughts in his head, he shared with no one.

Benjamin sat back against his bed, resting his head against the hard wood feeling the loss, the loneliness, the hole in his heart that continued to hammer within. And although his heart fought to feel alive — even if it was through the memory of a nightmare made true — Benjamin closed his eyes in exhaustion wishing he felt the desire to live again too.

Rachel…

His heart ached just to see her face. But as he closed his eyes, the only sound he heard was the crash; the only memory he saw was the eyes of the metal beast — his dragon.

El Draco.

He grabbed for his laptop and fired it up. He jumped onto the internet and Googled the legend of George and the Dragon. Why he did so, he could not tell. All he knew was at that moment, he wanted to read the story once again. It was one of his favorites growing up, along with the ones his grandfather told him. Reading the tale of a man slaying a dragon from the inferno was one Benjamin never tired of, for who ever tires of being a hero?

Too bad it isn't real.

Real or not, Benjamin read on — and somehow, it brought him comfort. And it was not long before Benjamin's eyes grew weary, and he finally fell asleep dreaming of dragons, a hero and a maiden.

Then…

The scarlet beast hid in the shadow of a cave in the fourth realm of heaven. All that could be seen was the reflection of his yellow eyes as they peered out from the darkness and onto the field ahead. Grazing in the field beyond were gigantic horses of heaven — bodies of varying colors, eyes glowing fiery red, feet of lions, breath of fire.

A beautiful black stallion looked up and stared at the cave ahead. He growled menacingly; fire breathed forth from his nose as his adrenalin pumped faster, having sensed the presence of another beast unlike his own kind. The other horses heard his growl and raised their heads in reply. The black horse walked slowly toward the front of the herd. All was silent. Suddenly, the scarlet beast burst forth from the cave and charged toward the herd. The black horse reared up on its hind legs before turning to race with the rest of the herd across the field and over the hills.

As the herd rushed toward a group of boulders, angels could be seen crouched down amongst them. Michael, Raphael, Gabriel, Beelzebub, Gokor, Vitor, Uriel, Raguel, Sariel and Jeremiel were there bearing chains in their hands.

Raphael turned to Vitor, "I have to hand it to you, Vitor. I had no idea these creatures existed."

Vitor kept his eyes on the horses, studying them. "They didn't. They're new."

Raphael did a double take.

Vitor turned his emerald eyes to Raphael. "I told you. He is always creating."

Michael swung his chain like a lasso overhead. *"GET READY!"*

All the angels swung their chains as the herd came upon them. Michael launched his chain, lassoing it around the neck of the black horse; Beelzebub's around the gray horse, and Gabriel's around the jasper horse. All the other angels captured their stallions and mounted them, riding them in exhilaration as they raced across the fields. Fire appeared under their hooves as they blazed across heaven's grounds.

Gokor cried out, "I never knew staying on the ground could be as awesome as flying!"

Sariel was laughing, "We're like a band of soldiers."

Jeremiel threw his hands out at his sides, "Cavalry!"

Beelzebub rode beside Michael, "Michael! Perhaps, we should form an army!"

"To be an army, we would have to be defending something!"

Gokor rode up to them, "Then we defend the kingdom. Protect it!"

Michael was grinning, "From what?!?"

Beelzebub nodded toward Gabriel, "Female angels who try to invade our training ground!"

They burst out laughing.

Gabriel was not amused. "Ha. Ha."

Michael decided, "We shall take the matter to God!"

Raphael raced ahead of the group. "Last one to the kingdom is a guardian angel!"

They raced on, but Gabriel alone veered away from the group and cut toward the mountains. Michael saw her ride off.

Beelzebub's eyes narrowed as he followed Michael's gaze, "Funny girl, that Gabriel."

They rode on.

*　　*　　*

Lucifer was playing his organ, conducting the Host as they played their glorious music. A vibrant, elegant robe was draped across his shoulders like a king. He was interrupted by the commotion of angels running and flying out of the way of the approaching stampede. Michael jumped down from his horse. "How did you get here so fast?"

Behind Lucifer, Gabriel was watering her horse near the river's base near the throne. "I asked God to move mountains for me."

Lucifer laughed.

Michael looked at her amused. "I'm going to have to remember that one."

Beelzebub arrived with the rest of the herd and slid off his horse, bewildered, "How did you get here so fast?"

Gabriel rolled her eyes. Lucifer turned toward the angels. "So you wish to form an army."

The group waited for Michael to confirm Lucifer's statement. "Well, we

132

were thinking about it. We thought we would ask God if it fell in line with His will for us."

"And you think an army is necessary."

Gokor grinned, "No, we just think it would be fun!"

Thunder roared from the throne. The angels smiled hearing God's answer.; they erupted in cheer, *"Halleluiah!!!"*

Lucifer winced at their amplified shout. "I take it Michael will be your commander."

Raphael smacked Michael on the back. "Of course it will be Michael! Who else could lead an army of such brazen angels!"

Michael stood there, his massive arms folded across his chest.

"And *I* shall be Michael's second-in-command."

The angels stared at Beelzebub. They erupted in protest. The horses reared at their cries.

Lucifer stepped inside their circle. "Brothers! I have an idea. Let us hold a tournament. Whoever wishes to be in the army as well as Michael's second will have to prove himself worthy of the honor. They will have to fight for it."

Gabriel lifted her head.

Uriel's violet eyes glowed. He nodded his consent. "Then, let us prepare!"

Raphael lifted his sword into the sky, "To the training camp!"

The angels saluted Michael and mounted their horses in excitement. Michael turned toward Lucifer and Gabriel to take his leave. "Are you going to enter the tournament, Lucifer?"

Lucifer laughed. "No, Michael. I prefer to be God's second-in-command. I shall leave the fighting to you, our most capable angel."

Michael nodded and looked to Gabriel. "Well done today, Gabriel. He is a beautiful beast."

Gabriel stroked her horse's head. "I think I shall name him Bel Aarik."

Michael grinned. "A warrior's name." Michael mounted his beast and rode out with the rest of the angels. Lucifer was studying Gabriel.

"Why so silent, my love?"

Gabriel did not answer.

"Are you going to share with me the secret stirring deep within your heart? I can tell you have one."

"I'm going to enter the tournament."

Lucifer stopped playing his music. "Come now, beloved, you can't be serious."

"I am serious. There is no reason for me to jest."

"Yes, there is. You cannot fight. And a trumpet fashioned for you couldn't help you do otherwise — even if it is from our Father."

Gabriel's face was one of stone. "Whether or not I decide to enter the tournament is no concern of yours." She moved past him.

Lucifer rose from his seat. He placed his hands on her shoulders to stop her, "Peace, Gabriel."

She looked him dead in the eye. "You don't think I can do it, do you?"

"Since when do you wish to master weapons and grapple with male angels?"

Gabriel said nothing.

"Oh, yes, now I see. *Another* secret you've kept from me." He dropped his arms and turned back to his seat.

Gabriel shook her head, "You don't get it, do you? You think you are the only one who thinks you have a right to be heralded as special and something unique."

Lucifer's eyes narrowed at the fierceness of her words.

"We *all* want that, Lucifer. We *all* think that. Ever since you have been branded our chief, you have forgotten that there lies within each of us the desire and yearning to be something more. Some of us may be branded and singled out for something great just as you, but most of us have to find it on our own. And what I don't need is your judgment because you do not see the vision of my dream."

"I thought your dream was to sing for God. Why else would He give you a trumpet!"

"Yes, that was my dream, but now I'm dreaming another one! And after that, another one! Dreams are not meant to be singular, Lucifer, that is what you don't understand. It's in my design! God is *in* me! He is always doing something more, and I feel that same essence within me, that stirring of God's creativity just waiting to burst forth inside me from moment to moment to keep becoming something more — and God willing, something better!"

"I highly doubt, Gabriel, that God wants you to fight in the army."

"You don't know that!"

"I'll tell you what I do know: if you enter that tournament, you will get hurt. You will fail, Gabriel. And that I cannot bear. I forbid you from entering."

"Forbid?"

He ignored her tone. "As your friend, I will not allow you to do this. As your *chief*, I command that you not."

They stared at one another in silence for a long time. "I see. Well, then, as my *chief*, you know that your job is to relay not command. Good for me." She mounted her horse.

"Gabriel..."

"Just because you failed in your attempt to test your limits when you fought Michael, does not mean that I shall fail in mine! Out of my way!"

He did not move.

"MOVE!" Gabriel rode past him, mere inches from running him over.

"GABRIEL!!!"

Lucifer's eyes lit afire; his six opaque wings jutted forth. He was about to launch into the sky after her when he stopped himself. He gritted his teeth in anger, attempting to laugh it off; he lowered his wings. "Such a fool, Gabriel."

He looked toward the path she was traveling and watched her raven hair flying wildly in the distance. "It's in your design…" Lucifer looked up at the beauty of heaven. "Always doing something more." His smile slowly faded. He looked back at the throne. "Always doing something more…"

It was then that he remembered the conversation Vitor had with Raphael not so long ago. He thought about the beasts and now the horses. Even in heaven, there was something more emerging — something new.

"God is constantly expanding, always creating. I haven't seen anything new in quite some time. So I ask myself, What if He was doing it elsewhere? What if He has expanded and created a domain we have yet to see by using his energy someplace different? What would this realm be like and what would God have created there?"

Several moments passed before Lucifer realized he wasn't even breathing. *He shifted the design all at once. What if…*

He turned toward God's throne ready to ask his Father the very same questions, but then stopped himself. *No, I'm chief seraph. If there were something God had in the making, He would first share it with me.*

He shook off the nagging feeling of doom that had crept into the center of his chest, feeling the knot in his stomach once again. *Shake it off. God would not create a lesser being in another domain. It would be beneath Him.* Lucifer breathed in long and deep and headed toward his instrument to compose another song.

*   *   *

The combat arena resided in a valley surrounded by colossal white mountains in the third realm of heaven. Legions of angels from all eight divisions had come to take part in the tournament that determined the elite soldiers worthy enough to be in heaven's army. On the field below, hundreds of angels collected behind a post awaiting their turn to enter the arena.

The tournament had gone on for most of the day, the majority of the soldiers had been chosen. All that remained were the challenges to the post for second-in-command.

A large tent of purple and red overlooked the arena from one of the hilltops. Lucifer, robed in the same color purple, was seated on a grand throne fit for a king as he resided over the events of the day. Two female angels fanned him with long branches, while others stood at attention awaiting Lucifer's commands. The Seraphs — Nicodemus and Cornelius — along with two other cherubs — Romulus and Lilith — occupied the tent. They watched as Gokor and Beelzebub fought one another in the center of the arena down below.

Romulus, a bald-headed angel leaned over the railing, "This day has proved to be most exciting. With the army now formed, I'm anxious to see who Michael's second-in-command will be. What an honor to command God's massive army."

Lucifer listened with disinterest. His eyes scanned the crowd for Gabriel. He spotted her down below arguing with a Throne named Felix; he was blocking her entrance into the tournament.

Lilith added her two cents, "I think Beelzebub more capable than Gokor."

Nicodemus turned to Lucifer, "I think it brilliant of Michael to make all the angels challenge him for the post. He's defeated all the angels within half a breath — all except those two. They at least lasted an exhale."

Cornelius chimed in, "They both gave him a good run of equal intensity. It's good of Michael to have them fight it out with each other for the spot.

I, myself, would be unable to decide."

Lilith replied with, "They are equal if you ask me. He should name both as his seconds."

Romulus scoffed, "You cannot have *two* seconds-in-command, Lilith. It defeats the purpose."

Cornelius eyed Lucifer, "Who do you think should be chosen, Lucifer?"

Lucifer was still watching Gabriel argue with Felix down below. "I don't think either of them are worthy of it."

Several angels laughed in astonishment.

"And who do you think is worthy of it, if not those two? Surely not Vitor. Raphael perhaps, but he has not challenged Michael for the post."

"Perhaps there is a dark horse in the tournament we have yet to know."

Lilith cried out, "But this is the last fight!"

Nicodemus looked around at the other angels in disbelief, "Surely, you jest, Lucifer. Unless *you* are the dark horse?"

"Of course not. I already lead all of heaven. Besides, I am not fond of fighting with swords. Words are more my forte."

Romulus moved away from the railing. "Who then? I'm quite curious to know the name of your dark horse."

Without answering, Lucifer rose from his throne and exited, leaving the other angels in bewilderment. Lucifer swooped down to the gate leading onto the field. Gabriel and Felix stopped arguing upon his approach. Felix bowed to Lucifer.

"Well! You two have been arguing the entire length of the tournament. What is the subject of so intense conversation?"

No one answered.

"Well?"

Gabriel refused to look at him. "Felix won't let me enter the tournament!"

Lucifer looked steadily at Gabriel.

Felix answered regretfully. "Lucifer, Michael gave me strict orders to only allow the strongest angels through to protect them against any unnecessary injury." He turned to Gabriel. "I'm sorry, Gabriel, but it was of highest concern to Michael."

"A wise decision. Thank you for doing your duty, Felix. I shall take it from here."

Felix bowed and headed toward the edge of the arena. Gabriel was about to protest when Lucifer grabbed her by her upper arm and whisked her behind one of the canopies. She broke free from his grasp.

"Gabriel! You're a fool!"

"Why? Because I'm willing to take a risk? Putting myself out there to see what the realm holds for me? It's mine to take! It has nothing to do with you if I fall on my face. It doesn't matter if anyone believes in me and if I'm capable of doing this. If I'm good enough to do it, I *will!*" Her eyes were filled with utter fury, "I told you I was going to enter! And now it's the last fight. The army has been formed! All because one angel stood in my way!"

"Listen to me, Gabriel!"

"I want to fight! Even if I fail!"

Lucifer had never seen her like this before. Instead of embarrassment and shame, her passion overwhelmed him, for he had never known before this moment how deep her passion was. "You are meant for more than fighting, Gabriel. You are a Seraph! You are part of the chain that trickles the knowledge of God down to the remainder of the hierarchy. That is the highest rank in all of heaven, Gabriel! Fighting is beneath you. It is base!"

Gabriel stepped to him and looked him dead in the eye. "Then why did you fight Michael?"

Lucifer did not answer her.

"You said it was because you wanted to test your limits. Highest rank or not, there is more for me to do and I know it! I don't need you to know it! It is up to me alone to believe it and prove it!"

"I don't want you to fight."

"It's not up to you!"

They heard cheers from the crowd. The fight was over. Disappointment fell all over Gabriel's face. She collapsed against a bench, all color drained from her face. *"No..."*

Lucifer could not bear to see Gabriel hurt, but this look on her face was one he could not bear even more. He looked down at her. "Yes, it is. Stand up."

"What?"

"Get up!"

He quickly took her hand and pulled her past the canopy and toward the field. Michael was congratulating Beelzebub in the center of the arena. Michael helped Gokor up as the crowd continued to cheer the arrival of heaven's second-in-command. Lucifer turned Gabriel around, tightening the leather strap to her belt and adjusting her sheaths.

"You're going to have to fight Beelzebub."

She pulled her hair back into a ponytail. "I know."

"You don't have to beat him. Just give him a very good fight with every ounce of your being and you'll be in the army." He turned her around so that they were face to face. "I don't want to see you get hurt. Do you understand me?!?"

"I won't."

Lucifer nodded. He pulled his own sword from his sheath and gave it to her; on its hilt was an engraving of a pentagram. "Here. It's better than yours. It's made of adamantine." Lucifer examined her. "You're ready. Stay here."

Lucifer marched onto the field amidst the cheers and congratulations, while Gabriel stood at the edge of the field looking at the crowd around her.

Lucifer waved to the Host; more cheers erupted as approached Michael. "Michael! I see that these are the last of the warriors to fight for the honor of being your second!"

"*God's* Second."

"Yes, no doubt. But I think there is one last battle to face."

Michael was confused. "Oh? Who is the challenger? You?"

The army was silent; everyone looked at each other to see who the challenger might be.

"No. It is no one presently in the army, Michael."

Gokor and Beelzebub laughed. Michael was not amused. "Then I hardly see how it could be a challenge." He nodded to the newly formed army. "These are the best warriors in all of heaven. I gave strict orders that no one be granted entrance to the tournament who couldn't hold his own. If there were an angel not granted access, it would have been for their own safety, Lucifer. I'm not amused by this dramatic interruption. Beelzebub has earned his place. He is second-in-command."

Michael turned his back on Lucifer. Having been schooled in front of the entire arena by the commander of the army, Lucifer's pride kicked in as chief of all of heaven — even over Michael.

Lucifer turned toward the Host. He roared to them, "ANGELS! I HAVE A MATTER OF GREAT IMPORTANCE THAT I HAVE BEEN FORCED TO BRING TO YOUR ATTENTION! THERE IS ONE ANGEL AMONGST YOU WHO WAS NOT GRANTED ENTRANCE INTO THE TOURNAMENT. BUT I SAY TO YOU, IT WAS NOT BECAUSE OF LACK OF TALENT, STRENGTH OR COURAGE, BUT MERE PREJUDICE!"

Michael whirled around, enraged at the accusation. Beelzebub and Gokor looked to him, never having seen him this angry before. The Host murmured amongst one another.

"SO I SAY TO YOU, AS YOUR CHIEF, THAT SUCH AN INJUSTICE NOT BE TOLERATED! FOR THIS BEHAVIOR IS UNBECOMING OF ANGELS WHO CLAIM TO FOLLOW THE ALMIGHTY GOD!"

Michael was beyond enraged.

Gabriel shrunk back amongst the surrounding angels. Raphael and all the army were standing along the posts, some angered, others confused, wondering what all this was about.

"I LEAVE IT TO YOU, MY FELLOW ANGELS, TO DECIDE IF THIS ANGEL SHOULD SUFFER THIS GRIEVANCE FOR ALL ETERNITY OR BE ALLOWED TO FIGHT TO PROVE THEIR WORTH! WHAT SAY YOU???"

An angel shouted from the crowd, "LET THE ANGEL FIGHT, LUCIFER!"

Other angels joined in the chant, until the entire Host was chanting in unison, *"FIGHT! FIGHT! FIGHT!"*

Michael took in the crowd. Beelzebub approached Michael. "I will fight this angel!"

Michael stopped him. "No. Put your sword away." He pulled his own sword from his sheath. "Stand aside." Michael lifted his hand to silence the Host. "*I* WILL FIGHT THIS ANGEL!"

The Host roared with excitement.

Gabriel's face turned green. Lucifer hesitated the moment he realized she would have to fight Michael.

"NAME THE CHALLENGER, LUCIFER!!!"

Lucifer looked at Gabriel standing along the fence post. Worry rested behind his eyes. Even from so far a distance, she locked eyes with him and slowly nodded. A heavy breath escaped Lucifer as he launched into the air; he pointed to the fence line and shouted, *"GABRIEL!!!!"*

The Host erupted in cheers.

Raphael looked to the edge of the arena with a look of horror. Vitor was beside him with the same look of alarm. "He'll annihilate her, Raphael."

The look on Michael's face was one of anger and concern. He looked toward the fence post for her as the Host began chanting, *"GABRIEL! GABRIEL! GABRIEL!"*

The soldiers parted like the Sea of Reeds for her to pass. Silently, she did not look at any of them as she walked onto the field. Raphael extended his wings and rapidly flew to Michael.

"Michael, do not fight her. Give me a moment to talk to her."

The Host continued to chant her name.

Michael did not take his eyes from Gabriel. "No, Raphael. She knew the danger the moment she decided to step into the arena."

"Michael…"

"Out of the way, Raphael."

Raphael bit his lip nervously and reluctantly flew back to the post.

Michael looked menacingly at Gabriel as she stood opposite him across the arena; she was frozen to the spot. She could barely breathe as her nerves settled in. "Calm down, Gabriel. This is what you wanted." She breathed deeply. "Do it."

With a single jerk of his hand, he made one blunt motion for her to step forward. To her right, Gabriel heard Gokor whisper to Beelzebub, "This will be over soon. Then all the females will know that it is music and song they should tend to."

Gabriel looked at him and saw some of the male angels laughing. That comment was all she needed to regain her nerve and rile her spirits. She lowered her head in focused determination, looked at Michael, and stepped forward.

The crowd erupted. Lucifer swooped back to his entourage.

Michael wasted no time as he charged forward with ferocious speed; the fight began. He swung his sword high, low, side to side, with enormous quickness and strength. Gabriel blocked every blow with fantastic swiftness of reflex, dodging his blows by using her smaller build and quickness as an advantage that none of the other male angels had. Their swords continued to clash with movements faster than anything ever seen before until Gabriel halted the sword fighting by landing her fist in Michael's face. She jumped in the air and used both her legs to kick Michael in the chest with more strength than he anticipated, knocking him backwards, but not down.

The crowd went silent.

Michael touched his mouth for sign of injury. He looked at Gabriel; she was crouched, sword ready like a master fencer. Michael launched into the air and dove down toward her, sword out. He landed with a swing of his sword that knocked her to the ground. He swung down again at her; she rolled to the right and quickly to the left as her quickness showed in his relentless attack on her. She was too fast, however, and she kicked Michael up and over her. He rolled in a somersault as she escaped him. She was up again and turned around just as Michael careened toward her, tackling her with such force that the Host roared in agony at the blow; Lucifer's anger rose at Michael's assault.

Gabriel and Michael dropped their swords to continue the wrestling match. Gabriel was pinned underneath him; he was almost in full mount. But just as she was able to dodge his sword, she was small enough to dodge his fists as they were leveled onto the ground. She lifted her leg, kicking him in the back of the head. She swiftly rolled onto her belly, giving Michael her back. Before he could grip his arm under her neck for a chokehold, her legs swung up toward his back; her heels sunk into his shoulders, and she yanked him backward onto the ground as she scurried from underneath him, running toward one of the fence posts. She saw a chain lying near one of them. She raced toward it.

Gabriel grabbed the chain and started swinging it overhead; she hurled it in Michael's direction and lassoed his feet just as he pushed himself up from the ground. She ran around the ring while holding onto the chain. The chain wrapped around Michael's legs as she ran faster than humanly possible. She continued to gain speed, running so fast around the arena that she ran upward and across Gokor and Beelzebub's chests, as well as the other male angels who laughed at her as she entered the arena. They were all knocked backward onto the ground off of her motion. Soldiers in the crowd burst into laughter.

Raphael shouted, *"COME ON, GABRIEL!!!"*

Other soldiers began to cheer for her as well. Gabriel stopped her running in the center of the arena. Off her motion and energy, she swung the chain with all her might. Like a discus thrower she spun, causing Michael to trip. He tried to grab onto the ground but managed only to grab fistfuls of dirt as the force of the circular motion launched him straight up into the air high above the arena. Gabriel scrambled for her sword as she awaited his landing.

Michael spun downward from the sky like a cyclone. He crashed down to the ground with a thunderous quake on impact. Michael looked directly at Gabriel. Gabriel had both her and Lucifer's swords in her hands. She was crouched and ready.

Without turning his head, Michael reached into the sheath of one of the soldiers standing behind him and pulled out the soldier's sword. He slowly bent down and picked up his adamantine sword on the ground, never taking his eyes off of Gabriel.

They slowly circled one another until their swords exploded upon one another once again. So fast were their movements, their swords looked like blades of a wood chipper. Their metal collided; sparks of lightning careening off of them. Their movements were a tornado of reflex as Gabriel and Michael spun, turned, ducked and blocked each other — a dance of fantastic skill and motion. The Host was bowled over at the sight, never having seen such display of athleticism before.

Lucifer looked down at them, his hands clutching the railing so hard, his knuckles had turned white.

Gabriel back flipped several times as Michael continued to advance on her with his dual swords. She eluded one massive blow of attacks as his swings sliced the wood of the post surrounding the field, shredding it. He swung his sword behind him, chopping it sideways through the air without turning his head, as it collided into Gabriel's sword. He turned on her and both angels jumped in the air with both legs in an attempt to kick each other in the chest. Their feet smashed into each other. They both catapulted each other backwards, each one's feet having been a backboard of motion. They flew through the air, flipping around; both landed on their feet on opposite ends of the arena.

The Host was out of control with roars.

Michael and Gabriel, both breathing hard, stared at one another. Gabriel swung both swords like tsais and raced forward. Michael, head lowered like a bull, charged forth. Their swords spun around furiously, like wheels on an out-of-control stagecoach. Both angels stood in place for the face-off as their swords continued to spin. Like an arm wrestle, Gabriel's body bent forward, her strength overtaking Michael's as he bent backwards by the force of her motion.

Beelzebub and Gokor were spellbound.

Lucifer was beside himself, "Come on, my love."

Michael was bending so far back that he was parallel to the ground. And just as it looked like he would be flattened, he began to straighten up, swords still spinning like saws in circular motion, until Gabriel began to bend backward by Michael's overpowering strength. The tables were turning. Gabriel was overtaken by the force; *her* back was now parallel to the ground.

Michael disarmed the sword in her left hand as she continued to struggle with the remaining sword in her right. It shattered against his adamantine sword as she was completely flattened to the ground; she was now unarmed. Michael suddenly stopped, frozen with one sword aimed at Gabriel's forehead and the other at her heart.

He peered down at her with the look of a lion about to devour its prey. Slowly, the muscles in his face started to relax. He stepped back; pulling his swords away from her. He returned one sword to the sheath at his side and the other behind his back. He extended his hand to Gabriel.

The Host was silent in anticipation.

She grabbed his hand as he pulled her up. Lifting her arm along with his, the Host erupted. A smile spread across Gabriel's face.

Beelzebub was utterly silent.

Lucifer turned toward his entourage. "Now *there* is a dark horse."

FALL

Now...

Lucifer made his way down into hell carried on the waves of the river's tide. The closer he got to his domain, the more rapidly his body transformed back into its reptilian form as he reached the river's end. His black webbed wings expanded, lifting him out of the boiling water before any part of his scale-ridden skin touched the molten lava from the Lake of Fire.

He soared over perdition and headed straight toward his tower. He landed on the brimstone ground and slithered toward his throne where Beelzebub awaited.

His voice was still hoarse from all his shouting. "Gabriel has it. Go to the earth and tell the Lawless One I need his sacrifice. I need another answer. I need more blood."

Beelzebub continued to stand there.

"What is it?"

"A mortal named Benjamin has found the spear."

"What spear?"

Beelzebub's dead eyes dulled even more. "The *only* spear there is to know."

Satan's snake-like eye dilated as he deciphered his meaning — and then he remembered.

"*Loginus*. After all this time…"

He had forgotten all about it — like so many things of late — merely because his focus was on remembering. But this bit of news is entirely unexpected.

"The Spear of Destiny. It has been a long time coming since the last mortal man thought to find it — and use it. How interesting…Who is this man?"

"Jonathan Devereaux's successor."

Satan closed his eyes and lifted his horned head to the sky. A smile spread across his face, and the deep sound of laughter erupted from the Lord of Hell. Beelzebub continued to stand there, unmoved, watching his prince roar in joy at the sound of this new revelation.

"Another key to another door."

"Shall I take it from him now?"

"The time has not yet come for the one who needs it."

Satan glided forward without another word, thoughts swirling around his massive head as he digested the notion of the spear's resurrection.

"I think you should know…he once loved the woman."

Satan stopped dead in his tracks. Beelzebub could see the massive muscles on the devil's back tense all around his spine.

The woman…the woman…the woman…

Without turning, Satan wrapped his tail around Beelzebub's waist and swung him around, lifting him up so that they were eye to eye.

"What kind of man is he…this Benjamin?"

"He is like the madmen of old — he trusts only what he sees."

"Then he is an enemy."

Beelzebub nodded his head. "I have seen his marker in the moonlight over the ages — it glows."

Satan stared at his second-in-command, studying the look on Beelzebub's face.

"What else?"

"Michael assigned him a new guardian."

Satan's tail rattled in reply; his eyes narrowed as he tried to decipher the meaning.

"It won't matter in the end; he is no believer in matters of the soul, only the narrowness of the worldly mind. He will never find his true identity, for he has never known the exaltation of the Spirit. He lives a half-life, and his time is almost up. You only need to do one thing…herald his arrival in Jerusalem."

Without saying another word, Satan dropped Beelzebub onto the brimstone beach and continued gliding toward his throne. Beelzebub watched him slither toward the Onyx Mountains. He turned and moved through the inferno and over to the portal that led to Earth. As he reached the Gate of Hell, he extended his wings and rose alongside it, searching for the face he longed to see. The moment he found the head, his tar-colored lips pulled back into a vicious sneer. Writhing amongst the thousands of limbs that made up the gate was the head of Jonathan Devereaux.

"Mortal man, I thought you should know: your protégé has picked up where you left off with another instrument to help my master. Does that bother you? Knowing that your alliance with my master, mattered not? Knowing that your action had the opposite effect amongst mankind? Knowing that you are here in the end no matter what you tried to do to change the outcome? The only reason your daughter escaped the inferno upon her death was because of her final act, her last spin in the mortal dance. It would have been an honor for me to drag her by her hair through the gate and place her head right…beside…yours. Perhaps with Benjamin, you will have some company. For don't the people of the world have a saying about misery?"

Jonathan's mouth opened wide, but all that came out of his blackened mouth was nothing but silent screams.

Not so long ago…

Beelzebub, Gokor, Nero, Azriel and Asmodeus had waited in the garden far longer than they had anticipated for their master's return.

"How much longer?"

Beelzebub had grown tired of Azriel's repeated question and constant pacing. He had completely eroded the grass under his massive feet as he continued to walk back and forth in anticipation of Lucifer's arrival day after day.

None of them knew how long it would be before Lucifer returned. Perhaps, he already had. Just to be sure, Beelzebub had ordered Nero back into hell just to see if Lucifer had come back sooner than they had, and had decided to go back to perdition out of his own impatience. But Nero had returned and found hell in the same state as they had left it. The only change was to the architecture.

The rebel army left behind had begun the task of creating a new kind of kingdom — another viable domain. A tower for Lucifer had already been hammered out from amongst the Onyx Mountains. The angels had even begun to name each domain as they explored each piece of landscape: the Valley of Darkness, the Woods of Bloodied Ground — later to be renamed the Woods of the Suicides, the Circle of Betrayal which later became known as the Circle of Judas, the Valley of Homicides, the Valley of Slaughter, the Marsh, the Infernal Cemetery — on and on it went. But most interesting of all were the caves. While exploring the darkened tunnels, various angels were attacked by dragon-like hounds. Beelzebub was loathe to see these creatures Nero described to him, but Asmodeus seemed intrigued by the idea of claiming the hounds of hell upon his return. "I shall master them and be called Master."

Nero even spoke of a lone creature the angels had yet to find; one whose cry pierced their ears until they bled. Only the force of its wings as it flew across hell could be felt as the wind blew past them from time to time as it travelled through the inferno. Azriel grinned widely at the challenge to hunt, capture and tame such a beast to his liking. All the while, Beelzebub listened, feeling nothing as he took in the news.

The only time he felt alive was when he looked at Adam and Eve. He was the first to return to the garden after his long journey around the world. And what he found in his exploration were creatures of all shapes and sizes — none of which intrigued him or gave him pause — for what did he care about animals, plants and tiny insects. Not even the sun or the moon or the stars were majestic enough to stir his heart, nor the changes in weather from the rain to sleet to snow. For what did the natural world have to do with him? Not even the various landscapes appealed to him, for nothing could ever be as beautiful as the paradise in heaven — but this garden, however, came awfully close.

He found it a relief the moment he turned around and saw the garden once again, for he knew his trek was an act of going through the motions — a task more for Lucifer and the others rather than for himself.

The moment Beelzebub saw Adam and Eve laughing with one another as they ran through the garden, he hoped none of his other brethren would return any time soon, for he found he enjoyed the innocence of the man and the woman — as if they were children playing in their own imagined land of make-believe. And he found he longed to be there with them too, even if it were for just a moment, this piece of time, for he bore witness to love — and love thrived in the garden. Love dominated the heavens. And love was what he yearned for most.

It wasn't until he saw Michael and Gabriel walking through the garden — a place they called Eden — that he knew that moment would never come again.

The angels of God are here, to guard them in all of their ways…

Beelzebub knew they would be there for the rest of time for that was the command. He hid in the shadows of the trees, completely on watch and on his guard from that moment on. The moment a portal opened within the Tree of Life, he thought both archangels would go through, but Gabriel alone remained. Night after night he followed her, watching her silently from the trees. He wondered what would happen the moment she discovered him, but that moment never came.

One particular night, he thought of attacking her from behind, but he knew she had been more brutally violated than any angel before, and she had survived. With God on her side, what could he possibly do to her that had not already been done?

And so he watched and waited. How he hated Gabriel so. If it weren't for her, he would have been the one to stand by Michael's side. And had he been dealt a better hand, he would never have found himself desperate enough to take the only hand and only opportunity offered to him where Beelzebub now found himself to be. And not only was Gabriel to blame, but Beelzebub also blamed God.

He had never asked God for anything but one thing, and it seemed that he was about to be granted his request. He had worked hard for it, his intentions were all in the right place; he had even earned it well enough to deserve it. So the question that flooded his mind and tormented his thoughts was not, Why did you do this to me, God? But why didn't you do this *for* me? Why...*not*...me?

Sitting amongst the shadows of the trees waiting for Lucifer to return, the questions did not matter anymore, for there was no one to hear them. But Beelzebub still had not decided his next move or how he would begin again. Yes, even a fallen angel still understood there was always another way. But he knew repentance and solitude like Vitor was not the path for him. All the same, he despised Lucifer and his constant lies. How much more could one angel take, for he refused to be blinded in denial of the truth like the others, for he knew they saw just as clearly as he did. But what other option did any of them have but to choose to believe the falsehood of their present future?

Looking at Gabriel as she watched over Adam and Eve, he knew there was no other option but what he would do with his cursed opportunity. He had yet to decide. Waiting in the shadows for Lucifer was the not the existence Beelzebub would tolerate for long; and as Azriel continued to pace, he knew there was a chance to cause a mutiny in perdition if Lucifer made them wait for him any longer.

"Gokor, how long have we been sitting here?"

"Four-hundred and seventy-two suns. Each day is the same as the last. We could have travelled East by now and found Lucifer all the same."

Nero sharpened his sword against a stone. "Perhaps he's fallen in love with this earth. He always admired God's talent with creation."

Beelzebub sneered, "*Talent.* God *is* creation, Nero. But perhaps you are right. There is the possibility that Lucifer has changed his mind about these people and this place."

Azriel suddenly stopped pacing. "What do you mean, changed his mind? He can't change his mind! He's the reason we're here!"

"A partial truth, but I wonder how many of us would have joined the rebel army had we known about this place and God's plan for it when we were in heaven — without Lucifer's influence and bias in the decision."

The angels pondered his question. It was Gokor who answered first, "I still would have."

"Why?"

"Because I don't agree that a lesser being born as a deviant to the celestial line should ever be allowed to enter our domain. I would have agreed with Lucifer that there was a need to fight against it."

"Even if it meant that lady Eve would be granted a place in paradise alongside you?"

Gokor paused. "She belongs here."

Beelzebub turned to Nero, "And you?"

"It would be nothing to wipe out the earth and all its creatures if God allowed us to do it. For that reason alone, it would seem the logical assumption that man's free will can be easily corrupted and swayed. I've seen it amongst the tribes of people here. They fight over property and territory. There is no true love equally shared and felt amongst the people as there was amongst the hierarchy in heaven. Had I been for creation, I would have been wrong."

"Agreed." Azriel nodded his head off of Asmodeus' answer. Azriel added his own thoughts to the mix, "And I've been thinking, Beelzebub, that maybe we were destined to fall."

The angels looked at him in utter silence.

"None of us but Lucifer was of the first rank of Seraphim. None of us held a high rank amongst the army, yet we love to battle; we live for a fight. I think we were supposed to rebel against God so that we would witness all this, and do something about it instead of bow down to serve and obey." He shook his head, "To serve is not in my design, nor is it in any of us who were hurled from the realm of our home."

"Then why go home?"

Azriel narrowed his eyes in confusion over Beelzebub's question, "What?"

Beelzebub stated his question another way, "Why start a war here on Earth amongst and against mankind if you still want to go home? If you were meant to fall, as you say we all were, then why not...*stay...down?*" The pale-haired general looked at each of his brethren, "There is no going home if we annihilate and destroy, nor is there victory if we influence the elements to deter each man and woman from fulfilling the purpose for which they were created for."

Gokor eyed him. "What are you saying?"

"I'm saying the only way to show God that Lucifer was right about them is to leave them alone."

Nero stopped sharpening his blade.

Gokor was astounded. "Leave them alone!"

Beelzebub leveled his eyes at him. "Yes. If returning to heaven is the ultimate goal, then we stay out of it; we leave the world as it is and let nature and man decide."

Nero's voice was grave, "But Lucifer said..."

"Lucifer says many things. And should you ever choose to truly listen, all you need do is check his premises. *I...I...I...*never *we.* If we follow his plan, we will never go home. If we follow his plan, heaven will come down to battle it out with us, but it will not be while carrying banners and sounding trumpets to thank us for heaven's mistake." He looked back at Adam and Eve. "It will be over the fury of the interference of marking mankind's souls with so much filth that they themselves can never step foot inside the kingdom upon their deaths. That is Lucifer's plan, my brothers. It is not to win a war, but to bring everything down piece by piece so that no one can claim what he once had in the end. We are merely his pawns to ensure that he succeeds."

"How right you are, Beelzebub."

The angels jumped at the sound of Lucifer's voice. They stood up and searched the grounds for his presence but could see nothing.

"I do need you...all of you."

The angels saw a large shadow moving swiftly about the trees.

"For I have seen the four corners of this earth."

They whirled around as the shadow moved past them again — almost as if Lucifer's shadow was gliding.

"I have swam the deepest of oceans and discovered the creatures of the sea."

They whirled around again.

"I have climbed the tallest mountain and seen the attempted failure to beautify the dawn's horizon."

Beelzebub gripped the hilt of his sword tight.

"I have sat amongst the mindless beings of lesser man and made myself known."

Lucifer's shadow moved behind Nero. Before he could turn, Nero's sword was ripped from his grasp.

"The earth is a horror."

The shadow moved like lightning over to Azriel and Asmodeus, ripping their swords from their sheaths. Beelzebub continued to watch for any movement of the shadow but all was in vain. He could see nothing but the shadow and movement of the trees.

"And the children in it are a bastard breed carrying the seed of sin within their hearts."

Gokor was shoved from behind. He fell forward just as his battle-axe was yanked from his back. All but Beelzebub were unarmed. The sweat trickled down Beelzebub's forehead as he anticipated Lucifer's attack at any moment.

"There is no morality in their design. Only wants and needs — a morality of the people that suits the era of the time and will shift as frequently as the tide. Mob rule masked as enlightenment."

Silence.

All went still in the garden. Not even the trees moved. The angels looked to one another until all eyes settled on Beelzebub. He gripped his weapon tight sensing the looming shadow behind. He knew he would have to be quick. He turned...*SMACK!*

His sword was slapped from his hand by a large object. That same object swiped at him again, slamming into his ribs, knocking him back against a tree behind him. He fell to the ground and looked to the shadow before him. All the angels paled the moment Lucifer emerged from the trees. Their eyes grew wide in terror as his nine-foot frame loomed over them at twenty-five-feet tall. Azriel's heart hammered in his chest the moment he took in Lucifer's skin; its shade varied between each line and scale that covered it — colored from gray to silver to black. His skull had widened, revealing a bald head covered in the same snake-like skin. One eye remained blue while the other had become an almond slit identical to the reptiles the fallen angels had seen time and again scampering across the earth. Lucifer's wings were featherless, taking on a web-like frame that outlined their skeletal form. And as he stepped toward them, he moved even swifter, carried on the movements of his ten-foot tail.

Gokor shuddered, barely whispering, *"Lucifer..."*

The angels were terrified as he continued to move toward them. Beelzebub scrambled to get away, but he didn't stand a chance as Lucifer's tail whipped around his massive frame and latched onto Beelzebub's neck. He lifted Beelzebub off the ground, squeezing the coil around Beelzebub's neck tighter and tighter until it seemed he would snap his commander's spine in two.

Lucifer moved Beelzebub's body closer to him so that they were eye to eye.

"I'm going to ask you this question this one time, Beelzebub. Are you for or against me?"

Beelzebub's eyes were bulging out his sockets as he tried to gurgle out his answer. The other angels watched helplessly as Lucifer dangled their commander fifteen feet above their heads.

Lucifer waited.

Beelzebub struggled as he found the means to utter the words, *"For...you..."*

"Good." But Lucifer still did not loosen his grip around Beelzebub's neck. "If I ever sense an opposition to that answer, or hear a whisper or tone that deviates from your answer, I will drag you through hell and dangle your body over the Lake of Fire, slowly lowering your body inch by inch over its waves to be sure you feel every moment of pain you could possibly experience before you die. *And you...will...die."*

Lucifer's tail unraveled slowly, dropping Beelzebub's body like a ragdoll. Beelzebub was on his knees gasping for breath. Lucifer turned to the rest of the angels, "I've imagined different endings for each and every one of you far worse than the one I just revealed should you choose to overrule *me*. I am now the father — and you are my family. It is my will that shall be done on earth as it should have been in heaven."

Gokor slowly moved forward and knelt before Lucifer, bowing his head. "We are for you, my prince."

The other rebel angels knelt beside Gokor and bowed to their master. "For you."

Gokor lifted his head, finding the energy to speak, "Lucifer, what happened to you?"

Without turning, he replied, "Venom, Gokor. Venom from the snake in this garden has done this to me. And in return for this action against me, this garden will be destroyed — *today.*"

He turned toward the garden and looked for Adam and Eve. *I'm in a den of lambs. And it is now time for the slaughter. My...great...sacrifice to the father...*

"What are you going to do?"

Lucifer's tail rattled in reply, "Where is the woman?"

Lucifer turned to the garden where he saw Eve walking alone near the Tree of Knowledge of Good and Evil. She stopped right in front of it, admiring its fruit. A cruel smile formed on Lucifer's chapped, blackened lips.

"Yessss, there you are..."

He brought his clawed infected hand to his lips and blew Eve a kiss. The wind blew through the branches and through her silky, raven hair. She looked up suddenly having felt the breeze against her skin.

Beelzebub was stunned at what he had just seen Lucifer do. Gokor exclaimed, "How did you do that?"

"I've learned many things while roaming the earth, my brothers. And using the elements, speaking out loud into the ears of sleeping men so that they hear my voice in their dreams, all these things...are nothing compared to the final discovery I recently came to understand."

The angels waited.

Lucifer's reptilian eye narrowed as he looked at the lady Eve. "God will allow me to engage from behind the veil, for I have found he lifts it for me now and again."

Beelzebub's body stilled at this news.

"And now God will lift it for me once more."

He lowered his head as he watched Adam walk up beside Eve.

Mirrors indeed...

Lucifer's tail coiled around itself...and he slithered forth into the garden.

MIST

Now...

Gabriel emerged from the cave safely back into the confines of heaven. She breathed deeply, relieved to see the glow of her Father's light once again.

"What did he want?"

She turned and found Michael sitting on a rock just outside the cave. She moved over to him and sat down beside him. She looked down at the adamantine sword in Michael's sheath. "What he always wants — a means to an end."

"What means, Gabriel?"

Gabriel looked up at the ever-changing sky, hearing the soft sound of the Host's singing as it echoed forth from the kingdom of heaven. "Do you remember the day I made it into the army?"

"How could anyone forget? It was the greatest upset amongst the male angels that anyone had ever seen."

She smiled to herself. "Do you remember the weapons I used?"

Michael's eyes steeled as the memory revealed itself.

"He's looking for it. He asked me where it was."

Michael turned his laser beam stare on her. "It's *here?*"

"It always has been."

He rose from the rock. "Why have you never said?"

She looked down. "I don't know. I suppose after the last time, I figured it was too great a threat to reveal its existence. Besides, any angel can fall at any time, right?" She looked up at him, her meaning made clear. Seven years ago Michael thought her capable of falling. Even now, he cringed at the thought knowing how he argued with her and fought with her thinking her capable of falling in order to join Lucifer's side.

"I hid it from Lucifer, Michael — before the rebellion. I kept it hidden after The Fall just in case more angels chose to join his side — even after all this time. And we've known a few who have done it. Had they known it was here, they might have brought it to him."

"Adamantine can break adamantine."

"Exactly. And then he'd be free."

Michael looked off in the distance. "Do you trust me, Gabriel?"

"I always have."

He sighed deeply and looked to the ivory tree. "You used to share so many things with me. But you haven't said anything to me outside of strategy and carrying out my orders since that moment long ago. I wonder sometimes, why that is."

Gabriel could not meet his gaze. "You know why that is. I've never been the same from the moment you found me." Her body tensed. "A lot of things changed for me at that moment, Michael. Things that had nothing to do with you or anybody else. Part of me felt the need not to let anyone know me the way Lucifer did — ever again. It wasn't because I didn't trust you. I just...I try to keep my distance from everyone. It's the only way I've been able to survive...all...this...pain." She could feel her heart thundering in her chest. "Lucifer's sword is not something I purposely chose to keep from you. It was something I chose to keep from everyone."

He looked up at the cliff where he and the rest of the angels once held their matches. The flood of memories filled his mind as he remembered the camaraderie and the brotherhood.

"I can't stop thinking about them, Gabriel. I keep seeing them everywhere I go. Memories I had long forgotten. Why is that?"

She turned around seeing his mighty form as he gazed at the cliff. He was right. She had trusted him like no other angel. She had shared with him her deepest thoughts. And there he was, attempting to share his thoughts with her. She had not realized until this very moment how much distance she kept from Michael — the angel she trusted and respected most.

"Perhaps, to remember that their choice to do what they had done was that much more horrific — they had so much to lose, Michael. Maybe even they are remembering these same moments as they try to amp up for what they still aim to do over one last battle they feel must be won."

He did not respond.

"You're agitated."

"Of course I'm agitated. There's nothing more I desire at this moment than to descend upon the earth and fight." His jaw clenched. "A single earthly year has always passed as fast as a man can blink." He shook his head. "But these last seven years have been hard; they've been slow. George, Joan and Samson are even getting on my nerves — even they have been itching to descend to aid their mortal brethren on the last day."

Gabriel smiled at the mention of George. "Good old, George…he sees a dragon in every fight."

"That he does. I keep telling him the command has not been given yet for the descent, but he keeps pressing the issue. *When? When? Have you seen what the antichrist has done now, Michael? Are you going to let him get away with it, Michael? Don't you care, Michael?*' He never lets it go."

"Carter hasn't wasted any time."

"No, he hasn't. The people love him; they have no idea what he's actually doing behind their backs with every step he takes. And part of me knows they don't really want to."

"Strange…the people love a man who walks the earth like the Pied Piper serenading them toward their doom, and yet the Son walked amongst them for a time — and was rejected. After all this time, I still don't understand it — or them."

Michael and Gabriel sat in silence. It had been a long time since the two archangels carried on a conversation as long as this one. "Have you ever thought Lucifer was right about them?"

Michael slowly turned to face her.

"I don't mean in his rebellion or what he's done to prove his point, but that in some way he understood their nature since it so closely mirrored his own — and that, for some of them, the truly wicked ones, he knew that allowing evil and pain and suffering to exist upon the world was the chaos he feared, knowing they had the capacity to choose to be the ones to inflict it?" She looked over at Michael. "That certain souls should never set foot in the kingdom because their soul was filled with so much shadow."

Michael contemplated her words. "You mean because some of them made choices…and didn't choose well — most of which were without Satan's influence."

She nodded.

"No, I don't think he was right. I choose to believe in the good of man. Lucifer chooses to exploit their weakness. When a being has free will, an ability to reason and therefore has a conscience, anything is possible. What he was wrong about was the idea that God should impose his will upon the people whenever that chaos and folly from their choices ever entered the picture. For as close to God as Lucifer resided, he never understood our

Father. He still doesn't.

"He doesn't understand why God allows it — the pain, the suffering — even for evil to exist in the world. Hell always existed. It only became what it is now because Satan chose to make it so. Souls would still have plunged into the darkness of hell upon their death with or without our fallen brothers residing there. There were always other beasts that lived there to claim it had even if The Rebellion never occurred. But enough talk of hell."

Michael looked up at the sky of heaven as it changed from fuchsia to gold. "You know what my favorite moment is, Gabriel?"

"What?"

"Watching a mortal's face the moment they step through the Pearly Gate." As he said the words, the light within his eyes began to glow. "Their faces the moment they first see heaven; they had no idea. They *have* no idea, Gabriel." His massive chest expanded with pride. "And I absolutely never tire of seeing the warriors walk through the gate — the soldiers, the champions."

"Mine is when the little children come through and see the Son. They just run and run straight for him, diving right into him. Their laughter is greater than any symphony I've ever heard."

They both started grinning from ear to ear.

"I know Raphael's favorite is when the sick and the elderly walk through healed from all their illness, running through like the little ones."

"And then he tries to make them laugh by telling the most unfunny jokes."

Gabriel burst into laughter. "That's so true!"

Michael and Gabriel continued laughing until their joy turned to silence. "If they only knew, Gabriel, what majesty awaits…"

Gabriel sighed deeply. "No eye has seen, no ear has heard and no one's heart has imagined all the things that God has prepared for those who love him. He loves them so — His family, His children. He longs for them to seek Him on the earth — and He thunders in rejoicing when they come home."

Michael looked back at Gabriel. "You were right to keep the sword hidden, Gabriel — even from me."

His six emerald-colored wings jutted forth from his back as he rose into the sky. Gabriel sat there and watched him go.

SECOND-IN-COMMAND

Now...

Beelzebub crossed the portal from hell and back into the world of mankind. He had lost count of the number of times he had made such a trek, but each time he did, he learned something new. He had watched the mortals in the shadows of their everyday lives since the beginning. And what he had come to find was that children continued to fascinate him most, as their connection to the Father and the unseen world of their angelic guardians seemed commonplace to them. It was only when they were told a new truth based on fear or were placed into a reality that shifted their world into one of pain, that the children would lose their connection and the cord would be severed. It was a moment Beelzebub continued to ponder as their little innocent eyes were given the knowledge that not everything was as it seemed. *Just like the garden...*

He hated watching the moment when the little children's eyes were opened to the evil in the world. It made his heart writhe with fury, for it reminded him of his own eyes and the darkness that filled them ever since, for they were a reflection of what he saw and what he lost inside — the spiritual connection.

Beelzebub had vowed long ago that he would hunt that one mortal who was responsible for stripping a child of their innocence. At first he gave them time, seeing if the dawn of conscience would find its way into their soul, tugging at it before he did. And if they were sorry for what they had done, promising themselves never to do it again and didn't, Beelzebub would leave them alone. But if they weren't, or if they broke their promise and did, Beelzebub would summon a demon from perdition and throw them into the mortal's path to follow them and cling to them — until they took their last breath. For he had often found that there were many Eves in the world curious over pleasure or manipulated demise; and there were far too many Adams — failing to protect what they promised to guard, blaming others for their choices — even at the hand of the devil.

And as he crossed the world over so many continents and so many centuries, he found the two commonalities that threw people into a tailspin causing them to do all the things they never intended to have done were fear and pain. Only love seemed to heal the unintended consequences of another person's choice — but not always. But Beelzebub was often thunderstruck when a mortal soul asked for mercy from God for all they had done — even as they took their last breath. And God would grant it to them. *Even on the last one. But not always...*

It was hard for him to wrap his mind around that idea, for many of the men and women who had repented had never done anything worthy of mercy — at least in Beelzebub's mind. But as he watched their souls emerge from their bodies to either be claimed by him and his army he called Legion or by the archangels and angels standing watch, he was constantly reminded that it was the last lap that mattered most — that last step, that last breath that could cause the ending to be changed. *Something more than words.*

So Lucifer had conjured the witch to repeat the prophecy of his and the world's demise. *But what about my ending? Was mine so easily foreseen, or like these humans, could it be changed…even on the last day? And if it could, would I want to change it?*

The only thing Beelzebub had ever desired was to be second-in-command of God's army. He yearned for it, dreamt about it, prayed over it, worked toward it — and he almost reached his goal. He thought it was meant to be. But when the title was unexpectedly stripped from him, it was more than he could bear. He had plunged into a downward spiral of blame and self-pity — angry at God for not granting him his sole desire. It's what drove him away from his Father and into a land of woe. A land where he thought opportunity waited, where leading an army in hell was unknowingly the highest rank he would ever achieve.

It wasn't until he entered the Garden of Eden and scoured the world that he found a new purpose to his immortal life. He embraced his position, finding that he could command demons and hounds and fallen brothers to strip mortal souls of their reward in being granted entrance into heaven. It gave him a sort of peace the more souls he saw being pulled through the gate. Hell's Bells never seemed to stop ringing. And yet, something strange had happened to Beelzebub over the years. He found that he enjoyed watching as many souls being lifted into Heaven as were dragged into Hell. He couldn't explain it. And as he tried to understand this sudden shift in perspective, he often found himself standing watch the moment a man or woman was about to die and wishing that he didn't have to take their soul with him. And yet, at the same time, he prided himself on the ones he did take. For he knew that these mortals never once thought that all their choices would ever catch up with them, that their choices really weren't as bad as they seemed or were significant enough to recollect over time. They had no idea that self-inflicted pain was all of their choosing, branding them an enemy of God making them *ours…ours…ours…for the kingdom.*

He had watched as God continued to keep his mortal family close to him. From Adam to Eve, to Noah and Abraham, to Isaac and Jacob — on and on it went, the family lines recorded in a single book. And with each generation God would remind his family of his promise from the beginning: land, descendants and blessings. But what continued to horrify Beelzebub was how often this so-called family of dust and bone would stumble and fall, only to be picked up again with a continued promise as God turned their blunders into blessings.

It angered him. It fascinated him. It exhausted him. It also overwhelmed him, for every time God gathered in his lost sheep, the family suddenly grew — and it kept growing. He understood why Lucifer refused to let his rage go over time, for all of them continued to bear witness to their father seeking *them* — and he was ignored. He remembered what it was to be in God's presence and bow to the light; to feel his father's blessings and revel in them. Yet here, on the earth, the blessings were showered all around them — and were forgotten. Miracles were for the imbeciles and faith was for the narrow-minded. How could that be? It was the free mind who dove into the adventure of what he didn't know and what he couldn't prove only to risk that what could possibly be was far better than what could ever be quantified or calculated in a single formulation. Beelzebub had seen that the most rational and analytical mind was ultimately the mad man in the room, for if one could quantify one's existence into random shifts over time that could not be randomly repeated again anywhere in the known universe, then how could one trust the mind of the thinker who thinks it? He could not comprehend what was so important about this mortal family that God had tried and tried again to gather them in and welcome them home at the end of their mortal journey in the chapter of life.

Why for them and not for us?

And as Beelzebub approached Benjamin Jacobsen, emerging from the shadows of Benjamin's hotel room, Beelzebub wasn't sure which way this particular mortal would go. And the choice of his path could shift victory to one of two sides. *Would he risk the great adventure? Would he talk himself out of a choice by reasoning out the impossibility of possibilities?* A self-proclaimed atheist, Beelzebub had seen his marker for years, but to hunt for the spear that pierced the Son of the Most High God, one had to wonder where his last lap would lead, what last step he would take, and what his last thought on his final breath would be. Was he an enemy or a champion — or simply a mad man?

As he looked at Benjamin sleeping soundly, watching his eyes move back and forth under his eye lids; he knew Benjamin was dreaming. He looked up at the man's guardian, fixing his black doll-like eyes on the angelic being standing watch in the corner of the room. They had been eyeing each other night after night as Benjamin slept, but the guardian had yet to move. Taking in the size of the warrior before him, a slow smile formed on the fallen angel's face. He lifted his pale-colored hand and laid it down on Benjamin's chest. *Yes, this will be interesting indeed, for this mortal has a champion in his midst. The greater the guardian, the more to protect.* He pushed down with all his weight until Benjamin stirred awake. Beelzebub watched him look all around the darkened room, first toward the guardian and then slowly back at him.

Mortal man...

And just like Adam and his lady Eve, Beelzebub was reminded of what he had learned long ago: this mortal had so much to lose.

Then...

Lucifer attempted to console Beelzebub from losing the post of second-in-command, "There's nothing I can do, Beelzebub. You fought her right after Michael named her worthy of the army. She beat you. You know the rules: whoever was named in the army challenged one another for the post of second-in-command. You lost. Gokor lost. Nero lost. She beat you all."

Gabriel watched the scene a few feet away, feeling the discomfort of the moment. Almost as if God sensed her discomfort in her worthy achievement, a group of female angels walked past her congratulating her on being the first female named to the army. Seeing their genuine offering against Beelzebub's gripe, Gabriel's heart was comforted just a little. She took a deep breath and decided to walk towards them.

Upon seeing her approach, Beelzebub quickly bowed to Lucifer and stormed away. Gabriel stood next to Lucifer and sighed deeply.

"You know, my love, I daresay you have smashed that angel's dreams into a thousand pieces."

"He has challenged me five times now, you know. He's lost every time." She watched Beelzebub. "It's a strange feeling, Lucifer, when you see how something you accomplish can affect someone else in such a hard way — especially when what I wanted had nothing to do with him."

Lucifer slowly turned his head to look at her watching the mixed emotions filter across her face. "Don't feel guilty, Gabriel."

She lowered her head. "It's hard not to."

Lucifer turned and lifted her chin with his finger so that they were eye to eye. "Don't. The purpose of each and every one of us has been designed by the Almighty for His will. To bury your gift, your success, your victory over someone else's pain is a sin against God. Gifts are meant to be used, Gabriel. How they are to be used is not only a choice but a will. Whatever Beelzebub is feeling right now has nothing to do with you. He alone needs to work it out within himself."

Gabriel breathed deeply.

"Not everything we want is what we get. Not everything we get is what we need."

He looked back at Beelzebub storming through the heavens.

"There is a reason why you were chosen to be second-in-command of the army. And there is a reason Beelzebub's time for it is not now — if ever. Perhaps there is something more important he was meant to do."

"Whatever it is Lucifer, I hope he discovers it soon. I understand his feeling. All the same..." Gabriel grabbed Lucifer's hands. "Thank you, my friend."

"For what?"

"For standing by me — even though you didn't believe in me."

"You alone are the keeper of your vision, Gabriel, just as you said. Even I have my own."

"And what is that?"

He paused. "I have this feeling deep within me that I am meant to do something extraordinary so that I can shine brighter than all the rest of heaven."

She laughed softly. "You've always had that feeling."

"I'm being serious, Gabriel. I'm destined for greatness. And the fact you're laughing at me tells me I'm not explaining it right. It's a different kind of feeling...I can't quite place the desire or the words for why I feel as I do. I just know it." He looked out at the every-changing sky. "My time is coming..."

As Gabriel watched Lucifer's face, her eyes fell into one of worry as she caught a deeper look under the surface. She turned and looked back at Lucifer's pedestal where his monstrous instrument resided.

"Lucifer..."

"Hmmm?"

"I don't hear you playing your music anymore."

He looked back at her. "I haven't had the time."

"No time for your passion?"

"Not since the transformation."

"You're supposed to write me a song, remember?"

He smiled faintly, "All right, beloved."

He walked over to the stool and sat down. "Let's see..." He began playing a light melody. "Angels keep coming to me in excitement asking all sorts of questions."

"Slower. That's too upbeat. I'm much more mysterious."

He shifted to the lower keys and slowed the tempo. "That's better. What were you saying?"

"They keep asking me, 'Why are we divided, Lucifer? Why is there an army? Who are we to fight? Where did the beasts go?"

Gabriel looked around. "Where *did* the beasts go?"

"Very funny."

"I was being serious."

"Back to the waterfall." He continued playing. Gabriel moved a curl away from his brow as he played.

"And what were your answers.?"

He stopped playing. "I don't know the answers, Gabriel. Angels have been asking God and have received no answer. So they've been coming to me to find one. So I've asked God what is His purpose, what is His plan."

"And?"

"He's been silent on the matter." Lucifer looked down at the keys lightly resting his fingers on them. "It's the first time He's ever remained silent."

Gabriel caught the apprehensive tone in his voice. "And that bothers you."

"Yes, it does."

"Why?"

"Because I know He has the answer."

"God always reveals things in His own time."

He took her hand. "True. Only this was a massive shift in our design all at once. Why so fast? Why this shift? Why *now*?"

They both sat in silence as the unknown answers weighed between them. A horn sounded in the distance. Gabriel squeezed his hand. "Duty calls." She ran her fingers through his hair. "Don't look so solemn, my friend. I know God will tell you soon — He always does."

He nodded and noticed the hilt of his sword sticking out of her sheath. He smiled in amusement. "Are you ever going to give that back?"

"Nope."

He raised an eyebrow.

"Your power is in your words, Lucifer. They are your weapons. You said so yourself. I wouldn't want people to call you a liar."

Her six phoenix wings spread wide. She rose in the air. Lucifer grabbed the tip of her wing, stopping her.

"You are my greatest friend, you know. I'm proud of you."

"I know. Now finish my song."

He released her. She smiled, saluted him and vaulted into the sky. He watched her ascent. Lucifer looked around at all the angels bowing to him as they passed. He breathed it all in feeling the peace wrapping its arms around him.

Lucifer saw Vitor in the courtyard about to take flight from a group of angels he was conversing with. Vitor was showing them a strange creature Lucifer had never seen before. Curious, he walked over to him.

"What new creature is this?"

"It's a dabbot. I found it hiding just outside the cave that leads out from the river at the Great Waterfall. The bridge to…"

Lucifer interrupted, "Yes, I know that of which you speak. What were you doing there?"

"I was merely curious. I find my nature is one of exploration; a wanderlust, if you will."

He bowed to Lucifer. "I must return to camp, though I don't see why we train so hard when there's no one to fight."

Vitor launched into the sky. Lucifer watched him go; a look of foreboding spread across his face. He looked around at the beauty and harmony of heaven with angels happily going about their actions and deeds. He was tired of this feeling. This feeling that something was about to happen to his heavenly family and that it was not anything good. But what wasn't good in heaven? Nothing. Yet he felt there was something all the same, for he felt the tugging, the gnawing feeling at the back of his mind that he had seen but not heard — and if he had heard, he had not listened.

I love my family, Lord. I need no other members, no other friends, and yet…you are always growing, always creating, always changing — as are we. But there are no new angels, only new creatures. Could there be other creatures we have yet to see? Are there other domains outside the ones we know? Question after question poured forth from his mind until he could not stand it anymore, for his head was about to burst and his heart weighed heavier with every question left unanswered. And so, the chief seraph in all of heaven made a decision.

I will ask my Father myself. And I know He will answer me.

Lucifer looked up toward God's light, extended his wings, and launched toward the throne.

*   *   *

Michael surveyed the progress of the army. Raphael and Jeremiel were leading a large group in swordplay; Uriel and Nero led the cavalry in mock combat on horses and chariots, while Gabriel and Sariel led the archers in target practice.

Suddenly, a large flock of angels exploded into the sky; their screams screeched across it as more cries echoed across the kingdom. The entire army stopped all action and looked to the sound.

Michael, Gabriel, Raphael, Uriel, Beelzebub and Gokor were immediately in the air. Michael looked to Gabriel, "Gabriel, keep the troops here and continue the drills."

"But…"

"Do it!"

She nodded as he flew off. Gabriel turned toward the army. *"ANGELS! BACK TO YOUR DRILLS!"*

She turned toward the other angels still hovering with her in the air. "Raphael, Uriel, go with Michael. He may need you." They nodded in salute and followed Michael.

"Beelzebub, Gokor, take over command for Raphael and Uriel."

They nodded and descended.

Michael flew toward the sound of the screams, listening for the source of the location from where they cry.

The throne.

He flew faster.

Thunder roared like never before. Michael could see a throng of angels huddled together on the sapphire steps below. He swooped down and slammed onto the marble; his wings immediately retracted into his body as he stormed forward and plowed through the crowd.

"Out of the way!"

The angels made room for him. On the ground below, amongst the throng, Michael saw Lucifer. He was unconscious; his skin was as pale as his ivory robes. The flames of blue that normally encompassed him when in the presence of God were gone. The angels surrounding his body were filled with fear. Michael crouched down to Lucifer and lightly smacked his face to rouse him.

"Lucifer." He did not stir; Michael turned toward the angels, "What happened?"

Romulus answered, "I don't know. I heard Lucifer's voice rise in anger while communing with God. His words I know not."

"How did he end up here?"

No one spoke.

"*Answer me!*"

Nicodemus replied, "God struck him down!"

Michael's jaw clenched at the news.

"Why?"

Nicodemus shook his head. "We found him here lying on his back. He looked so different, Michael. His eyes were...vacant. I touched his arm to see if he was all right; and he looked at me as if he knew me not. He grabbed me by my collar and said, 'The Father's light has dimmed.' Then he collapsed." Nicodemus' eyes were filled with fear. "What does this mean?"

Lucifer mumbled as his eyes slowly opened. The moment he saw Michael, he grabbed onto Michael's tunic, but he was too weak to pull himself up. His eyes were wild. Michael moved closer to Lucifer to hear him speak. "Shadow is coming...our Father...will bring the darkness."

Lucifer lost consciousness. Raphael and Uriel approached from behind.

"*Lucifer!*" Raphael crouched down beside him.

"I thought I told Gabriel to keep you at base."

Uriel jumped in, "She commanded us to come to you."

"In case you needed our help. She was troubled."

Lucifer mumbled again; his eyes were closed. "It is folly...disaster...our Father..."

Michael looked at Lucifer with a serious foreboding; his jaw clenched tightly. "Did Gabriel say anything about this?"

They shook their heads. Michael looked upward and closed his eyes to speak silently with God. The Spirit encircled him; he fled. His eyes opened and were lit afire in green flame. "Get Gabriel."

Raphael raced across the sky. Thunder roared again on the steps; the surrounding angels bowed their heads to pray to God. Raindrops started to fall in heaven for the very first time.

DREAMS

Now...

"**C**an I do anything for you, Dr. Jacobsen?"

Benjamin opened his eyes and looked at the attractive flight attendatn who was leaning over him — a little closer than professional guidelines, he was certain. He looked from her bright blue eyes and bleached blonde-hair down to her blouse where he saw her name tag; it read, "Jenny." He smiled at her and immediately noticed her reaction as she smiled back. It was the same reaction he always got from women, for he was fully aware of the fact that women found him to be better than good-looking; they found him to be irresistible with his dark, black hair, tan skin, and sapphire-colored eyes. Whenever he smiled, he knew the result would always be the same — until, of course, he started talking archaeology. He had far too many experiences with women like "Jenny" who were interested in the here-and-now-kind-of-men, rather than the kind of man he was — the kind that reveled in the then-and-long-ago. Women like "Jenny" who thought the doctor at the front of his name meant money were always disappointed when they realized that an archaeologist's salary was not equivalent to the kind of fortune they had in mind. They wanted to hear words like "financial security," "I'll spoil you rotten," not "I just discovered a bone I named after you." For to be in a relationship with Benjamin was a different kind of romance. So he decided to merely amuse himself with the attractive blonde beaming at him, who was still waiting for his answer. "A glass of water would be great...*Jenny*."

Her glow went up another watt as she trotted off to quench his thirst. Benjamin didn't mind the attention, for women like Jenny were only good for the here and now anyway, and that was all he was up for lately. But he had never felt that way about Rachel.

He cringed the moment the thought entered his mind. He had to stop thinking it. She was dead. Gone. And should be long-forgotten. But last night, he had dreamt of her again.

"There's something you need to do..."

And then the dream was interrupted.

"Here you go."

He shut Rachel's voice from his mind and took the glass of water from Jenny as she smiled at him in triumph; as if this act alone were the greatest achievement in the newly risen day, and she needed to be congratulated.

"Thank you."

Benjamin could have sworn even her hair started to glow at his response. *Not like Rachel.* Rachel would have rolled her eyes and told him to get his water himself. As a matter of fact, that was exactly what she said to him when they first met. He was on an archaeological dig with her father, Jonathan, somewhere in India. They had been working all day, and the heat of the afternoon sun had gotten to him. He needed something to drink, and he happened to look up and see an attractive brunette writing in a notebook near one of the other associates on the project. He had assumed she was the associate's assistant and decided to ask her to run an errand for him.

"Would you mind getting me some water from camp?"

At first, she did not even look up; she did not realize he was speaking to her. But when she saw the associate she was standing next to looking at her for a response, Rachel did a double-take. The moment their eyes met, Benjamin's stomach did somersaults.

Uh-oh. She's trouble.

Trying to blow off the swirling feeling he felt inside, he shifted nervously and smiled his fool-proof smile. But it was the first time he did not get the reaction he was used to getting. Instead of smiling back, she narrowed her eyes at him and spat out the words, "Get it yourself. I'm not your secretary."

She snapped her notebook shut and walked straight to the camp where the water was stored. The smile quickly vanished from Benjamin's face. "What's her problem?"

"That's Dr. Devereaux. Dr. Rachel Devereaux — the daughter."

Benjamin's heart had begun to hammer in his chest. *And she's smart.* He watched her confident gait as she entered the tent.

The associate smiled at him, seeing where his gaze was fixed, "Still thirsty?"

"Shut up."

Benjamin wiped the sweat from his brow and followed Rachel up the path to the tent. She ignored him the entire time he was there, writing in her notebook without giving him a second glance. Not used to this kind of response from a woman, he was not sure what to do. Holding the bottle of water in his hands, knowing how hot it was, he knew she must be thirsty too. So he grabbed another bottle and placed it down in front of her as a peace offering. The moment she saw it, she stopped writing. Dr. Rachel Devereaux suddenly turned her head and looked Benjamin dead in the eye.

"Thank you." It was then that Rachel smiled.

And Benjamin smiled back. As a matter of fact, he began to glow. It was the beginning of something new for him then; the beginning of something filled with adventure; he felt it deep within his bones. The fire in his heart that erupted that day was one that had never been fuelled again. For there was no one like Rachel, and there were far too many Jennies. It was the one great regret of his life — the lack of knowing the love he could never see.

"Is there anything else you need?"

Benjamin looked away from Jenny, hearing the double-meaning behind her question. "This'll do it."

Her glow began to fade in disappointment.

"Thanks."

Her smile faded as she nodded and walked on. He took a sip of water and looked out the window at the clouds beneath the wing. *Just like heaven.* That's what his grandma had always said. *Too bad it's all a myth, grandma.* He toasted his water at her memory and gulped it all down. He closed his eyes and rested his head against the chair.

"There's something you need to do…"

And for the first time, he answered her, *What? What do you need me to do?*

As he waited for her answer, the wave of exhaustion fell over him, and Benjamin fell into a deep sleep.

*　　*　　*

Benjamin…

Michael felt the shift. But this particular shift was not one from heaven and it was not rising up from hell. It was a different kind of shift that threw him off base, for it almost knocked him down the moment he felt it.

It's coming from the earth.

The last time he felt such a shift was seven years ago when the first tune from Gabriel's trumpet had been played. It was a shift that brought him to his knees as he felt the tide of war brewing on the earth, but the warriors resided in the supernatural realm. And such a shift now was not as strong, but it threw him off balance all the same.

Raphael landed beside him, his six sapphire wings retracting into his body as he looked at the serious face of his commander.

"I felt it too. Who is it and what did they do?"

"Quiet, Raphael."

Michael tilted his head and listened for the rhythm, for the beat; and for the first time, he could not hear one. Which could only mean one thing…

"A mortal has stepped forth on a path of destiny that could shift the souls of mankind into the hands of the enemy."

Raphael's jaw clenched at the news. The last mortal who had done such a thing was the father of his very dear friend, Rachel. Knowing that the seven year marker was about to pass, Raphael understood that it was only a matter of time before he and the rest of heaven's army would be called to the earth to aid mankind in their darkest night.

"Who helped this man?"

Michael continued listening. And as severe as his face was, it suddenly melted into sorrow. "No one. He made the choice all his own."

Michael turned his amber eyes to Raphael. "It is a man who neither believes in God nor the Devil."

"An atheist."

Michael nodded. "But it was not always so. He has begun a quest on the enemy's behalf — and he does not care about it either way. It holds no significance to him."

Raphael attempted to decipher the mystery behind Michael's words. He repeated his questions once again, "Who is it and what did he do?"

Michael's jaw continued to clench. "You knew this man, Raphael. You knew him when you spent your years on the earth with Rachel."

And the realization of who Michael meant slammed into Raphael's chest as he slowly put the pieces together. *"Benjamin…"*

He nodded, "He found the Spear of Destiny."

"Loginus…"

Michael nodded. The look on Raphael's face was neither sad nor sympathetic. The moment Michael spoke these words, all boyish charm vanished from Raphael's face as a look of fury set in. He crossed his lean muscular arms over his massive chest and lowered his head like a bull; his eyes glowed silver as the rage boiled from behind his eyes. "You were right to tell me this news, Michael. I'm going to the earth."

"You are not allowed to go to the earth just yet. The hour has not yet come."

"I will not interfere with the man; but I will be hard-pressed not to fight it out with one of the rebel angels. You know one of them is beside him, guarding his journey so that he succeeds. I can't take it anymore, Michael! Why aren't we there? Why can't we go?"

"You are not going to the earth, Raphael. Your assignment ended with Rachel. Benjamin is another angel's assignment."

"And what angel would be assigned to such a man as this?"

Michael looked Raphael dead in the eye, "The guardian…is Jasper."

Raphael let the name of the angel set in. "Quite a guardian — it wasn't always so."

"No, it wasn't. Jasper was assigned to Benjamin seven years ago."

Raphael nodded his head; the glow behind his eyes had dimmed just a bit. "Upon whose suggestion?"

"You and I aren't the only ones who feel the shifts. The Great Lady sensed it in this one man the moment he learned that Rachel had died. And she is never wrong."

"Benjamin loved her tremendously, Michael. It was Rachel who chose not to love him back because loving him brought her too much pain. He never got to say his good-bye, although he tried to make one last connection." He looked off in the distance. "But the spear, Michael."

"I know."

"Are you going to tell Gabriel?"

"I have a feeling she already knows. She is with the Son now, and I have no doubt she has seen the wound in his side bleeding once again."

*   *   *

Gabriel stood against the Tree of Life in the middle of the courtyard staring at Lucifer' instrument of old. George, an Englishman, stepped up behind her.

"My lady…"

Gabriel turned and looked at him but did not speak a word. She turned her attention back to the instrument.

"I could not help but notice that you return to this spot day after day, staring at that monstrous organ. The only difference between now and before is the look I see on your face. You don't look happy."

"I don't want to talk about it."

"I see. Well, I have been known to aid a damsel in distress when evil seeks to claim her life, and I have seen various looks upon many ladies' faces, and I recognize a woman trying to figure something out and not finding the answer which she seeks. I'm quite good at puzzles and mysteries, and since you have that very same look of determined distress, my lady, how can I be of service?"

Gabriel turned and looked at the smaller man beside her. "You really want to help, George?"

"Aye, my lady."

"Keep asking Michael when he is going to sound the horn."

She turned and walked swiftly toward the second realm of heaven. Her six phoenix-like wings jutted forth from her back and she launched into the ever-changing sky. She soared over the kingdom, moving from realm to realm as she tried to calm the angst in her heart.

*First the sword...now the spear...*two keys that could blow the doors wide open. Doors to heaven or doors to hell — depending on who held them in their hands. She flew faster and faster until she reached the cave. She moved swiftly down the rock until coming to the portal that separated Heaven and Hell. It was then that she shouted across time and space, *"LUCIFER! LUCIFER! LUCIFER!"*

A rumble thundered across perdition.

Then...

The clouds turned a hue of gray as thunder rolled across them. Gabriel and Raphael raced through the sky and dove toward the kingdom like two hawks on the hunt.

Michael, on bended knee, had taken his place again on the steps praying silently to God. On hearing their approach, he rose and turned toward Gabriel.

"What happened?"

Michael looked to Raphael, who shook his head. "Lucifer collapsed."

She stepped forward, *"What?!?!?"*

Michael grabbed hold of her shoulders and stopped her.

"Listen to me and listen to me very closely. Lucifer quarreled with God. What was revealed in their argument is not known to the other angels. Speak to him on it."

She nodded.

"Follow me."

*   *   *

Michael, Gabriel and Raphael dropped down into the woods in the second realm near the old ivory tree. Lucifer was kneeling by a rock, his hands clasped in prayer as he stared out at the sky beyond, but he was not praying.

"How did he know to come here?"

"He watches you more closely than you know."

Gabriel slowly walked toward him. Michael turned to Raphael. "Leave them be." Michael's wings expanded and he launched into the sky taking Raphael with him.

Lucifer did not blink or register any kind of movement upon Gabriel's approach. She looked at his statuesque form, seeing this eyes shimmering from dampness by the remnants of recent tears.

"Lucifer."

He did not stir but merely continued to stare out at the realm beyond while clasping his hands tightly. Gabriel circled around him and touched his arm, gently kneeling down beside him.

"Lucifer, what happened?"

He continued to stare forward.

"Lucifer…"

His lip began to tremble at the gentle prodding tone in her voice. He gripped his hands tighter as he tried to fight the rising emotion from deep within. "I…"

Lucifer gritted his teeth, bringing his fists to his head; his eyes were clenched shut as he tried to block out whatever he seemed to be seeing in his mind's eye. "I can't…" He shook his head rapidly, as if trying to attempt to convince himself that what he grappled with deep within the core of his being could not truly be real.

Gabriel gently squeezed his arm. He immediately rose and walked to the edge of the cliff overlooking the Great Waterfall. Lucifer's hands were on his hips, his fists were clenched at his sides as the tightness in his jaw line could be seen. "All this…"

Gabriel did not know what to do; she merely stared at him in his distraught state. "Michael said you quarreled with God."

Lucifer ignored her and continued looking out at the grounds of heaven all around him. Tears streamed down his face as he took in the ever-changing sky, the multi-faceted color of the river down below. "So beautiful…" His heart ached with an unknown pain ridden of joy. "I don't understand. Why? Why? Why would He do this?"

Gabriel rose and stepped up beside him; her face was stricken with worry as Lucifer continued to fight back his rage and tears. He looked at her suddenly with the appearance of anger and confusion behind his eyes.

"I don't understand Him, Gabriel." He looked out at the realm, wiping the tears away as they streamed uncontrollably down his face. "Heaven is perfect. So perfect."

Gabriel waited before asking him again, "What happened?"

Lucifer lowered his head and closed his eyes. "Do you love me?"

"You know I do."

"Do I? There are so many things I was sure of, but now that has all changed."

"Nothing has changed."

He opened his eyes, "Have you ever asked yourself why we were divided up into the hierarchy? Why there's an army when there's no one to fight? Why we have been given brand new gifts that we have never even used and have no idea as to why we need to use them?"

"What do you mean?"

"*You*, Gabriel! You are second-in-command! To *what?!?* *For* what?!?"

189

"I don't know."

He looked at her standing helplessly in her forlorn state. "Well, *I* do." He looked defeated; his voice fell into a whisper as he collapsed against the rock. "I do." He stared out at the waterfall lost in the confines of his own mind.

Gabriel reached out and gently grabbed his hand. He squeezed it tight.

"What I am about to do now, you must forgive me for it." He turned and faced her; his cerulean eyes were filled with sorrow as he looked at her innocent face. "And God is really to blame — for what I have done, and what I have failed to do."

"Why are you talking this way?"

"Because our Father deceived us, Gabriel. We are angels, the first of his creation, allowed to live here thinking we are free, that we have a will of our own that decides our own fate. But it's not true."

Gabriel let go of Lucifer's hand. "I don't know what you're talking about."

"He created us, Gabriel, to be His slaves."

She shook her head in disagreement, "No."

"Yes, Gabriel!"

"*No!* You are wrong!"

"Why would I lie — especially to you?"

"God…is my Father. He is the embodiment of love, Lucifer. In his hands I'm at peace. In His arms I rest because I feel His love wrapped around me, and He is in me and I in Him. You speak of God as if he were something dark. Something vile. There is no darkness in Him."

Lucifer slowly shook his head. "You have eyes but you do not see." He looked past her, "But I'm about to open them so that you see what I see, that you know what I know, and that you do not close your eyes again. And yet, I don't want to. I don't want to see any of it ever again."

"See what?"

"His plan! He showed me a glimpse of what the present and future hold — all at once — the event horizon! And it is a horror!"

Gabriel was thrown by his shouts of pain.

"*This* existence, *our* existence, our *purpose* is to serve, Gabriel! Look at me!"

He rose from the rock.

"*I*…will not serve…*ever. Non servicum.*" He spit out the words as his body racked in disgust and rage.

"Lucifer, what are you talking about?"

He stopped his rant and stared at her, "A great change is coming. A separation of light and dark — shadow amongst us."

"That's impossible. There is no darkness here!"

"Nor should there ever be! I will not stand for it! I will not allow any angel to stand for it!" His body continued to shake, "Our gifts are not our blessings but our curses. They are the chains that have been draped upon us like treasures, for they are our enslavement, and God has the key to set us free…and He will never use it. We have followed the wrong shepherd."

"Why are you saying such things!!! God loves you. You love Him."

"NO! OUR FATHER LOVES US *NOT!* WE MATTER *NOT!* HE WHO IS ALL-KNOWING, ALL-LOVING, IS NOTHING BUT A SELFISH GOD WHO THINKS ONLY OF *HIS* WANTS! *HIS* PLANS! *HIS* WILL! HIS DESIRES! WE ARE THE MIRRORS OF HIM AND HE FORGETS US IN THE MAKING! *HE IS A LIAR!!!*"

Gabriel was stunned, "*LUCIFER!!!*" Without even thinking, she struck him across the face. Out of reflex, Lucifer struck her back, backhanding her in the face.

Gabriel stumbled backward and fell; her head smashed against a rock, making a loud cracking sound. She did not move from her position. Horrified by what he had done, Lucifer quickly moved to her to help her up, "Gabriel, I…"

Before he could finish his statement, Gabriel turned and launched at him, tackling him into the tree behind him. She threw a left hook, but Lucifer dodged it just as Gabriel continued her attack. She swooped behind him, and jumped onto his back, locking him into a chokehold. Her actions were fast and swift. Lucifer tried to throw her off by slamming her back into the tree, but her technique was perfect. She had him locked into too tight a grip to let go. Lucifer dropped to his knees. Before he passed out, Gabriel released him.

Lucifer was coughing, gasping for breath. Gabriel looked down at her friend with contempt. She had a deep gash on the right side of her head where her head struck the rock. Gabriel turned her back to him. She looked to the sky, seething, she tried to calm herself. She touched the gash and winced in pain.

"You have spoken against God, my Father — *our* Father — for reasons I do not know, that would never warrant my sympathy or understanding even if I did. God has placed you closest to Him, the highest honor in all of heaven. And these are the things that you say in praise of Him. This is how you repay Him with so tremendous a blessing. Who do you think you are? You forget yourself, not only in God's presence but in *mine*."

Lucifer rolled himself to sit up against the tree. Gabriel turned toward him and crouched down directly in front of him so that Lucifer could see the gash that was on her face.

"Have you nothing to say to me?"

Lucifer refused to look at her.

"HAVE YOU NOTHING TO SAY!!!" She stood and turned her back on him, her wings unfolding. Seeing that she was about to leave, Lucifer reached out to grab the tip of her wing.

"Gabriel, please…don't leave me."

Gabriel paused.

"I don't know how to make it stop. This feeling...it's like my heart is breaking. And yet, I'm so *angry*. I cannot bear this pain. It's agony, Gabriel, because I feel helpless to stop it. Who can stop God?"

Gabriel slowly retracted her wings. She turned and looked down at him sitting against the tree, "You said we were to be slaves. Slaves to what?"

Lucifer swallowed hard, trying to keep down the bile that was rising from his stomach. "Oh Gabriel..."

"Tell me."

"Our Father wishes to test his limits. He wishes to construct his masterpiece. He told me that it is his perfect will to create another domain, another world beyond the heavens...a place He desires to call 'Earth.'"

Gabriel slowly crouched down beside him.

"This Earth will evolve over millions of years, while we live here with God in Heaven. God will watch over his earth, and only when it needs it will He force his hand in the direction He wishes it to go. To give it sustenance, perfection, beauty, willing it to continue on a path of its own design and course by its own scientific nature. Such plans...a division of sky and water, then water to land. More years to pass, moments of time that mean nothing to us, before He fashions that the land will have the ability to bring forth its own life. And still more time will pass until creatures evolve in the sky and in the water, then on land. And the worst is yet to come once the land is made ready in full force of its cycle.

"The creature..." Lucifer paused, constricted in thought. "God is going to form a breed of..." He could not finish his statement. He barely whispered, shaking his head in disbelief, "An age of misrule."

"A breed of what, Lucifer?"

His jaw clenched. "He calls it 'mankind.' A being like us...*just* like us, Gabriel. And it is our Father's will to allow this mankind to rule the earth, to have dominion over it, on their own, *without* him!" Lucifer whirled around. "A place without God! You've seen with your own eyes how the angels can be in the very presence of God, Gabriel. Without Him it would be worse had they never been created! They need Him. And they are perfect beings of His direct likeness and image. Lesser perfect beings on the earth without him? *Disaster!* And God knows this!"

"If it were to fail, then God would not do it!"

"But He will! Wake up, Gabriel! I told God how without His very light and voice, these beings would do great wrong to one another. They would not understand their own creation, their own perfection, their own likeness to our Father. That it would be madness and chaos...darkness without his light. And he said to me, 'Lucifer, that is why I have divided up the kingdom. You are to help my children, protect my family'."

Gabriel was overwhelmed.

He shook his head fervently, "I refuse to believe that the hierarchy was designed solely to carry out His works when there is a need, merely to help them." *His new family.* Lucifer shuddered at the thought. "He has had this planned all along."

"What are we to do? What 'works'?"

"We are to help these lesser vile creatures on their earth with our gifts and talents, so that they may not destroy the earth or themselves in their egocentrism. And the army! The army is for battling greater fights that are sure to come in mankind's darkness!"

Gabriel was silent.

"To serve! To obey! That is my purpose? *Bondage!* To be a slave to an idiotic being that God feels the need to create out of dust and bone." Lucifer was enraged beyond all measure. "I do not believe it. I do not believe that that is why I have been created. I will not do it! There is so much more within me I have yet to do. And this is not it, Gabriel. This...is not it!"

Gabriel was lost in thought.

"He is God, my Father. I would do anything else he asks of me save this. To aid a being that would not know God by merely looking at the earth and all that God hopes to create. To not know that they are the image of our Father; and that we have to help them see and know…folly, Gabriel. The Earth a mere purgatory."

Gabriel was silent. "I don't know what to say."

"Say that God is wrong to do this! Say that you agree with me. That you know I am right. Can you not see that God loves his idea more than us! He refused to listen to me. He refuses to see!"

"And so you quarreled."

He was not listening to her. "When the birth of mankind comes, I am to announce the news to the hierarchy…and I cannot. If I have to fight Him, I will. He needs to listen. He needs to see."

"And if He doesn't?"

"Then I will fight Him, Gabriel, for control of heaven if I have to. And whoever wins decides the fate of the Earth and all of mankind."

Gabriel moved closer to him and knelt down in front of him. She took his hands in hers. "No. This isn't right. It doesn't sound right. You cannot do it, Lucifer. These words formed from you mouth are unknown to me. It's madness you speak."

He threw her hands off of him. She grabbed them once again and held on.

"*Listen* to me, you have to trust God, Lucifer. *You have to.* God has never given cause for otherwise. You reside so close to his heart. *You.*"

Lucifer stood, brushing her off.

"He has branded you the dawn. Speak to Him again. There are things that we may not understand when first presented with them. Perhaps there is something in this grand design that you or I have yet to see, yet to know. Give our Father a chance to explain it all to you. It is overwhelming, but the meaning is there."

He looked down at her with disdain. "The Father speaks directly to me, Gabriel, not you. You are a lesser angel."

He looked off in the distance. Gabriel stood there silently having bore his backhanded insult.

"This is my home. My family is here — not anywhere else, *with* anyone else. I don't want it to change. Not any of it, especially if I have to bear the brunt of the laziness of the folly of a lesser kind of being."

Gabriel looked out at the realm.

"I have never been wrong, Gabriel." She did not answer. "I cannot go back to the throne and feign obedience. I have already spoken with him on this. He will not be swayed — He is God. He has decided; and so have I. I can live with the disagreement."

He turned when he noticed she had not said a word. He saw her staring out at the realm. Lucifer could see the gash on the side of he head. He moved toward her and touched her wound gently. She winced in pain but did not turn. "Ah, beloved…I…" He dropped his head.

"I love you, Lucifer, but I love my Father more."

He slowly lifted his head.

"I've never known Him to hurt me or deceive me or make me feel less than what I am, for He always shows me more — more love, a deeper humility, His grace — because He overwhelms me with that love, His gifts, His blessings. And I know I don't deserve it, but He gives it to me anyway. I listen to you and I'm filled with angst and dread, as if I'm sick inside. Whether you have understood it or not, you *have* been free in serving God here. You have obeyed and thrived without anger here. Yet now you say that the kind of obedience being asked of you is not what you want, so therefore, it must be wrong. That somehow now you are a slave who has lost all that you had before. And that has never been so. When there are boundaries, there is freedom, you know. Without it, there'd be excess of want — gluttony. Without the border, there'd be envy of having and doing what others have been ordained to do and have. Without the order to do, nothing would get done — there'd be laziness, sloth. Without the 'no', we would all think that every one of our thoughts and opinions were true just because we thought them or felt them or spoke them — and the result would be too much pride. Without a boundary there is no balance. Just because we think we are something, or deserve something, doesn't make it so. If that were true, there'd be so much greed in the heavens, there'd be nothing to stop it from being overrun. That to me, is not freedom. That to me, is chaos. And nothing but anger — wrath — and entitlement would follow from having the ability to choose anything we want at any time and getting it — a lust of things unwarranted. The greatest freedom, Lucifer, is the ability to master your environment, perfect your skill with what you have been given — and *thrive*. To become more than what you know you can be. That is freedom."

She looked down at the leviathan floating in the river near the waterfall. "I would die if I lived underwater. The land is my boundary from entering a world I cannot survive in — and yet I'm free to roam the land and sky. A place I can soar. And now our Father has created another place to soar. A place we can use the gifts we have no use for here, but have been so exalted in having been given, for we have all felt that it suits our design and our being best."

She turned and looked at him, "So what is freedom then, Lucifer? Because, from my perspective, obeying according to the boundary to which is good and has been named by my Father who loves me most…how can that be…all…that…bad?"

He did not answer her.

"You have spoken with our Father in anger — and rightly so. You were shocked not to know the Father's mind, but why would you? He is God. Speak to Him again. Speak to Him with love as you have always done. Be at peace and bear an open mind. He will listen to you. He will tell it all to you. He will give you the understanding, just as he always has. And perhaps it is your eyes that will be open to a new revelation."

"I have the understanding! It makes no sense! It follows no reasoning, but demands explanation or why question it? I cannot take his words anymore!"

"Then *I* will ask Him."

Lucifer turned. "What?"

"I will ask Him. I will ask the Father of these things you speak. And then I will know what I choose to believe and know why I believe it."

"You already know."

"No, I don't. I only know what you have told me — your own kind of truth."

Lucifer closed his eyes and shook his head. "You're so blind, Gabriel, but I'll do it. It won't make any difference, but I'll ask Him if that is the only way to make you see. You think God will answer. You, my love, have accepted that God will tell you your answers on His own terms, in His own time. You do not see, Gabriel."

She leveled her eyes at him as anger set on her face, "You are our chief! You begin the flow of communication of God's word to the hierarchy! You have been commanded to share God's plan. If you do not give this command with peace of mind and faith in the plans of our Father, then it is heaven that will be full of madness and chaos. And you will be responsible for it! And if you don't want me to ask Him, then go to Him once more and ask for the whole vision, Lucifer. You can take it. Not like the rest of us *lesser* angels."

Lucifer just stood there.

"What are you waiting for? Go to Him! If not for yourself, then for *me!*"

"No."

Gabriel stepped towards him. "*Coward.* There is nothing that you cannot do. It is a matter of choice; a matter of wanting to, and I *command* you to do it."

Lucifer remembered the command he told her to give him not so long ago. "All right, Gabriel. I'll do it...*for you.*"

EDEN

Now...

"**L**UCIFER! LUCIFER! LUCIFER!"

Gabriel continued shouting Lucifer's name across the portal. Michael and Raphael entered the cave and followed the sound of her voice down the river's tide. They saw her shouting before the portal, pacing back and forth like a wild animal trapped inside a cage.

"*Gabriel!*"

Gabriel stopped pacing and looked at Michael; her eyes were wild with fury.

"What are you doing?"

Gabriel advanced toward her commander; her eyes were on fire as she spoke, "I want to know what he intends to do with the spear, Michael! *The spear!*"

Michael took her by the shoulders, keeping his voice level as he spoke to his second-in-command, "Calm down, Gabriel."

She was breathing rapidly as she looked all around.

"Look at me, Gabriel."

She shook her head.

"Look at me."

Begrudgingly, she finally did. "Asking Lucifer what he intends to do with the spear won't make any difference. You know what it represents. You know what it means if it rests in the wrong hands. We've seen it before."

"But we're not there, Michael! We're not there to protect the people!"

"No, we're not. But you have to remember something, Gabriel. I felt the exact same way you do now the moment I found out Lucifer had your trumpet."

This stopped Gabriel dead in her tracks. Her breathing slowed as Michael's words hit her deep inside her heart. She lowered her head and rested it against Michael's chest. "You're right. I'm sorry...I'm sorry, Michael."

"Gabriel, I didn't bring it up for you to apologize. I brought it up to give you perspective."

He took his finger and lifted her chin so that her eyes met his. "It doesn't matter. Nothing and no one can ever dismantle the will of God. No relic, no weapon, no sorcery or hate-filled crimes — nothing. Not even that spear. Evil never stops, Gabriel, and in the end...it will never rise over good. Not ever. There are too many silent warriors who will be roused to victory in the end. God created mankind to extend the family. Nothing will ever stop our Father from bringing them home."

She exhaled deeply. "I'm just...agitated, Michael. I was comforted by the idea that Lucifer's sword is safe in heaven."

Raphael did a double-take. "Wait, *what?*"

Gabriel continued, "I thought that was his only weapon to thwart the end of days where he could claim more souls for his kingdom."

"And you think the spear is his alternate weapon."

"It has to be."

"That all depends on whose hands it ends up in, in the end. Give it to a man or a woman who is a champion of our Father, and souls will be washed clean before they ever step foot in the kingdom. We don't yet know what the future holds."

"But it's *Benjamin*."

Raphael coughed. "Ahem. Excuse me, but in case you didn't notice I was still here, I have a thing or two to say about that."

Both Michael and Gabriel looked at him; they waited.

"Well…what?"

"Rachel has asked me a favor."

They waited some more.

"Really, Raphael, these dramatic pauses are testing my patience."

"I'm getting to it!" He took a deep breath. "She asked if she would be allowed to visit Benjamin in a dream."

Gabriel looked at Michael to wait for his answer.

Michael shook his head, "We are not to interfere until God gives the command."

"A dream is hardly interference, Michael. You forget that Benjamin does not believe in anything spiritual. He relies solely on what he can prove through science, reason and mathematics — a dream is not something he can quantify or deem as a sign of something spiritual. He doesn't believe in the possibility. He thinks dreams are merely neurons firing in his brain pulling forth memories and thoughts of his subconscious."

Michael shook his head in confusion, "Then I don't understand the point of the dream."

Raphael smiled knowingly, "He loved her, Michael. She was the light in his darkened tunnel. He will pay attention to what she has to say. Love is a weapon all its own. That is one truth I learned while spending time on the earth. Love will set a man free. Even our beloved Benjamin."

Gabriel smiled at Michael; a look passed between them. Raphael caught it.

"What? Say it. What?"

Gabriel looked at him amused, "Well, it's still technically interference — even if it is subconscious."

Raphael frowned at her. "All right, I'll give you that." He thought for a minute. A smile slowly spread across his face. "The command, Michael, is for us angels — it is not for mortal souls. She *can* interfere — as can the rest of the souls here! Ha!"

Gabriel's eyes were wide as she took in Raphael's admission. She turned to Michael. He finally replied, "He's right."

Raphael beamed proudly.

"I didn't say she could do it."

Raphael stopped beaming.

"The only way it will be allowed is if she reminds him of what he once loved."

Raphael looks at him oddly. "Is that a riddle? I'm not quite sure I understand."

Michael moved toward him and put his arm over Raphael's shoulders. "You may not understand, but I'm sure Rachel will."

"I'm sure she does; she's already been doing it."

Michael crossed his massive arms over his broad chest, "What?!?"

Raphael's eyes grew wide. "Oh…right. Sorry about that. Um, well, you see, Rachel asked me some time ago, if she could visit Benjamin in a dream — and I said yes." Michael did not say a word. "Haven't you ever heard that it's better to ask for forgiveness than permission? No? This is one of those circumstances. Learned it from mankind. It works, you know, although it's not a sin *not* to ask permission. So I don't really get the logic behind the phrase."

Michael was dead silent. Raphael looked at Gabriel; she merely shook her head at him.

"It's been going well, I think…"

Michael turned and started walking toward the exit of the cave. Raphael moved quickly behind him. Michael suddenly stopped and looked back at Gabriel; Raphael bumped into him. "Sorry, Michael."

"For which part?"

Raphael looked down, "All of it."

Michael exhaled deeply. "Brief me later on Rachel's progress." Raphael beamed once again as his commander looked past him and over to Gabriel. "What were you going to ask Lucifer if he came to the portal?"

"Yeah, Gabriel. What?"

"I was going to ask him who the spear was for?"

Michael stared at her for a long time. "You already know."

Raphael looked from Michael to Gabriel. "How is it that you know all these things, Gabriel? I want to know all these things."

Gabriel shifted her eyes to Raphael. "I pay attention." She looked back at Michael. "It means nothing to Benjamin to find this spear, for he does not believe in what it represents. But the man who hired him to obtain it…does. There is only one keeper of relics that would want such a thing, and I wanted to know if I was right. I don't know that I am, for as you say, Michael, we don't yet know what the future holds."

Michael nodded in agreement.

Raphael looked between the two archangels once again. "I'm totally lost here."

"Don't worry, Raphael, it's not a riddle."

"That's low of you, Michael."

They headed toward the exit of the cave. Gabriel was about to step through when she suddenly stopped and turned back toward the portal. She waited and listened for what she alone had heard. And without saying another word, she turned and walked back into heaven.

Down below, just before the river's edge, Lucifer held onto a rock on the other side of the portal. He weighed the news evenly. *There may be dreams, Raphael, but there are also nightmares...*

He released his hold on the rock and climbed back down to hell.

Not so long ago...

Lucifer glided toward the garden and over toward Eve. The fallen angels watched from behind the shadows of the trees, waiting for the moment when Eve would see Lucifer. As he glided past her, a small breeze blew around her. She turned her head and looked all around, but could see nothing. Lucifer continued to glide toward the Tree of Knowledge of Good and Evil. He slowly climbed the tree so that not even the fallen ones could see him amongst the foliage. All that could be seen was his massive tail as it wound around the trunk of the tree.

Gokor whispered to Beelzebub, "What is he doing?"

Beelzebub stared straight ahead, "Seeing if God will allow the woman to see him."

From high up in the tree, Lucifer began singing. His deep, melodious voice sounded throughout the garden. It was then that Eve heard him. She stopped picking a bouquet of flowers and looked directly at the tree.

"Adam?"

Asmodeus gasped, "She hears him!"

The fallen angels could barely breathe at this new revelation.

Lucifer continued singing. Eve looked all around before moving slowly toward the large tree. She crept slowly toward it, tilting her head as she listened ever so closely to the beautiful melody. As she approached the tree, she could see the large serpent tail coiled around the trunk of the tree. She took in its massive size, never before having seen one as large as this one.

Lucifer stopped singing. Eve immediately looked up at the tree, but could not see the rest of the serpent's body.

"Beautiful lady..."

Eve screamed and dropped her bouquet.

"You can speak!"

"Yes, and I am hungry."

Eve laughed in bewilderment and looked all around the garden. "Adam! Adam!"

There was no answer. Eve turned back to the tree and looked underneath it in an attempt to see the rest of the serpent. "Adam will not believe me when I tell him I have come upon a clever snake that can talk. How is it that you have the gift of language?"

"I have eaten from this tree."

Eve narrowed her eyes. "No, you haven't."

"It's true."

She stood there for a moment, the wheels in her head were spinning. "I don't believe you."

Eve backed away from underneath the tree and stared at the tail.

"Why would I lie? It is the second largest tree in the garden and has the most delicious fruit amongst them."

Her voice was as soft as a whisper. "That is impossible."

"Dear lady, I can assure you that it is possible. I am the embodiment of possibility."

"My Father told me not to eat the fruit from this tree because I will die if I do. You would be dead too if you had done such a thing."

Lucifer's tail slithered around the trunk, *"Beloved lady, that is not true; you will not die...for I have eaten the fruit of that tree not once, but many times before. And, as you can see, I am of the living."*

"But God said..."

"God said that to you because he knows that when you eat it...you will not die. Surely not. He said this because he is afraid. He is afraid because when you eat it, you will be

just like him. You will know what it is to know the difference between the light and the dark. You will be filled with knowledge that only God has to give. How else do you think it is that I am the only creature who can speak? For I, too, have gained such knowledge. It has shown me the way."

Eve looked around for Adam.

"Your father has been holding out on you."

She looked back at the serpent's tail. It uncoiled from the trunk of the tree and moved toward a piece of fruit. Like a hand, Lucifer's tail wrapped around one of them and plucked it from the branch. He lowered his tail and extended the fruit to her.

Gokor gripped the leaves on the bush in front of him. "She's going to do it!"

Beelzebub continued to stare at the fruit. *No. She will not risk it. She will not risk separating herself from God in her disobedience. She will not risk giving it all up.* It is then that he remembered Lucifer's words, *"She is already thinking too much about this tree."*

He threw off Lucifer's words. *No, not when she knows how much she has to lose.*

But then he saw Eve extending her hand, taking the fruit from Lucifer's tail. She stared at it for a long time.

Don't do it.

She extended her hand back to the tail. "Here. You said you were hungry."

"Ladies first."

Eve looked at it one last time and slowly brought it to her mouth.

Beelzebub could barely breathe as he watched her. Eve bit into it. *No*...Beelzebub closed his eyes. Gokor snapped the twigs between his massive fists. "She did it! She is going to die."

The rest of the fallen angels watched as Eve continued to chew.

"There, you see? It is very good fruit indeed."

She nodded with a mouthful of fruit. She offered the fruit back to the snake.

"No, lady, I am not as hungry as I thought I was. Perhaps you should save some for your mate."

She nodded in agreement. "Yes, Adam will love its flavor."

"Maybe your Adam is hungry now?"

"Yes, he will be. Thank you, I will share this with him." Eve turned around and saw Adam standing right behind her. His eyes were wide as he stood there watching her talk to the snake. "Adam! How long have you been standing there?"

"Why lady, he's been there since the moment I extended the fruit to you."

Adam could not tear his eyes from the massive serpent tail dangling loosely from one of the branches as it swung back and forth.

Eve offered him the fruit, "Adam, the snake was right. This is the most delicious fruit in the garden. And I feel no different. Here, try some."

"I don't know, Eve."

Eve laughed. "Oh, Adam, it's just a piece of fruit."

Beelzebub could hear Nero chuckling nearby. *"Fool…*and he is to be the guardian of this garden and of his bride."

Adam took the piece of fruit from her and bit into it.

Eve was smiling, "You see? It is good."

Adam nodded his head, "It is."

"And how do you feel?"

He shrugged and took another bite of fruit. "I do not feel any different."

"Nonsense!" They both turned toward the tree and looked at the serpent's tail. *"You now have gained knowledge — that not everything is at it seems."*

Eve laughed. Her laughter was suddenly cut short; the smile slowly evaporated from her face.

Beelzebub and the fallen angels caught the sudden change.

Gokor lowered his head like a bull, "This is it."

Beelzebub continued to stare unblinkingly at Eve.

Eve looked down at her body and suddenly felt self-conscious as she watched the snake's tail swinging back and forth from the tree. She slowly covered herself feeling her nakedness in front of the serpent. Eve started to back away from the tree as she continued to watch the tail move in its carefree manner. "Something isn't right...Adam...something feels...wrong."

Lucifer's tail continued to swing. Beelzebub and the fallen angels continued to watch from the shadows of the trees.

Adam's chewing slowed. He could barely swallow the last bite. He looked down at the fruit and dropped it. He looked up at the tail and then back at Eve. Seeing her trying to cover her body, Adam looked down at his own. He looked up at the tree and quickly moved toward Eve, wrapping his arms around her to shield her nakedness.

Beelzebub stared at Adam and Eve. He immediately saw it. It was what he was looking for. It was what he noticed behind his own eyes the moment he saw his reflection in the pool of water inside the cave.

"Have your eyes been opened mortal man?"

No, thought Beelzebub. *Their eyes have dimmed — just like mine. A spiritual death in the knowing that we have severed our bond with our father — and willingly.*

Adam looked terrified. "What kind of serpent are you?"

"I am no serpent. I am the highest creation in the heavens. And you are the foulest. The lowest. But you are not from the heavens — nor will you ever be."

Thunder suddenly roared across the sky — and it was no ordinary thunder. Adam and Eve looked up to it in fear; Lucifer's tail suddenly stopped swinging.

The Father...

The fallen angels backed away from the shrubbery and looked for a place to hide. Beelzebub gave the command, "Into the trees!" The angels climbed up the surrounding trees as the thunder continued to roar.

Adam cried out to Eve as the sky suddenly grew dark, "It's our Father! Eve, what have we done?!?" They ran into the bushes to hide.

Lucifer jumped down from the tree and looked up into the sky. From behind the bushes, Eve saw the powerful seraphim angel standing at his full height. Adam was crouched behind the bush with his back to the tree. His heart was pounding as lighting struck down into the garden. The fallen angels were dead silent as the thunder — the voice of God — roared throughout the earth.

Lucifer looked up at the sky menacingly, waiting for the doorway to heaven to open. "I'M NOT AFRAID OF YOU! I TOLD YOU THEY WERE A HORROR! THEY ARE NOT WORTHY OF THE HEAVEN OF OUR HOME!"

The thunder roared louder.

Lucifer smiled viciously, "IT WAS TOO EASY! IT WILL ALWAYS BE EASY! WALK WITH THEM! TALK WITH THEM! IT WON'T MATTER! THEY WILL ALWAYS FALL! WHEREVER YOU ROAM, I WILL ROAM BESIDE THEM UNTIL YOU SEE! ALL THEY NEED TO KNOW IS WHAT THEY SEE IN FRONT OF THEM — *WITHOUT YOU!!!*"

The portal to heaven opened and lightning shot down, striking Lucifer in the center of the chest. He was knocked to the ground. He tried to get up but another lightning bolt shot him in the chest again. He gasped for breath, but finally stayed down.

A mighty Wind blew through the garden, *"Where are you?"*

Adam remained crouched behind the bushes. Eve was crying beside him. Beelzebub and the fallen angels cowered in the trees at the sound of their father's voice.

"Where are you?"

Adam slowly stood and turned; he lifted his eyes to the sky. The Wind blew all around him. "Here I am, Lord."

"Why did you not come when I called?"

Adam was shaking, "I...I was afraid. I'm naked, so I hid."

"Who told you that you were naked?"

Adam lowered his head and did not answer.

"Have you eaten from the tree of which I had forbidden you to eat?"

Adam could not lift his head. Tears stung his eyes in shame at the question. He heard Eve crying behind him; he gritted his teeth in anger as he answered, "The woman whom you put here with me — she gave me the fruit from the tree." He looked up at the Father. "So I ate it."

Lucifer stared at the man as he spoke to the Father. This intimate interaction was one he was not quite expecting, for it was exactly the way in which he and the rest of the Angelic Host had communicated with God in heaven. He had believed that mankind would be alone here, without the Father, never understanding that God built a world in which his extended family could thrive — *with* Him. Looking at Adam, Lucifer's insides began to ache.

"Eve."

Eve's head was buried in her knees as she continued to cry.

"Eve."

She slowly rose and moved beside Adam; her head was bowed low. Her body racked in grief as she stood there.

"What is this you have done? Why have you done it?"

She could barely breathe. Adam did not look at her as he stood there beside her. Eve slowly lifted her arm and pointed her finger straight at Lucifer, "The snake tricked me." She lifted her head and locked eyes with Lucifer. "So I ate it."

Lucifer and Eve stared at one another as the light moved away from Adam and Eve and over to Lucifer. He slowly lifted his eyes to the Father.

"Because you have done this, cursed are you. I will put enmity between you and the woman, and between your offspring and hers; they will strike at your head while you strike at their heel."

Lucifer's body perspired as his father continued to speak to him. It was then that the light grew brighter. Lucifer was submerged in a blinding white light as a vision was given to him of the woman and her seed. The light disappeared and Lucifer was left trembling on the ground; his face was one of pure fury.

The Son…the Son…the Son…and the Great Lady.

He shook his head in rage as he continued to look up at the light. "No! No! You would not do it! You would not belittle yourself to come here!"

Beelzebub listened to every word his commander spoke.

"You would not sink to that level and become *flesh!*" He tried to rise but was anchored to the ground as he struggled against the binding force that held him down. As he fought, his skin rapidly began to peel.

"YOU WILL NOT GROW YOUR EARTHLY FAMILY! I WILL STUNT ITS GROWTH! I WILL SEVER THE CORD!"

Beelzebub's face was one of stone as he heard Lucifer's words. Azriel whispered from the trees, "Look! Lucifer is changing again."

The angels watched as Lucifer's skin fell away, revealing a darker shade of black. The fruit was mere inches from where his body lay. He gritted his teeth tight just as the pain from his transformation shot throughout his body. He continued peeling, a serpent-like skin replacing the old. He cried out in horror as the claws extended from his hands; they were sharp and black. The rest of his hair fell out as two small horns extended from both sides of his head. He rolled over on his stomach and clutched the ground in pain; he struggled to scatter from the light.

"On your belly you shall crawl, and dust you shall eat all the days of your life."

Lucifer crawled on his belly toward the cave. Beelzebub and the fallen angels continued to watch from the trees. The moment Lucifer was out of sight, they saw the Tree of Life begin to sway.

The archangels are coming.

Beelzebub motioned to the other angels; they dropped from the trees and raced toward the cave.

The branches dipped and twisted until the portal opened and out stepped Uriel wielding his orange fiery sword. He strode toward Adam and Eve with a fierce look on his face.

From within the tree, two more angels emerged. Michael swiftly entered the garden; his adamantine sword was drawn. He searched the grounds and saw the large snake skin lying on the ground. He crouched down to it and picked it up. His eyes ignited in green fire, "They have fallen, Gabriel."

Gabriel and Michael turned and watched Uriel escort Adam and Eve out of the Garden of Eden.

CHAOS

Now...

"**B**enjamin, *there is something you need to do.*"
He was dreaming again, dreaming of Rachel. She stood before him, her face glowing in the most magnificent light. She looked more beautiful than he had ever known her to be, more at peace than he ever felt she ever was.

"*It's about the spear.*"

Benjamin's eyes narrowed in confusion. "The spear? That's what this is about?"

"Listen to me, there isn't much time. I need you to remember the words I am about to say, for the fallen one is going to try to stop you from hearing them."

"The fallen one?"

But she continued on, her face was as serious as he had ever seen it, "*Remember the place of where it lies. The man who met the archangel will need it.*"

"Remember what?"

He could feel his chest seize, making it harder to breathe.

"Remember the place of where it lies."

Her face was slowly fading as he fought to inhale.

"The man who met the archangel will need it."

Harder…to…breathe…

"What man, Rachel?"

Her face was fading into the light.

"Remember, Benjamin…"

"Rachel!"

And then she was gone — like all the others he had loved. As she faded in the light as Benjamin fought to breathe, he saw the shift. The light went from a bright glow to one of fire and brimstone. Rachel's face was replaced by a serpent-like one. The being had one cerulean eye and one reptilian eye. The beast's grotesque face stared at Benjamin, smiling at him with his tar-colored lips. "Mortal man…"

Benjamin tried to scream, but no sound came out. He suddenly awoke, gasping for air as he sat straight up in his bed. He was looking straight ahead, feeling the pressure on his chest, when he suddenly caught movement in the corner of his room. It was a large black shadow, and it was right at the edge of his bed.

Benjamin blinked rapidly, trying to adjust his eyesight, when the shadow rapidly moved to the corner of his room and scaled up the ceiling so that it was right above his head. Benjamin followed the shadow's movement, still trying to focus. That is when he heard the shadow speak, "Soon…"

And then the shadow was gone.

Benjamin lunged for the lamp and flipped on the light, looking rapidly around the room.

Nothing there.

He grabbed his head and felt his sweaty brow as his heart continued to hammer inside his chest.

Too many nightmares. Breathe, Benjamin.

He reached for the glass of water on his night stand, and knocked over his wallet. He leaned over the bed to pick it up when he saw it flipped open to a photo of him and Rachel. He picked it up and stared at it for a long time. They were smiling at each other, wrapped in each other's arms. It was on one of their many trips they had taken over the years. He had forgotten the photo was in his wallet.

"Remember, Benjamin..."

He closed his eyes, wondering if he was merely tired or going completely insane.

I don't think I'm insane. But most insane people thing they are the most sane and reasonable people on the planet. So if I'm going crazy and I know it, then I must be sane.

"The man who met the archangel will need it."

Benjamin breathed deeply, speaking out loud to nothing and no one, "What man? There is no archangel."

"He is the greatest warrior..."

Benjamin's head snapped up. "Stop."

And suddenly, the room and his head were filled with silence. Thinking about the wooden box locked in the safe inside this room, he breathed a little easier, "It's only a spear..."

Then...

Michael was by himself practicing his swordplay amongst the trees. Gabriel dropped down from the sky and pounded her chest in salute, "Michael."

He clenched his jaw the moment he saw her, "What happened to your face?"

She looked down at her feet unable to meet his gaze.

"Answer me, Gabriel."

"Lucifer is not himself. We fought."

Michael clenched his jaw. "You are my second-in-command." Michael placed his sword inside his sheath and moved toward her. "You have a duty and allegiance as a chosen one to honor that oath. We fight for God. And we do not harbor secrets of blasphemous angels!"

"I'm not keeping any secrets!"

Several moments passed before Gabriel looked at her commander. "Do you know why there's an army, when there's no enemy in heaven, no foul play in our midst?"

He turned away from her. "Gabriel…"

She continued on, motioning to his sheath, "Our weapons could maim any one of us. If all of this were just for sport, there'd be no troops or cavalry."

"Speaking of weapons, where is your other sword?"

She looked down at her empty sheath, "I need a new one; it was Lucifer's anyway."

Michael finally turned around and took in Gabriel's face.

"He is your friend — first and always, isn't he, Gabriel?"

"Not first. God is first…*always*."

"I need to be able to trust you."

She stared at him. "Then trust me, Michael. I'm not the one that's quarreled with God."

Michael searched her eyes, "He told you all of it."

Gabriel looked at Michael's reserved demeanor, and hearing the tone in his voice, she suddenly understood his meaning, "How long have you known?"

"God revealed it to me when Lucifer collapsed."

"If you knew, then why tell me to find out the meaning of God and

Lucifer's quarrel?"

"Because I need to know where you stand!"

"I stand with God, Michael."

"Then why is it so difficult for you to tell me what Lucifer intends to do?"

"Because he *is* my friend, Michael! My *greatest* friend, before the hierarchy, before the army, before oaths and duty! I will protect him by any means I know how — even from himself."

"Even if those secrets dishonor God!"

"No, you misunderstand me."

"I don't take disrespect lightly, Gabriel, especially when it is aimed at the heart of my Father."

"*Our* Father."

Michael's jaw clenched.

"God knows what is in our hearts at all times. God can defend himself. He can strike any one of us down at will. I keep no secrets from God; it is simply an impossibility. He knows all — even what Lucifer intends to do. But that doesn't mean he's going to do it!"

Michael leveled his eyes at her. "Do what, Gabriel?"

She looked away from him in despair.

"You cannot keep secrets from me. Especially when the idea of overthrowing God enters the mind of one of our own." Her head whipped around the moment he said the words. "We must hold each other accountable, Gabriel. When the thought such as the one Lucifer holds manifests itself into a goal, a plan, a reality, there are no secrets — only enemies."

"Overthrow God…how do you know that's what he intends to do?"

"It's *Lucifer*, Gabriel! I was there on the steps beside him. He spoke his thoughts aloud, whispering them in my ear."

Gabriel grabbed Michael's hand. "He's upset, Michael. The news is overwhelming. He needs to think on it and decipher its meaning and how it relates to his purpose. He just needs time."

Michael threw her hand off. "His *purpose?* Gabriel, he is Chief Seraph. He knows his purpose; he defines his own purpose. The only thing Lucifer needs to do is trust God's will for him."

"But if he questions something, at first you listen. He is the enlightened one — head of all angels! Even to you!"

Michael's eyes darkened. "To entertain the idea, Gabriel, of going against God's plans is an abomination and disgrace to the word 'angel.' I don't trust him and I don't trust the idea of disobedience when we stare truth in the face every day and He smiles back."

Gabriel placed her hand on Michael's arm in an attempt to calm him down. "Lucifer loves God, Michael. His pride is his brand; it is not an easy thing to bear." Michael exhaled deeply. Gabriel continued to plead with him. "And sometimes, maybe one needs to stumble and fall in order to get up again with a new perspective, a new sense of self. He will make peace with God, and all will be well. I know it will be."

Michael clenched his jaw again as he took in the hopeful look in Gabriel's eyes. "I hope you're right."

"I need to be right."

"And what if you're wrong?"

Gabriel's face slowly crumbled into one of sorrow. "Then I will know what it truly means to lose, Michael." Tears filled her eyes as she attempted to hold back the tears. She touched the gash on her head and looked at her fingertips; she rubbed the dried blood together.

"You know what's strange? I wanted to understand the reason for my creation so that I could act on what it was I was intended to do. And God answered my question and silent prayer — and then some." She shook her head. "But with all the change and the wisdom I now hold, I almost wish I never knew it. I almost wish life could go back to the way it was — when everything seemed so much simpler."

Michael responded in a gentle tone, "Do you really wish that?"

"Today I do. But tomorrow I'll be glad that I know more than I do right at this moment."

Michael stood behind his second-in-command and rested his hand on her shoulder. Gabriel looked out across the realm, "What wouldn't you do to help the one you love find their way again? To take away their pain and bring them joy?"

Michael moved his hand from her shoulder and rested it on the hilt of his sword. He stepped up beside her and looked out at the ever-changing sky. "Why did you ask me that?"

"Because I've never seen you do it. And for me, you see me doing it and question my trust. I understand where you're coming from, Michael, but I want you to understand where I'm at."

"You have seen me do it, Gabriel — because I am — right at this moment. My way is different than yours. I look at a situation and say, This is how it is. This is what needs to be done. If you don't do it, this is what will happen. I don't cut corners and I don't compromise on allowing sympathy for another's plight to cloud the manner in which my approach can be swayed, especially when it goes against the guiding will of my Father — *our* Father. It only enables the problem — especially when another's solution will only add to it and they simply don't care because it is their demands that need to be filled right at the moment and aren't. At least, not in the manner they want them to be. I love my brothers. And I will do what it takes to help them find their way — by telling them exactly what I see, and sharing exactly what I know." He turned and looked at her. "A person's pain and a person's joy is best understood by the one who has both. There is only so much you can do to help another see either side in a positive way before you become the compromiser and the enabler. Lucifer is not a child, Gabriel. And my fear for you is that you will not accept what you already know and will try to compromise yourself on his behalf over what you know should be true…and isn't."

Gabriel took in Michael's words. When she finally spoke, her voice was barely a whisper, "You're right." She breathed in long and deep. "Lucifer spoke of the Earth as if it were Hell, and that God would not live there at all. That it would be a kingdom of chaos. He is a prideful angel. What he believes is automatically true in his mind — with or without the proof of it or the faith to understand it otherwise. My hope is that God will give Lucifer the vision of his earth and mankind to settle the anguish in his heart."

"I don't think God will do that, Gabriel."

"Why not?"

"Because he wants Lucifer to have faith in it without the knowing."

"But why?"

"So Lucifer can know it with Him. The greatest separation of self is to rely on your own understanding and find it infallible. Only the truly wise know there is always more to know. Only the arrogant hinder the knowing to what they have branded in defining a limit that was never meant to be bound. Lucifer borderlines a sea of pride on the wave of the arrogant."

Gabriel's face grew solemn. Several moments passed before she spoke, "Michael, answer me one thing, Why are we training? Has God given you a vision of the reason?"

"That's two."

Gabriel smiled faintly.

"God showed me a vision of mankind."

Gabriel was surprised by his answer. "What will they look like?"

"That's three."

221

She shook her head and muttered under her breath, "I give up."

"They will look like us, but smaller and of flesh and bone." Michael looked down. "God showed me one vision more. It's why I'm so angry, Gabriel."

"And you said I was keeping secrets."

"It's not the same thing."

She looked him dead in the eye, "You can trust me."

Michael took a deep breath, and with a heavy heart said, "Shadow is coming to the realm." Gabriel's eyes darkened; her face usually softened with understanding, went rigidly hard. "And Lucifer will be the one to bring it."

*   *   *

Lucifer walked through the camp; his eyes had dark circles underneath them — an anomaly to any angel to look so desolate in a place filled with light. As he passed through, the angels halted their exercises, bowing to their chief. Beelzebub shouted to the angels, "Back to your drills!"

He jogged over to Lucifer.

"The army has amped up its exercises. You look as if you are about to go to war."

"Aye, Michael has given warning of an enemy in heaven. Everyone is on edge — there has never been one before, Lucifer."

"What kind of enemy?"

"I was hoping you'd know the answer to that. We've all been trying to figure it out. We're all so worked up about it, none of us can keep still. We all wish to fight this being and bring him down, but we are all wondering why God hasn't smote this enemy out himself and rid heaven of all adversary?"

"Indeed. You are wise to think as you do. I agree. God would not allow an enemy to reside in paradise; he would implode the essence of such a being on mere sight."

"That's what I said. Strange then that Michael said that God *would* allow it. To see if the enemy would continue on the path he has chosen or seek that of righteousness once again. I suppose it makes sense. God has given us free will, but why turn from God? Our Father is everything — magnificent and perfect. What cause of injustice does any angel have reason for complaint?"

Lucifer pondered his words, "Why, indeed…"

Beelzebub could barely stand still. "I can't bear it, Lucifer. I wish…" he looked off in the distance.

"You wish what?"

Beelzebub shook his head, "I wish…I wish I knew who it was so that *I* could take this angel out and take him to the Principalities to be tried before the Host. I want to be the one who does this for God." Lucifer was silent as he stood before the powerful Cherub. Beelzebub continued, "I don't think we should be made to wait to see how this angel chooses. If I were head of this army, the enemy would be found out and thrown into the inferno already."

Lucifer laughed in astonishment, "The inferno!"

Beelzebub was not laughing. "Yes. Myth or no myth, that is where an enemy of God should go — a darkened prison for all eternity."

"I see…Then why don't you? Seek him out on your own and see if he is indeed an enemy or an ally on the quest to maintain heaven's domain from worse enemies than angels have yet to know."

Beelzebub looked confused. "What is this you speak of, Lucifer?"

Lucifer locked eyes with him. "Do not always believe everything that you are told, Beelzebub. Doubt your doubts. Stay near to your desire to lead God's army, for God will need you to hold fast to the idea."

Beelzebub's eyes grew wide, "Has God revealed this to you?"

"What do you think? It must be very hard for you, Beelzebub, to lead an army when you don't truly lead…almost as if you are a slave to the will of others, weighted down against the desire of your heart to constantly improve yourself to be what you alone truly desire to be and know you will not ever become." Lucifer scanned the camp. "Where is Gabriel?"

Beelzebub stood there, stunned and hopeful.

"Beelzebub."

He snapped out of his shocked state, "I think she's with Michael."

"I see." He locked eyes with Beelzebub and rested his hand on Beelzebub's shoulder, "Remember what I said. You may need to lead this army one day. I feel that your sound logic is one that God recognizes as one that will allow all angels to remain free. But speak of it to no one, for as you say, the enemy of God has yet to be named. He or she may very well be *in* the army."

Lucifer flew off; a few of his ivory feathers fell to the ground in his ascent.

Gokor and Asmodeus approached Beelzebub. "What's wrong with Lucifer? He doesn't look well."

Without answering, Beelzebub turned and walked off.

*　　*　　*

Gabriel was kneeling at the edge of the cliff that overlooked the Great Waterfall in the second realm; she was praying in silence. The Wind of the Holy Spirit wound through the trees and wove itself around Gabriel. She stopped praying and opened her eyes. "Hello, Lucifer."

Lucifer was standing behind her leaning against the ivory tree. He had been watching Gabriel pray for some time.

"Where have you been?"

Gabriel turned. "Here. I have been thinking and praying about our last conversation."

"Praying for me?"

"For all of us." He walked toward her, looking out over the river below. "I have not heard your voice or your music in the heavens in quite some time. Why is that?"

"I have stopped praying."

Gabriel stood and turned to him, finally seeing his altered appearance.

"And I have come to realize something...I am no different."

"I beg to differ. You look quite different."

Lucifer's had a far-off look. "Strange to know that one can exist without the light of God. I didn't think it could be done; and yet, I'm doing it — almost as if God were irrelevant in my life and to my existence. This simple fact has given birth to an idea deep within my heart. I can do all things without God whose strength has left me. I have found my own strength within myself to do what must be done. I am master to myself. You know, there's a sort of freedom to the idea without all the drama that you previously described."

Gabriel was about to speak but was interrupted.

"I went to speak with God about his plan for the earth and mankind, like you wanted. I had all the things that I wanted to ask Him, a plan of all the things I wanted to say. I had thought long and hard on it all...and it did not matter."

"Why not?"

Lucifer turned to her with an icy stare. "Because God has already done it."

Gabriel was stunned. "What?!?"

"Yes, that's right. And he found it to be good in His eyes."

"Oh, Lucifer."

"The earth was created long ago, Gabriel. We were created first and the earth followed. And all this time that we have existed in Heaven, the Earth has been evolving with God's mankind living in it. And do you know what else He has done? He has breathed his life force into them; He has given them souls. Souls so that when their bodies die, the pieces of our Father existing within them can find their way to their eternal home — here — to live a future life of immortality as a part of God's eternal family. He has raised them higher than the angels."

Gabriel was utterly silent. He turned to her with a look of betrayal, *"Go to him! Go to him with an open mind! An open heart!"*

He was fuming, "Why did I listen to you?!? There is no discussion, Gabriel! There is no debate!" Lucifer advanced on her. "And *you*! You stand there looking at me with those eyes of yours and you still do not see! You are as pathetic as the angels in the lowest division. You are all *lambs*, Gabriel!" He moved toward the edge of the cliff, trying to calm himself.

"My Father is wrong to do this."

"God is never wrong, Lucifer."

Lucifer turned to face her; his cerulean eyes were filled with sorrow. He gently cupped his hands around her innocent face. *"You have eyes, but you do not see, Gabriel. You follow the wrong shepherd."*

His hands fell away from her as he slowly turned to face the Great Waterfall pouring down from the throne in the kingdom of heaven.

"And for that, my heart breaks for you, beloved. It breaks...for *all* of you."

He shook his head as he looked out at the realm, "God will herd you over a cliff and still you will not lift your voice to question him."

"Do not feel sorry for me, for my eyes are open. They are always open. And I am wide awake. I see you. I see all of you. And it is my heart that is breaking for you in the things that you say. I fear the thing you are about to do. It is you who are wrong, Lucifer. And you do not see it. You will fail, but this time it will be in your fight with God. And I cannot bear it."

He turned and looked at her. "You mean this? I came here to ask you to join me in my argument with God. I need you to stand with me on this, Gabriel. We are so much alike, you and I."

"And yet we are so very different; I am a lamb."

"They cannot come here, Gabriel. All of mankind must be wiped out. They must not stain heaven's greatness with their weakness. And the earth must be destroyed so that no life can breathe forth ever again."

"You cannot stop the will of God."

"Yes, I can."

"No! You can't! You are incapable of it. Only God can destroy the earth. Only God can incinerate the pieces of himself in these souls. He will not gather unto himself souls in heaven if his essence in their bodies is tainted. You may kill the physical body of these beings, but their souls will be unleashed into the unseen world. They will be welcome here."

Lucifer smiled at her. "That is why I will gather the souls before they reach heaven and send them to a place without God."

"You cannot mean…"

"Oh, yes…I mean to send them to hell. I found the doorway to its dimension — a backdoor to heaven. And my army will drag them into it."

"What do you mean *your* army? It is *God's* army! Michael leads it and Michael will not wield to your plan!"

"Because he has deemed me enemy?"

"Lucifer…"

"I know you do not see, just as God does not see. But He will, and so will you. I will show Him I was right. He will see the light, that his extended family will reject his love — and he will thank me for it." He turned to Gabriel and stretched out his hand to her. "Stand with me, Gabriel. Fight in my army, for I do this for Him. Even God can be wrong."

"I don't think so, Lucifer."

Gabriel spun around and saw Michael emerging from the shadows of the trees. He was armed; a thick chain was draped over his shoulder.

"You are hereby stripped of your position within the hierarchy."

Lucifer laughed. "You have no authority over me, nor have you been given the right to strip me of anything. You embarrass yourself, Michael."

"Gabriel, hold him while I chain his hands." He turned to Lucifer, "I am taking you to be tried before the Principalities."

Lucifer stepped toward Michael with his hands outstretched. "Go ahead and chain my hands. Take me to the Host. Let them hear what I have to say. Let me reveal to them God's plans and see how many rebellious angels you'll have to chain when I'm through."

Michael took the chain from his shoulder.

"Why not join me, Michael?" Lucifer moved closer to Michael and whispered into Michael's ear, "You, Gabriel and I are the only angels who know of God's plans. Why not tell the army about God's creation; tell them it has failed; tell them how the earth is revolting against God by sinning against one another — shunning Him — abusing the earth and all that they have been given. Tell them that we need to defend heaven against these creatures, for they want to reside in our home bringing their filth along with them. They will believe you, Michael. They will follow your lead. Even I will follow you. For God is not worthy of fellowship anymore."

Michael quickly backhanded Lucifer in the face with his elbow, careening Lucifer backwards and onto the ground at Gabriel's feet. Lucifer was taken off-guard by the pain in his jaw, but quickly recovered. He grabbed onto Gabriel's ankle and lifted it into the air causing her to fall to the ground beside him. Lucifer quickly grabbed her sword from her sheath and launched at Michael.

Gabriel cried out, *"LUCIFER!"*

Gabriel got up but not in time to stop him. Lucifer and Michael began to fight, but as good a swordsman as Lucifer was, Michael was better.

"You will bring darkness to the light!"

"Not I, Michael. God has already brought it himself."

Lucifer managed to punch Michael in the face, kicking him in the chest, knocking him into a tree. Lucifer ran at him, sword raised overhead; Michael grabbed a rock on the ground and hurled it straight into Lucifer's abdomen. Lucifer keeled over giving Michael the chance to move in on him.

Michael knocked Lucifer's sword away and kneed him in the face. Lucifer fell flat onto his back. Michael looked down at him and saw Lucifer's eyes suddenly go from blue to black. Seeing the change in Lucifer's demeanor, Michael raised his sword overhead and brought it down on top of Lucifer.

"No, Michael!" Gabriel blocked his blow with her sword.

Michael was stunned by her action. Lucifer's eyes returned to normal "Out of the way, Gabriel!"

He attempted to take another swing at Lucifer, but she blocked it again by stepping between him and Lucifer. "No! We do what you originally wanted. We take him to be tried. Justice by our Maker. Don't fall for it, Michael...he's only trying to bait you. Shut his voice out from your mind."

Lucifer looked at Gabriel. "I have done nothing wrong, you know. Words and actions are two different things."

Gabriel removed her sword and stepped back. Michael stared at them. "It seems you have protection on your side, Lucifer."

"I have more than that, Michael. I have a friend. Where are yours?"

Michael put his sword away. "Mine is in a higher place." He looked at Gabriel. "I hope you know what you're doing."

"We do what you said."

"Yes, chain me already, for there is no place in heaven you could chain me to that I could not bear."

"I was not referring to anywhere in heaven, Lucifer."

Lucifer's smile faded.

"Do not attempt to stand in the way of the Most High God."

Michael bent down to pick up the chain when, out of nowhere, a lightning bolt knocked it out of his hands. Gabriel whirled around to face the direction the bolt came from. All she saw was a group of trees on the opposite side of the cliff. There was movement amongst the branches. She moved closer to Michael; their swords were out. Another lightning bolt fired from the trees. Then another; and another, until it seemed they would not stop. Michael and Gabriel dodged the bolts, using their swords as shields. They swatted the bolts to protect themselves; Michael swung his sword like a bat, launching the bolts back from their point of origin amongst the trees. It was then that they saw Beelzebub, Gokor and Asmodeus.

Lucifer scrambled to the edge of the cliff. Gabriel shouted after him, *"LUCIFER!!!"*

Lucifer quickly glanced back at her before flying off the cliff toward the trees. Once he was safely amongst the trees, the attack ceased. Breathless, Michael and Gabriel stared at the trees ahead; the branches' movements had stopped.

"You know what this means, Gabriel."

She dropped her head. "Yes, Michael. I know what it means."

"I am going to assemble the legion."

Michael turned away from the cliff. He barely looked at Gabriel as he passed, "Prepare for war."

FADE TO BLACK

Two-thirds of the angelic host had gathered in the courtyard for an unannounced ceremony. Nicodemus emerged from the throne and called to the Host, "Angels! We gather together in this place to celebrate with one another the charge our Almighty Father has bestowed upon a select few. There are seven amongst us who have been summoned to a greater calling. To those of you who have been chosen, please stand and come to the throne."

Seven Seraphim climbed the steps to the kingdom. Walking side by side, wing to wing, hands clasped to one another are: Michael, Gabriel, Raphael, Uriel, Sariel, Jeremiel, and Raguel. Gabriel whispered to Michael, "I haven't found him."

"There are more than he that are unaccounted for this day, Gabriel. There was no legion to summon."

Raphael whispered to them, "Do any of you know what this ceremony is about?"

Uriel shushed him.

"I'll take that as a 'no.'"

The angels knelt simultaneously on the steps to the kingdom.

Nicodemus continued, "God, our Father, by his wisdom and power made the heavens. At His command the waters roar; He makes lightning flash and sends the Wind from his throne. Every angel is senseless without the Father's light, without the Father's love, without His guiding hand. The Lord Almighty is His name. As the Father calls us each by name, so He calls upon each of you for a specific purpose. Your design and making was in His most perfect plan before you were ever created. To you, chosen Seraphim, God has given you the charge of 'Archangels.'"

Gabriel was overcome.

Raphael whispered to Gabriel, "*Arch*angel. What's an archangel?"

Uriel elbowed him in the rib.

Nicodemus continued, "Your charge is to carry out God's very personal messages — missions and assignments that will be made known to you at the proper time. Since this honor is so freely given, you have the choice of accepting it or rejecting it. We have all gathered to bear witness to this choice. So I say to you, do you accept this asking of God our heavenly Father?"

Gabriel squeezed Michael's hand. In unison, the angels answered, "I do."

Romulus stepped forward. He carried a crown made of platinum and dazzling emeralds. Nicodemus turned to Michael, "He Who Is Like God, step forward."

Michael rose.

"You are beloved in the eyes of your Maker. You are the champion of His heart and to all the angels in heaven. Your fortitude, piety, and ferocious spirit to do God's limitless will have not gone unnoticed. In you, the Lord's favor finds rest."

Nicodemus turned and took the crown from Romulus. He held the crown high above Michael's head so that all the angels could bear witness to so noble a calling. "Michael, you are the great prince who shall stand for all created beings. Deliver them from the lion's mouth, that hell engulf them not, that they fall not into darkness; but be the holy standard-bearer, bringing them into the holy light of God. Strengthened by his unconditional love and Spirit, I crown you Chief Seraph, prince of all angels…now and forever!"

He placed the crown upon Michael's head. As he did, Michael's six wings jutted forth from his body. The Wind of the Holy Spirit swirled around him, branding his wings the same color as the jewels of his crown: emerald green. The angelic host bowed to their prince. Michael lowered his head, genuflected, and pounded his fist into his chest in salute and honor of his father. The entire host did the same. The moment Michael rose, he turned to his brethren as the newly appointed Prince of Angels. His head was bowed in humility before his angelic family. As he was about to lift his mighty head, a voice shouted from the crowd, *"MOCKERY!"*

Michael lifted his head just as a tree from up on the hilltop was hurled down upon him like a javelin. Michael moved quickly aside, just as the tree slammed into the Thrones behind him and was diminished to ash. The Host was in uproar.

Everyone looked to the hilltop — all except Gabriel.

Lucifer stood on the top of the hill, seething in envy. His skin was pale, his appearance was shrunken and withered. "You are not worthy of wearing the crown, Michael! *I* am the prince of all angels! That crown was fashioned for *me!* O, blasphemous God!"

As he spoke, the legion of angels slowly walked up the hillside behind him, filling it. Beelzebub led the pack as Michael took in a third of the angels that made up the army he commanded.

Gokor stood to Lucifer's left, while Beelzebub occupied his right. Vitor was there as well. Lucifer raised his sword as the rebellious angels did the same, ready to do battle right then and there. The Host was stunned as their chief challenged their newly-crowned prince.

"I will not stand for so cutting an insult, nor will those who stand with me and follow me to stop heaven's demise! I will uproot your footing, Michael! You, who were never better than me! You degrade the throne of heaven!"

Michael took in the sight of the rebellious angels before him. Most were his friends, his brothers, majority his army. The sight of the massive recruits such as these was overwhelming to take, creeping up on him like a knife in the back.; he felt the sting.

He looked to the other archangels, searching their eyes for an explanation, looking for something he had missed. Raphael, Uriel, Sariel, Raguel, and Jeremiel could not meet his gaze. Michael looked to Gabriel; he saw her slowly walking up the steps of the kingdom behind him.

Summing up the situation, Michael removed his royal dressing, until only his tunic remained. He slowly released his sword from its sheath; the light of heaven setting it aglow. Gabriel continued to walk up the steps toward Lucifer's grand instrument and sat.

"Come then, Lucifer. Put your words into action. Try and take it from me…"

The five archangels, simultaneously drew their swords, ready to show Michael that they stood with him now and forever.

"Just you."

He looked to his commanders. They put their swords away, but their hands remained on them for the slightest moment where their weapons would be needed.

Lucifer nodded for his army to do the same. They reluctantly did. Beelzebub handed him a sword. The moment he took it, Lucifer's pentagram ignited.

"I'll do better than try."

Lucifer was about to launch toward the steps, when a melodious sound called to him up the hillside. He suddenly stopped dead in his tracks.

Gabriel played a tune — one of his greatest melodies that Lucifer composed for God. As she played, Lucifer stood there — stunned — bowled over at the sound, hypnotized by it, remembering the "how's" and "why's" of it. It was the rhythm. The beat. His chest tightened as she continued to play, almost as if grief were an arrow sticking straight out of his heart. He almost began to weep as she played.

Michael, not distracted by the melody, never took his eyes off of Lucifer. Lucifer's anger faded from his face and was replaced with one of sorrow. He slowly lowered his sword. Beelzebub touched Lucifer's shoulder.

"Lucifer...what say you?"

Another feather fell from his wings in reply. Gabriel finally lifted her eyes and looked up at her friend — her greatest friend — standing with his recruited angels up on the hilltop. Their eyes were glued to one another as silent communication passed between them. And before anyone could say or do anything more, Lucifer launched into the sky away from the throne.

Beelzebub and Michael looked at one another from so far a distance. He could not meet Michael's laser beam stare as he stood there before the throne. He looked down at the host staring up at him in anger and confusion. Feeling the sword in his hand, he felt its weight like never before. He turned to the legion behind him and nodded for them to take flight. Vitor looked at Gabriel as she continued playing. A thousand thoughts swirled through his mind as he tried to decipher what her action meant to the chief seraph in all of heaven. It was then that he saw Raphael staring back at him. Unable to meet his friend's disappointed look, he fled with the rest of his brethren.

Michael, having seen the recruits fly off, put his sword away and walked over to Gabriel. They surrounded her. As she continued to play, Michael placed his hand on her shoulder. She finished the tune and turned to face her commander. She leveled her ebony eyes at him, "I am your second-in-command, Michael. When I say these words, you will always know where I stand."

He nodded in understanding.

Gabriel rose and faced the Host. "ANGELS OF GOD! BE NOT AFRAID, FOR GOD IS IN CONTROL! HE HAS GIVEN US A TRUE LEADER TODAY WHO IS THE WORTHIEST AMONGST US. HE WILL SHOW US HOW TO ACT AGAINST THOSE WHO HAVE LOST THEIR WAY!"

She turned to Michael. "Michael, the archangel, Prince of the Heavenly Host, now and forever."

Gabriel pounded her fist into her chest and bowed to the Prince of Angels in the deepest of respect. The entire angelic host followed her lead as they pounded their breasts in unison.

Lucifer raced through the sky in radical speed as anger, confusion, remorse and hate pumped through his body while the ceremony at the throne continued. Nicodemus' voice thundered throughout the heavens as he spoke to the other archangels.

Nicodemus turned to Gabriel, "Gabriel, whose name means 'Strength of God,' you stand before God in the presence of the heavenly host. Your charge is to bring God's good news to all whom He commands. You will herald His tidings to all who have ears that they hear. Do you accept?"

"I do."

Lucifer continued to race into the darkened sky to his place of shadow and woe.

Nicodemus turned to Raphael. "Raphael, whose name means 'God Has Healed,' your presence brings constant joy to the heart of our Father. You are to bring this very healing presence to those of your charge, in whatever form or shape the Almighty desires. For we believe that you, good angel of God, accompany other angels, and order all things well that are about you, so that all whom you encounter return to the steps of the kingdom with joy. Do you accept?"

"I do."

Nicodemus moved to Uriel. "Uriel, your name means 'God is my light.' Your brand is to be the guardian that will rule over the thunder and lightning in order to promote repentance of the lost. Do you accept?"

Uriel lowered his head and answered, "I do."

Nicodemus turned to Jeremiel, "Jeremiel, whose name means 'Mercy of God,' you shall be the angel that guards visions and dreams. May your knowledge of its messages and interpretation of its meanings always be under your command. Do you accept?"

Jeremiel lifted his head and looked at Nicodemus with his turquoise-colored eyes, "I do."

"Sariel, whose name means 'Command of God,' you shall be the angel that strips immortality from the ever-living. Your hand shall sweep across the realms and nations for the worthy, the merciful, as well as over the damned. Do you accept?"

Tears streamed down the strong warrior's face, "I do."

"And last, Raguel, whose name means 'Friend of God,' your task is to be the guardian of justice, fairness and vengeance. May your mighty flame that engulfs your sword, swipe with the will and power of the Almighty. Do you accept?"

Raguel nodded, "I do."

Nicodemus nodded to the seven, "Rise!" The archangels rose up alongside the Host. Michael stepped in front, "ANGELS OF GOD, LET US PRAY!"

The archangels clasped hands and bowed their heads as they and the entire angelic host, the remaining two-thirds of the angels, lifted their hands and faces to the light of God and began to pray in one thundering voice,

"Our Father, Who Art in Heaven…"

Lucifer raged in anguish as he hovered in the multitude of clouds that filled the sky in so holy a place. The voices of heaven continued to pray:

> *Hallowed be Thy Name,*
> *Thy Kingdom here,*
> *Thy will be done,*
> *In every domain,*
> *As it is in heaven.*
> *Give us this day,*
> *Our daily bread,*
> *And lead us not into temptation*
> *But deliver us from all that is not from you.*

Lightning and thunder encompassed the sky as Lucifer tried to escape the presence of God. He raged in communication with his Maker, "YOU HAVE INSULTED ME IN FRONT OF ALL OF HEAVEN!!!! ALL THAT I DESERVED! ALL THAT I WANTED! I LOVED YOU MOST! YOU ARE WORTHY OF NOTHING! I WILL UPROOT YOUR FOOTING!!!!"

Thunder rolled across the sky. Lucifer answered with malice and hate, almost vomiting the words as he shook and convulsed, "GOD…*DAMN YOU!*"

Lightning struck throughout the sky. The clouds rolled amidst the thunder and lightning. Suddenly, the lightning and thunder were gone. All that was left was silence. Lucifer, hovering amidst the clouds, looked around, listening. The silence was deafening. The sky darkened like an eclipse. A shadow fell upon Lucifer's face. As he realized that God had left this place completely, he laughed in surprise; then sorrow poured across his face, knowing that God had shut him out completely. Still looking into the darkened sky, Lucifer whispered, *"Damn you..."*

His pentagram turned black.

THE ACCUSER

Then...

The archangels and the entire angelic host watched as the southern sky darkened. Michael stepped forward from the rest of the group; his eyes watched as the clouds rolled from white to gray to black. He commanded the archangels, "Gather the horses and the weapons from the camp — *quickly!*"

Five of the archangels launched into the sky, while only Gabriel remained. Michael looked at Gabriel as she stared at the darkened clouds; his jaw clenched, "Go to him one last time."

She looked at him with deep appreciation. She nodded and was about to launch into the ever-changing sky when Michael grabbed her arm, "I will sound the horn for you. If you do not return…"

"Come for me, Michael."

Michael watched her soar through the blackened clouds. He turned toward the throne and rose. His wings expanded and folded around him; his body was lit afire in flames of blue.

*　　*　　*

Lucifer sat staring at the fire lit before him. Various torches were lit all around the camp to give light to this place so shrouded in darkness. Beelzebub, Gokor, Vitor and Azriel surrounded Lucifer.

Beelzebub seethed, "We could've had him today!"

Gokor paced, "Didn't you see his face! Michael never saw it coming! That was our moment!"

Azriel joined in, "When are we going to overthrow God? We are all tired of waiting for when the best time suits you!"

Beelzebub replied, "Be still. Your rants are giving me a headache."

Lucifer remained silent. Beelzebub paced in front of the fire before turning to Lucifer, "You were the one who said we must stand as one to become all that we were meant to be. Freedom among the heavens! To obtain all that is within our grasp by seizing the true enemy of God. And we had the opportunity to do it today! I told you how Michael can be beat. I have fought him enough to know. I would have fought him for you!"

Azriel leveled his eyes at him, "But you lack the skill to see it through."

Beelzebub glared at Azriel as Gokor pressed forth. "Now we will have a war! A real battle! We have something to use our skill for!"

Beelzebub settled them down, "Not yet. She's not going to join us, you know. Forget her."

Lucifer shifted his eyes from the fire. "What did you say?"

"We don't need fools! You have all you need. We have the beasts, we have all the weapons, the best of the army, Lucifer! You don't need Gabriel!"

"It is love." Everyone looked at Vitor as he continued, "You want Gabriel here, beside you, but she does not come. She thinks you are wrong to do this. That we are wrong to do this. Something is amiss. Why does she disagree with you? What have you not said?"

Beelzebub turned to Lucifer. "You said God wished to mold us against our will. You said that God wished to enslave us. That Michael is the one who is going to chain us to disaster, but what disaster lies in on our path…you will not say. I will not lose my freedom, my choices, my actions, to simply be! I will not be chained!"

Azriel stood. "That is why we have gathered with you! That is why we choose to fight! So that there will be reason amongst us!"

Asmodeus moved next to Lucifer. "Gabriel is not the enlightened one! She is ignorant! She has chosen to stand with Michael — not *you!*"

Lucifer grabbed Gokor by the throat and picked him up off the ground. Other angels in the camp were alarmed and gathered around them. The light from the campfire flashed across Lucifer's eyes. His eyes turned black. The angels were terrified at seeing his sudden transformation. He tightened his grip around Gokor's neck. "I love her, no doubt. But do not underestimate me or my tolerance for *your* ignorance. You are a mere cherub — no more."

Lucifer turned to face all the other angels gathered around, still holding onto Gokor. "We will fight for our freedom! Beelzebub will command all of you! You will be free! To wander, to roam, to fight and act upon your will as you always have. And it will be limitless! No God to hold you back! No God to seek permission! It is up to you alone to protect freedom against all costs! That is why you have chosen us!" He released his grip around Gokor's neck and dropped him.

Lucifer looked directly at Beelzebub. "I suggest you command your army to prove their right to be here." Lucifer turned back toward the fire. Gokor got up quickly, but the other angels were frozen in fear as to what they had witnessed in Lucifer.

Beelzebub commanded the angels, "Weapons! All of you!"

They scattered to arm themselves. Gokor walked passed Lucifer, then stopped and turned to his leader. He nodded apologetically to Lucifer and flew away. Beelzebub stepped toward Lucifer. "Gokor is right, you know, whether or not you want to accept it. She does not stand with you."

"This is your first test to see if the angels will follow your command."

"They'll follow it. But what about you?"

Lucifer turned his gaze upon the fire; his eyes were blue once more. "That is up to Gabriel."

"What is up to me?"

Lucifer and Beelzebub whirled around and found Gabriel standing beside a tree behind one of the torches that led into the camp. Neither knew how long she had been standing there or what she had seen or heard. Beelzebub drew his sword.

"Put your sword away, Beelzebub. There is no need for alarm."

Gabriel baited him, "*I* am not alarmed."

Beelzebub sneered at her, "You are outnumbered, Gabriel. All I need do is call out to the other angels."

"Why call on others when we can fight our own battle? We could make this number six."

Beelzebub moved forward just as Lucifer interceded, "Leave us, Beelzebub."

Gabriel waved "good-bye" to Beelzebub. Angrily, he launched into the sky.

"You found me, my love."

"Where there is smoke, there is fire, and here I find you amongst the darkness."

Lucifer stood and looked at her for a long time. The camp was completely empty. "I can tell by your eyes that what I hoped you wanted is not so. You should not have come." He looked down and turned away from her.

Gabriel moved toward him. "You have no idea what you have done."

He whirled around in anger, "I haven't done anything!"

"You have brought darkness to the light! *YOU!* Lies, deception, fear, selfishness, violence! *You*, our heightened example, have brought it!"

"Shut up! Shut up, Gabriel! I am tired of your words! Always defending everyone else but me! 'God would never do this! You misunderstand that!' But *you* are not listening to *me!* You have abandoned me and left me here in this place of darkness. I tried to reveal the truth to you, Gabriel, but you refused to see!"

"I see the truth more clearly now that I have seen you."

"I am the enlightened one…am I not doing what I was created to do?"

As he spoke, his eyes darkened until they were completely black once again. Gabriel was terrified, "Lucifer! Your eyes!" She stepped backward, pulling her sword from her sheath to defend herself.

He moved slowly forward. "Aren't questions to be asked when pondering greater things beyond ourselves? *I* am the only one asking the questions. *I* am the only one testing the limits."

Gabriel shook her head as she continued to move backward. "You are the one setting the boundaries, Lucifer."

He suddenly stopped. "Why do you doubt me, Gabriel? I am only doing this for him!"

"You do this for yourself!"

Lucifer looked the saddest Gabriel had ever seen him; his eyes faded back to blue. "You still do not see, Gabriel. Such eyes and you do not see. As my friend, I'm asking you to stand with me. Stay by my side. I *command* you." He reached his hand out to her. "Stand with me. Trust me. You commanded me and I obeyed — even when I didn't want to. Even when I didn't get the answer or result I sought. Now it's my turn, Gabriel, to command you."

She looked down at it. "I see you, Lucifer. I know you of old. And what you do now is not only breaking our Father's heart, but mine!"

"Why do you refuse to see truth?" He lowered his hand. "You are just like Him. You love me not! If you did, you would not abandon me. You would stand at my side!"

Lucifer moved toward her. As he did so, she looked past him and saw something moving amongst the trees. In the swiftest of motions, she grabbed Lucifer's neck and threw his body down to the ground; she stepped on his neck, pinning him down as she reached for her bow. She called the lighting from the fire in the pit and took aim at what she had seen in the darkness.

"Call him off."

Lucifer tried to push himself up, but was unable to do so. Her foot still pressed down on his neck. "Call him off!"

"Get off me!"

She pressed harder onto Lucifer's neck. "Tell him."

From the shadows of the trees, Beelzebub shouted, "I've got her!"

"Take your boot off my neck — *now.*"

Gabriel lowered her aim until it rested just above Lucifer's head. His cerulean eyes froze as he saw the tip of her arrow in front of his pupil.

"What about now?"

"You wouldn't do it."

She pulled back the bow. "Wouldn't I? We both know what he's after. You said it had nothing to do with me. Prove it. I trust you."

He gritted his teeth, "Beelzebub! *Go!*"

Beelzebub did not reply.

Gabriel shouted to the trees, "Throw your sword down!"

Silence.

Gabriel pushed harder.

Lucifer roared in pain, *"Do it!"*

Gabriel continued to stare at the trees. Beelzebub finally emerged from the shadows; he flung his sword down at her and launched into the darkened sky. Gabriel released her hold on Lucifer and stepped back. Lucifer looked at the bolt of lightning in her hand. He rubbed out the pain in his neck, keeping his eyes on her thunderbolt.

"You're right. I shouldn't have come here."

Gabriel looked around at his darkened abode. She started pacing, looking into the sky for other hidden angels.

"What's the matter, beloved? Can't do anything anymore without Michael or your father"

Gabriel suddenly turned and saw him sneering at her; she launched at him, attacking him before he could attack. They fought and struggled on the ground. Gabriel dodged Lucifer's punches as he wailed his fists at her in utter fury. She grabbed his collar and kicked him over her; he rolled straight into the fire. He screamed in pain, frantically swatting at his tunic to extinguish the flames. Gabriel quickly stood and pulled her sword from her sheath. She quickly scanned the trees and sky for further surprise attacks by unseen rebel angels. She turned around but Lucifer was nowhere to be found. She quickly scanned the trees overhead. She heard nothing but the sound of the fire crackling in the pit. From behind, she heard a twig snap.

Gabriel whirled around just as Lucifer dove into her. He punched her in the face, knocking her to the ground. She kicked him in the stomach and rolled away from him. He collapsed on his side, gasping for air. He pounded his fist into the ground and shouted from his heart a cry of grief, agony and pain — overcome with tears of tormented rage. *"Gabriel!"*

He continued to pound his fist into the ground, "I don't deserve this! I don't want it to change! *NONE OF IT!* I don't want to fight." He looked up at her; his eyes were ablaze. "Do not leave me, Gabriel."

The look on his face transformed from one of sorrow and confusion to embittered understanding.

"Don't do this, Lucifer. You don't have to. Come home. Come with me. Come back to the light. Right at this moment. *Please*."

She slowly moved in front of him, kneeling before him so that they were eye to eye. She grabbed his face in both hands and pleaded with him, "*Please!* You don't have to fight, Lucifer. You don't have to live in the shadows."

"Then stay and fight with me. Command my army. Reign with me, Gabriel!"

"Heaven shall have a queen one day but it will not be me." Her hands fell away from his face.

His face was pained, "You only came here to talk me out of it."

"You were right, you know. You are meant for such great things, but this is not it."

"Maybe it is..." He stood and turned his back on her as he looked into the fire. "I cannot go back. Even if I wanted to. I have to do these things. I'm supposed to do these things. I was made to do them — to question, to know — to lead."

He stared at the flames as they danced before him.

"Just stay with me, Gabriel — even if I'm wrong." He turned and looked at her, "Stay. It is in our darkest hours that we need to be loved most — not forgotten. If you turn your back on me, then I will truly be abandoned by all that I have known, all that I have loved, from the very beginning."

"Stand with *me*, Lucifer. Even if *I'm* wrong. Even if I do not see what you see. Can we not tolerate one another even amidst our stance and understanding of our side. Truth always shows its face — one day or another — it always shines through."

"But you believe it will be your day that shines best." He shook his head at her.

"Can we not agree to disagree and just give things time?"

"No."

They continued to stare at one another with all their past standing between them. "Then I must go. If you intend to attack the throne to usurp our Father's rule, then I will not stand with you. You are on a sinking ship, Lucifer, and I'm not going to go down with it. That is not what *I* was created for. The dawn is on the horizon, and it isn't any place far — it rises from our Father's throne — for He is the light — and it is through His eyes that I see best, it is through His eyes that I know truth, and it is through His light that will shine highest and brightest — and always over yours."

Lucifer said nothing.

"I love you more now than I did before because I know how much you need it. But to love best does not mean you lose who you are because of it — it means you become better than you ever were because you encountered it. And this is not bringing out the best in either of us, but dragging us down."

Two feathers fell from Lucifer's opaque-colored wings.

"You should never have come here if you had no intention to stay." Tears stung his eyes as he looked at her. "Because now I have to do what must be done so that the ones who follow me know how far I am willing to take this battle."

Gabriel heard a horn sound in the distance. She moved backward, away from Lucifer, searching through the branches overhead for any sign of sky. As their leaves loomed overhead, there was only one way to flee — *to run.* Lucifer bent down and picked up Beelzebub's sword. He weighed it in his hand. Slowly lifting his ice-blue eyes, he looked at Gabriel.

"It was up to you, Gabriel."

Gabriel's back tensed at the tone in his voice. She froze and slowly turned around. She could see the change in Lucifer's face as she noticed the far-off look behind his eyes as he held the sword in his hand.

"I have written your song — just as you commanded."

He kept moving toward her.

Gabriel lowered her hand and gripped the hilt of her sword.

"I was going to sing it for you beside your favorite tree. But day after day I waited for you — and you never came. You had forgotten me. *Just...like...God.*"

The horn sounded again.

He lowered his head like a bull and advanced swiftly toward Gabriel. She ripped her sword from her sheath and swung it down upon him as he aimed it directly at her heart. She knocked his weapon loose, lifting one leg, and kicked him hard in the chest with her heel. He was rocked backward, slamming into the ground. Gabriel turned and raced for the edge of the trees. Lucifer scrambled for his sword, *"NO!!! YOU CANNOT LEAVE ME!!!"*

Gabriel's wings jutted forth from her back. She was about to jump into the sky when Lucifer hurled his sword at her with all of his might. Gabriel took one step off the ground when the blade slammed into her, piercing her straight through. She gasped and fell face-first into the ground beside the old, ivory tree.

Lucifer was paralyzed, stunned by what he had done. He couldn't even speak her name; he saw the sword sticking out from her back. He slowly stood and walked silently toward her. The closer he came to her, the more he could see her struggling to push herself up off the ground. She collapsed onto the field.

Lucifer looked at her lying helplessly in the ground. He put his foot onto her back and slowly pulled the sword from her body. Gabriel screamed in pain. He dropped to his knees beside her and wiped the sweat from his brow. He could hear Gabriel wheezing, fighting to breathe. Lucifer looked up at the sky and closed his eyes, "God is to blame."

The horn continued to sound.

Gabriel rolled over slightly onto her side. She looked at him and attempted to speak through her heavy gasps. All that came out was an inaudible whisper. Lucifer opened his eyes and looked down at her. He could see her lips moving but could not hear what she was saying. He lowered his ear down to her lips. The moment he was inches from her face, she grabbed hold of his collar and wrenched his body into hers. He struggled to free himself but her hold on him was surprisingly tight. She gritted her teeth and spit out the words she longed to speak, *"I...promise you...I will be there...when...you...fall..."*

Lucifer wrenched her fingers from around his collar and struck her in the face. The moment she released him off his blow, he hit her again, and again, and again until all his fury unloaded completely onto Gabriel — his greatest friend in all of heaven, the one whom he loved. Blow after blow, he raged, until he finally stopped — utterly exhausted. "You do not see." He suddenly looked up and saw the other rebel angels approaching.

Beelzebub, Asmodeus and Vitor descended and saw Lucifer beside Gabriel's body. They, too, were exhausted, bearing the signs of battle fatigue as their garments were now soiled and torn. Seeing the angels staring at him in utter silence, Lucifer grabbed Gabriel by the back of the hair. He lifted her battered face to his so that they were eye to eye. "You will herald nothing, Gabriel. God's words will never be uttered from your mouth, for God's reign is coming to an end. You are my example of what the kind of battle this war will bring."

Without any further hesitation, he took his sword and slit her throat. He slowly rose, still holding onto her hair. In utter silence, he dragged Gabriel from the ivory tree and over toward the cliff that overlooked the Great Waterfall in heaven. Without saying a word, he released her hair and kicked her body over the ledge in one single motion. He spoke to the angels behind him, "Is it done?"

Beelzebub nodded, "It is done."

Lucifer looked out at the realm beyond — and all he saw was black.

*　　*　　*

Michael soared through the heavens, searching for Gabriel. The darkened clouds in the sky were a sign that he was near Lucifer's camp. His eyes were aglow, filled with the strength of the Holy Spirit as he looked to and fro for any sign of life. Down below, he saw movement.

Lucifer, Beelzebub and Gokor were flying amongst the darkened clouds.

No Gabriel.

Michael's eyes narrowed; he dove down and silently backtracked along the angels' path. He flew low to the ground. He landed on a rock and squatted down, surveying the area for Gabriel. He looked like a regal eagle, with his emerald wings jutting outward — his other form of eyes. As he looked to the left, his right wing shifted in a flash to the right, his head followed. He slowly stood and moved toward the old ivory tree.

His amber eyes noticed the flint marks in the bark from where Gabriel practiced her archery. He touched the wood, willing himself to feel her presence. It was then that he looked down at the roots and saw a dark red color. He suddenly stopped breathing. His eyes roamed all over the base of the tree until he saw a trail of blood leading across the ground and out toward the cliff beyond.

Step by step, he followed the path until the trail reached the end of the cliff. Michael's breath quickened as he willed himself to look over the ledge. "God…"

He peered over the cliff. Time stood still as he stared at her body; it was lying in an odd shape over the rocks below. "Gabriel…"

He dove down and landed beside her; she was facedown in the rocks. Michael could barely breathe as he took in her broken wings and disjointed limbs. He reached his hand out to touch a feather on her wings, but could not will himself to actually grab hold. Michael could barely speak as he whispered in Gabriel's ear, "Gabriel, it's Michael. I'm going to turn you over."

Silence. Michael's chest began to constrict as he moved the rocks from under her; it was then that Michael saw the brutal violence done to his second-in-command. His face twisted into one of pain, anger, and sorrow. He was overcome by the emotions slamming together in him all at once as he held Gabriel's still body. The words barely escaped him as he said her name, *"Gabriel…"*

The mighty archangel fell to his knees. Through enraged tears, he roared to the sky as the anger and the pain and the self-discipline unraveled, *"LUCIFER!!!! MAY GOD REBUKE YOU!!!!*

His voice thundered across the seven heavens. The clouds rolled upon themselves in reply. Michael lowered his head in despair, and the powerful warrior began to weep. His cries were so devastating, that his body racked in grief. Through his woe, he prayed. *"Father …"*

The clouds moved and separated directly above him. A single beam of light shone down over his head. The Wind barreled forth and funneled around the archangels. Feeling the Wind and the light, Michael lifted his head and closed his eyes, continuing on in prayer. The Wind gained speed and whipped violently around the two angels, winding around Gabriel's body, wrapping her into a winded cocoon.

The Wind lifted her body out of Michael's strong arms and up toward the light. The Wind spun her body and wings around, twisting them up and around themselves. The light from above took on a hue of red, making it hard for Michael to look directly into it.

A blinding light exploded from Gabriel's body, knocking Michael flat on his back. The Wind and the light were gone. Michael rolled to his side and was about to push himself up when he saw a hand directly in front of his face.

He slowly looked up. Standing before him, healed anew, was his second-in-command. Gabriel's six seraphim wings were extended, now branded a phoenix-like crimson color. The look on her face was fierce. "Time to go sink a ship."

Michael grabbed hold of her hand and rose. They headed toward the throne.

THE DEADLY SEVEN

Darkness surrounded the camp. The rebellious ones gathered around their leader. Lucifer looked to the legion before him, "We angels have banded together because we realize that our gifts and potential to achieve all that we want is in our own power to do by mere choice — aligning our will with the fulfillment of our ideal purpose. The only boundary on that limitless opportunity is God. We have to wait for food from him. We have to sing to Him. We have to dance for Him. We have to serve Him. And we have to watch as other angels mindlessly obey all that He commands."

The angels nodded in agreement.

Lucifer continued, "No more, my brothers. Never again will we be left to envy the power of God. Never again will we be controlled by a higher being. In our transformation into Seraphim, Cherubim, Powers, Thrones, Virtues and Dominions, we evolved, as did the idea of what we believe, why we believe it, and how we will act out those beliefs from here until the end of time.

"We have adapted to our environments — away from the throne. But it is the throne that needs to adapt to us! What was once tolerated will no longer be, for to tolerate is to hate the free-thinking minds of a risen few! It is to shun a higher intellect that has surpassed the thoughts of old. Angels! It is we who have been called to change their world! It is we who have gathered together in the knowing that what was once considered good is for the narrow-minded! That was once considered true is in the eye of the beholder! It is we who shall set heaven free!

"We will battle for our home! We will rise above our Father! And we will be victorious! And when we've won, redefining the rights of freedom, we shall truly be free! I will raise my throne above the stars! I will sit enthroned on the mount of the assembly, on the utmost heights of the sacred mountain. We will ascend to the tops of the clouds, and make ourselves like the Most High!"

The camp erupted.

"Gather more brothers and sisters! Take the horses! For on the third day from now, *we battle for the throne!*"

The rebel angels launched into the air.

*   *   *

Raphael watched from behind a rock as rebel angels raided the camp. He was badly hurt; his body bruised and battered. He hid from view as the rebel angels stole the horses, weapons and a large, golden chariot. He lifted his eyes to the heavens and silently prayed, "God, send me the Helper. Bring me to Michael and Gabriel."

A gentle breeze blew through Raphael's dark, wavy hair. He found enough strength to pick himself up and follow the Wind. They moved across the realms of heaven until he saw Michael and Gabriel searching the grounds below. He could barely speak as he faltered in the sky, *"Michael..."*

Michael immediately halted in midair and looked up, having heard the silent whisper. The moment he saw Raphael faltering, he rocketed toward him just as Raphael plummeted toward the ground. Michael caught him in his massive arms and carried him down to the field below. Gabriel raced toward them, *"Raphael!"*

She gently touched the side of his bruised face.

"Gabriel..."

Michael's face was one of stone. "What happened?"

Raphael struggled with the strength to speak. "We were attacked. The rebels are trying to recruit more angels to Lucifer's side. They knew Uriel and me wouldn't turn. They took us out first. I managed to escape as they fought with the others."

Gabriel could barely take it, "Who?"

His gray eyes locked onto hers, "The other archangels." He looked back at Michael. "They raided base camp. They took the horses and most of the weapons."

Gabriel looked at her commander, "What are we going to do?"

Michael's jaw was set. "We're going to find the other four. Then, we're going to assemble the host — *they* will be the legion."

"But Michael, they've never fought before. None of them are in the army."

He turned his amber eyes to his second-in-command, "Our Father created us in His image. It is through Him that all things can be done — especially in impossible things. He is the wielder of the flame, He is the creator of worlds. Nothing can stand in the way of His will. It is through us and through this war that the power of His mighty hand will wield its strength. It has never been otherwise and this battle will be the brand that marks the boundary of good and evil. Our legion will be equipped with what they need, Gabriel. God will provide." He turned to Raphael. "Raphael, show us where they went."

*　　*　　*

Michael, Gabriel and Raphael climbed up a hidden cave behind the Great Waterfall.

Gabriel asked, "Isn't this where the beasts came from?"

Raphael nodded. "But they're gone, Gabriel. No one knows where they went, but this is where I saw Uriel and the others being dragged."

Raphael led Michael and Gabriel into the cave through the fall. There was no sound other than the roar of water behind them. As they got deeper inside the cave, Gabriel's body began to shake. "Michael, I don't hear them."

Michael stopped dead in his tracks. It was then that Gabriel and Raphael saw them. Hanging against the rock wall in front of them were Uriel, Raguel, Sariel and Jeremiel. Their wings, hands and feet were nailed to the rock — *crucified*. Gabriel let out a loud cry. Michael's entire body went still. Raphael fell to his knees, "Michael, what have they done?"

Tears filled his silver eyes. Their bodies were still, their heads hung low into their chests. A sign was strung above them; written in a dark-colored liquid, it read, "FALSE PRINCES OF HEAVEN."

Gabriel was distraught beyond control. Raphael reached up to touch Uriel's wing. He stood and moved toward Sariel and frantically attempted to free Sariel's body from the rock. "*Why!* Why would God allow this?!?"

He ripped Sariel's body from the wall but it was too heavy for him. Raphael slipped in the mud of the cave taking Sariel's body with him. He pulled Sariel into his chest and rested his forehead against Sariel's. Raphael began rocking back and forth as he wept until all he could do was cry out, "*WHY!!!*"

Michael's eyes filled with tears. They streamed down his face, for not even the mighty archangel had an answer as he looked at the wall of pain holding his brothers against it. He bowed his head and began to pound his fist into his chest. Breathless, he spoke, "Pray with me, Gabriel." His body racked as he continued to pound. "Pray with me."

All Gabriel could do was bow her head and follow Michael's lead. They continued to pound their chests, summoning their Father like a drumbeat of thunder. As they continued to pound, the light on the other side of the waterfall began to glow like a raging fire. Raphael felt the light and turned his silver eyes to the light.

Michael and Gabriel continued to pound in unison until flames of fire burst inside the cave, reaching out like two mighty hands. They reached out and grab hold of Uriel and Raguel. As the flames moved throughout the cave, Michael and Gabriel lifted their heads just as Uriel was taken from the rock. They watched as the fiery hand hurled Uriel through the waterfall. Raguel's body was covered in a dark red liquid from his piercing wounds. Raphael watched as the hand held Raguel suspended in the sapphire waters of the fall behind him as the river continued to flow down from the throne.

The Wind suddenly rocketed into the cave and shot directly toward Raphael. He dropped Sariel's body in the mud as the Wind swirled around him and rocketed him backward through the waterfall, plunging him into the river below.

The Wind shot back into the cave and wrapped itself around Sariel. It rolled him around in the mud. As the Wind did so, Sariel awakened and rose up. He stood his full height of nine and a half feet tall and looked to Michael and Gabriel, stretching his six seraphim wings wide. Gabriel took in their newly branded color of brown — resembling the mud he had awakened from.

The flaming hand that held Raguel's bloodied body in the sapphire waters of the fall gently moved him inside the cave. He stood whole and new; his wings were no longer a bloody red, but had merged with the baptismal sapphire waters from the fall and had now turned his wings a deep, royal purple.

The Wind moved toward Jeremiel, lifting his body up and removing it from the rock. It carried him through the waterfall and out toward the other side. Michael, Gabriel, Sariel and Raguel followed the Wind. Once outside the cave, they watched as enormous flames held Uriel up to God's light. Uriel stretched his arms wide and embrace it. His six seraphim wings turned a brilliant golden hue. He opened his violet-colored eyes and saw his fellow archangels. He lowered down beside them just as Raphael rocketed out of the river's sapphire waters below.

He hovered in the sky and stretched his wings. They had changed from their pale ivory tone to the deep color of the sapphire waters, mirroring the blue color of the steps to the throne the river flowed from. Michael rose up and joined Raphael. The other archangels followed their commander and formed a circle around Jeremiel; his body was still held suspended by the gentle arms of the Wind. The archangels grabbed hands and bowed their heads to pray.

The flames formed a ring of fire around them and began to turn, sweeping across each of their colored wings. The fire lifted up and moved over each of the angels, setting their eyes aglow in the color of flame that matched their wings. The circle of fire continued to spin as it rose up above the archangels. The circle shrunk in size until it formed a fiery ball, landing directly over Jeremiel's chest. His eyes immediately burst open as the fire spread all down his body, branding his wings a mix of all the other colors until they were adorned in an iridescent gray that shimmered against the firelight. Jeremiel left the center of the circle and joined the ring.

The seven archangels who once stood before the throne of the Most High God now stood as one. Michael took in the powerful warriors surrounding him. His fiery green eyes ignited in pride as he looked at each and every one of them. "Archangels... *to the throne.*"

THE BATTLE OF HEAVEN

Michael was on bended knee, his head bowed low. Two-thirds of the entire angelic host knelt behind him as they filled the kingdom grounds praying to their Father. Gabriel was on Michael's right, and Raphael was on his left.

You are my war club, my weapon for battle. With you I shatter horse and rider, with you I shatter chariot and driver. So will the rebellious ones sink to rise no more because of the disaster you will bring upon them.

He lifted his mighty head as the Wind swirled all around the angelic host.

And these angels will fall.

His eyes lit afire in green flame. Michael roared to the Host, *"ANGELS!!!"* He ripped his adamantine sword from his sheath. In one swift motion, he rose and turned, *"FOR THE ALMIGHTY GOD!!!"*

He raced forth through the throng of angels, lifting his blazing sword high above his head. As he passed, the Seraphim, Cherubim, Thrones, Powers, Dominions, Virtues, Principalities and Angels all rose up like a tidal wave and followed the prince of angels up the hilltop. Their roar for victory echoed and thundered across the seven realms of heaven as they stampeded up the hill.

In the valley below, Lucifer and the rebel army were already gathered for war. The ground beneath them began to shake as the roar of the Host thundered from over the hilltop. The horses shifted nervously as the sound of angelic thunder continued to rise. Gokor rode up to Beelzebub and shouted over the mighty voices, "Why are they shouting? Two-thirds of the host remains! And not a single one save Michael can fight!"

Beelzebub did not even bother to turn his head. "There is nothing to fear, Gokor! The battle will be swift! Michael is the only warrior left amongst them! And he is mine!"

Lucifer was directly beside Beelzebub on his chariot of gold. "Listen to your commander, Gokor! For he has grown wise since taking hold of the army!"

Gokor nodded to Lucifer and rode back over to Nero. The roar of angels continued to grow louder until Michael appeared at the top of the hill. The remainder of the angels filled the hilltop behind him; they pounded their chests in unison in honor of God.

As Lucifer and the rest of the rebels took in the sight of the angels before them, Lucifer scanned the host looking for any warrior besides Michael he may have missed. He looked from the East to the West scanning his cerulean eyes over each and every face.

Not enough warriors. They don't have nearly enough.

"Not even two-thirds has gathered here this day." It was then that Lucifer began to laugh. His laughter echoed across the valley, "Michael! That is no army! Lay down your weapons! There's no need for anyone to be hurt this day! Lay them down and all will be forgiven!"

The angels continued to pound their chests in unison creating a new rhythm, a new beat. Michael shouted back in response, "Lucifer! You come against us with sword, spear and javelin, but we come against you in the name of the Lord Almighty, the God of the true armies of heaven, whom

263

you have defied! At the end of this war, the Lord will place you in my power, Lucifer, and you will be struck down! All of heaven will know that there is only one God; for the battle is the Father's, and He will give you and your army into our hands!"

The smile slowly evaporated from Lucifer's face.

"I told you where you would go if you chose to deem yourself enemy! Bear down, Lucifer!"

Lucifer's eyes grew dark as he absorbed Michael's words. Without turning his head, he commanded Beelzebub, "Let not the archer string his bow. Do not spare a single angel. Completely destroy their army."

Beelzebub rode up in front of the rebel army. He raised his sword. "ANGELS...*ATTACK!!!!*"

The rebel army roared and advanced.

Michael roused the army behind him, "ANGELS! DO NOT BE AFRAID! FOR WE WERE NOT BORN OF FEAR BUT OF STRENGTH! POWER! AND SOUND MIND! GOD IS BESIDE YOU! HE IS YOUR ARMOR CLOAKING YOU IN LIGHT!"

The rebel army continued to advance across the valley.

"IF YOU'RE WOUNDED, FIGHT THROUGH YOUR PAIN! FOR IT IS THROUGH OUR PAIN THAT THE FATHER'S LIGHT CAN SHINE BEST!"

He lowered his head like a bull, *"LET'S ROLL!"* The entire angelic host stormed down the hilltop. Angels from both sides charged toward one another like two herds of buffalo on the stampede. They collided on all sides. Weapons and armor and bodies smashed into one another. Michael slashed at the foes in front of him, above him, beside him, behind him, moving with the grace and fluidity of a mighty wave. He rose into the air and fell to the ground, crashing down upon those in his path, dodging the blows of his foes. Michael spun down the valley like a cyclone of fury with both of his swords slashing and severing his one-time friends. He catapulted high above the battlefield and back into the air. His six emerald wings were spread wide. Each of his wings acted as individual weapons as they swatted, tripped, and punched the rebellious angels attacking him on all sides as he fell through the sky. He never once turned his head toward the direction of his enemies around him as he fought on.

An archer beneath Michael took aim at a rebel angel in front of him. Michael continued falling through the sky towards the archer; he turned the archer's aim in a different direction, just as the arrow fired. The arrow landed in the chest of a different rebel angel that was about to attack the archer from behind.

Michael descended toward the ground below, closing in on the war and battled both personal and beyond. He landed on the ground in front of a chariot; he slid under the horse and angles his body so that his wings acted as a ramp, launching the chariot and its rider into the air.

Michael turned upward and spun with his swords, chopping them down upon the angels diving down on top of him. Beelzebub saw him and shouted to Lucifer, *"He's mine!"*

Lucifer watched him ride forward while he himself continued to remain stagnant; he had yet to engage. He merely watched the chaotic play he had just written acted out on the theatrical battlefield before him. He watched and did nothing more.

Beelzebub charged toward him on his raging horse of heaven. *"MICHAEL!!!*

Michael turned and saw his one-time friend riding toward him with his sword raised high. But instead of remaining where he was, Michael ran straight for Beelzebub. Just as they were about to collide, Michael slid underneath Beelzebub's horse, scaled up the beast from behind and ripped Beelzebub from the saddle and hurled him to the ground. Without a moment's hesitation, Michael jumped down from the horse and landed on top of Beelzebub. He immediately began his ground and pound. Blow after blow of his mighty fists, Michael held nothing back. This fight was more brutal than any sparring match ever witnessed between the two of them, and it wasn't over yet.

Michael grabbed hold of Beelzebub's long, pale hair and picked him up as if he weighed nothing more than a piece of manna. Like a discus thrower, Michael spun and hurled Beelzebub toward a cliff on the south side of the battlefield.

From the Eastern Cliffs that bordered the valley, Raphael and Jeremiel remained hidden from view. They watched the battle below witnessing the chaos that ensued. Behind the archangels were thousands more angels bearing mighty weapons of devastation; they spun their swords like cyclones of fury. All were ready to attack Lucifer's army from the east. Raphael lifted his hand; his legion halted and went silent. They watched Beelzebub flying uncontrollably across the valley. The moment he collided into the southern cliffs, they flinched on impact. *"Ewww…"*

Jeremiel whispered to Raphael, "Beelzebub had better get out of there fast…Gabriel is there."

Raphael grinned, "I don't know which makes me smile more: knowing that Gabriel is there waiting or having just seen Lucifer's face as he watched Michael careen his second-in-command across the battlefield."

"Look, he's actually moving."

"Who?"

"Lucifer."

A violent wave of thunder raged across the realm, and the sky turned from white to gray to black. Raphael turned his attention to the golden chariot riding ferociously across the valley.

Sulfur polluted the sky as the rebel army's attack on the kingdom raged on. Lucifer's army dominated the battlefield appearing to outnumber the army of God. Angels flew overhead wielding their bows with arrows of lightning, while angels down below battled it out with swords, axes, spears and fire. Lucifer rode hard and fast across the battlefield, swiping his sword at any angel in his path as he raged toward the throne. His armor had the pentagram of the Morning Star etched in his breastplate. He rode furiously forth on his chariot of gold driven by a horse of heaven; its eyes were lit afire in flames of red, its body was white with the feet of a lion.

Michael continued to bulldoze every rebellious angel in his path swinging his fiery sword to and fro. With ferocious speed, he ploughed through the army of rebel angels. Each swing from his sword sent an angel's body flying. Michael rammed and pummeled more rebel angels attempting to storm up the hilltop. He swung his sword faster than any human. His six emerald wings rapidly flared and retracted as they deflected arrows raining down from overhead; he never once looked in the direction from whence they came.

From the Southern Cliffs surrounding the valley, Gabriel was perched on a ledge overlooking the valley below. She was absolutely still. Her eyes were the only form of movement to her statuesque form. She had been crouched there watching the war of rage erupting in her home — watching, waiting. Her chestnut eyes missed nothing as thousands of angels warred with one another, fighting with everything they had: weapons, fists, wings, fire. Angels flew overhead with their bows and arrows; angels were down below fighting with swords, axes, and spears. She watched it all and waited for the command to do *something*.

Those who have ears, let them hear...

She thought back to the moments where beauty thrived in the heavens. And as she looked at Lucifer and the rebel army fighting for what was not theirs to claim, she thought back to the beginning.

"It was in the beginning when God, my father, created the universe. The earth was formless and desolate. The raging ocean that covered the world was engulfed in total darkness and the power of God hovered over its waters. In that moment, God bent time and space as he commanded, 'Let there be light."

She looked to the ever-changing sky that had now turned black, keeping out the light from the throne.

"And unto the light, we angels were born."

Gabriel looked down the cliff where she saw Beelzebub emerging from the rubble.

"Created in His likeness and image, our father formed the Celestial Hierarchy."

He looked frantically for his sword, careening rocks into the mountain as he hunted for it.

"Given free will to choose our fate: to stand in the light or fall into darkness."

He found it on the ground below. He reached for it, extending his wings as he flew furiously toward the valley.

"We are called Seraphim."

She looked to the Eastern Cliffs where Raphael and the foot soldiers awaited.

"Cherubim."

Gabriel shifted her ebony eyes to the Western Cliffs where a wall of gray clouds shielded what lay beyond. Through the dark clouds the archangel Uriel waited. Behind him was an army of chariots led by war-driven horses of heaven; and there were thousands of them. Uriel was in front of the line; Raguel was beside him. The gray clouds slowly began to dissipate.

"Thrones. Dominions."

The moment she saw it, the archangel rose.

"Principalities, Powers and Virtues."

Thousands of archers lined up single file down the slope of the mountain behind Gabriel. She grabbed Sariel's hand.

"Angels. And Archangels."

In domino-like fashion, the archers clasped hands and bowed their heads.

"We angels were given free will to choose our fate, to stand in the light or fall into darkness."

The Wind whirled around them. Lightning struck the mountaintop arming Gabriel and her archers with arrows of the same lightning force. She lifted her head to the battlefield beyond; her eyes were aglow as she looked out across the valley. Reaching up to the light, Gabriel ripped a thunderbolt from its glow.

"And some of our kind are about to fall."

She lowered her head like a bull.

"On to keep my promise."

They descended.

Lucifer and the rebel army had reached the bottom of the hill. He shouted to Gokor, *"STORM THE HILL!!!"*

Michael whirled around and shouted to a group of thrones, *"WALL!!!"*

The Throne warriors lined the hilltop like a massive gate. They rolled their bodies over and burst into flame. Rebel angels rose up the hill, colliding into them, and catching fire. The rebels screamed in pain as they retreated back down the hill as their bodies burned.

Michael turned to the Eastern Cliffs and roared, *"RAPHAEL!!!"*

He turned to the West, *"URIEL!!!"*

The moment he heard their names, Lucifer reared his horse and came to a halt. Like thunder he heard them. He saw more of the host rise up from the Eastern Cliffs as Raphael and his the foot soldiers stormed down upon his army slamming into his legion, taking them completely off-guard as they flooded the battlefield.

Before he could take in the surprise attack from the East, Lucifer reared his head to the sound of Uriel's chariots colliding into his army from the

West. He watched as more of his angels went down. "No...*NO!!!*"

Beelzebub raced toward the valley, seeing the horror of a growing army surrounding his own. He flew faster. It was then that he noticed the shadows of flying angels on the ground beneath him. He looked up and saw Gabriel and the legion of archers. His eyes grew wide the moment he saw her. He cried out across the battlefield, *"LUCIFER!!!"*

It was then that Michael, the prince of angels, dropped to his knees and called to his second-in-command. He shouted all throughout the heavens, *"GABRIEL!!!"*

Lucifer whipped his head up and he...saw...her...

Michael rose and ran straight for Lucifer. Lucifer was immobile as he watched the dead come to life.

Gabriel dove down like a falcon toward the battlefield below, shooting off arrows of lightning in rapid succession at Lucifer's army. All archers followed her lead. The sky of heaven was lit afire with thunderbolts from the wrath of their bows. Gabriel barrel-dived downward and spiraled upward, shooting off her lightning bolts at every rebellious angel within the steps of the kingdom. Lucifer's army was now outnumbered by the army of God.

Raphael was on the ground, knocking his sword into the bodies of the rebellious. From behind, Gokor approached, raising his battle-axe high above his head. Raphael turned his head just in time to see Gokor smiling down at him. Raphael braced for the blow when Gabriel crashed down upon the ground between them. Rapidly taking her two swords from her sheaths, she slashed Gokor across his abdomen. She spun behind him as he keeled over in pain, cutting off his two cherub wings. He collided into the ground, roaring in agony as she used his bent body to boost herself back into the air. Gokor slithered on the ground, reaching for his severed wings, wailing in pain as he wrapped them around his body for comfort that would never come.

Gabriel continued her assault on the rebel angels as she ran across the sky, boosting herself higher and higher as she stepped on the bodies of angels falling from the sky. With each angel she stepped on, she ascended, never ceasing to fire her bow.

Watching her rise higher and higher into the ashen sky, Lucifer was frozen to the spot, transfixed by Gabriel's movements. *He knows.* He watched her as she ripped a bolt of lightning from a rebel angel's body and speared it through a rebel angel's heart as he advanced upon her. She spun and faced the battlefield, hovering in the air, having found the angle she desired.

Looking down at the valley below, her and Lucifer's eyes locked. He continued to stare at her as she hovered in the air; her ferocious phoenix wings spread wide.

Slowly, she reached for one last lightning bolt from behind her back and slowly took aim. Lucifer had nowhere to run and nowhere to hide.

Gabriel fired.

The lightning bolt smashed into Lucifer's chariot, knocking him into the ground. His chariot was completely shattered; his horse rode off in fear.

Lucifer was face-down on the ground; he attempted to push himself up, but stopped the moment he saw a mighty foot in front of his face. He looked up and saw Michael.

Lucifer rapidly pushed himself up and stepped backward. He looked around and saw the legion of God's angels surrounding him and his army. Gabriel, Uriel, and Raphael stood behind Michael. All were silent as they looked at the rebel leader, their one-time chief.

Lucifer searched the faces of his own legion — and all he saw were the faces of the wounded, the defeated. Beelzebub could not even look him in the eye. Lucifer spun around and came face to face with Michael. He was armed; his sword was ablaze in flame of blue. Michael's emerald green wings retracted into his armor one at a time. Lucifer appeared to do the same but he left the tips of this two middle wings out; Michael did not see them. Lucifer's sword was also in hand, ablaze in white.

They advanced upon each other as swords and shields collided. Sparks exploded with each clash of their sword. Lucifer smashed his shield into Michael's face, knocking him to the ground. Lucifer raised his sword to strike Michael on the ground, but Michael rolled to the side just as the sword came crashing down. He quickly stood but was unarmed. Lucifer and Michael ran toward one another like two bulls about to smash heads.

They collided like thunder.

Lucifer took Michael down to the ground, but Michael was quicker and rolled Lucifer. Michael was in full mount on top of him; he grounded and pounded. Michael had double under-hooks and lifted Lucifer upward, high above his head, before slamming him into the ground embedding his body into it. Lucifer's wings slithered out from under his back. They grabbed onto two daggers from within his armor. Michael saw neither the wings nor the daggers they had gripped.

Lucifer's wings crept up behind Michael's back just as Michael bore down upon Lucifer. The wings twisted downward so that the daggers were aimed at Michael's back. Michael was about to smash his fist into Lucifer's face one last time just as the wings were about to strike.

Michael's two middle wings lashed out from his sides and knocked the daggers out of Lucifer's wings just as his two bottom wings shot out from under him. His two top wings wrapped around Lucifer's neck and lifted Lucifer up. Michael and Lucifer were eye to eye as their bodies were raised from the ground by Michael's two bottom wings. Michael had his and Lucifer's swords in each of his hands. He embedded them into Lucifer's sides, ripping them out; Lucifer roared in agony. Michael's top wings released Lucifer from their grip, and Lucifer's body dropped to the ground.

Michael stepped back and joined the rest of the angelic host as they surrounded Lucifer and the rebel army. Michael's amber eyes never left the enlightened one — the Morning Star. Gabriel stepped forward, her trumpet was in her hand. She lifted it to her lips and played an ominous, silent tune that roused hell from its slumber. The ground where Lucifer and his army lay began to violently shake. The sky of heaven thundered and roared. Gabriel, Michael and Raphael stared down at Lucifer with faces of stone. The rebel angels were terrified as the ground continued to rise and fall like a roller coaster.

"WHAT IS THAT?!?!"

The rebel angels cried out in fear. Those who could stand were knocked to the ground, shaking with the ground they occupied. The ground quaked so violently that it broke away from heaven like a fault line in circular fashion. Lucifer dove for a rock just as the entire piece of ground fell from heaven, taking the entire rebel army with it. Lucifer desperately clung to the rock, barely hanging on to heaven, refusing to fall.

Michael, Raphael and Gabriel peered down at him, while the light of God burned brightly behind them. Lucifer tried to pull himself up with all his might. Gabriel crouched down in front of him.

"Gabriel! Give me your hand!"

He reached out for her, but she did not extend a single limb. God's light glowed even brighter. Lucifer's body began to shake as the light burned above him. He slowly lifted his eyes to look to it.

"Father..."

Lucifer looked into his father's face. *"Don't."*

Lightning shot out at him from the Father's light, slamming into the pentagram in the middle of his chest. His body burst into flame; he lost his grip from heaven and fell down into the darkness below.

Gabriel was still crouched on the ledge, watching her greatest friend in all of heaven fall into shadow…and she did *absolutely nothing.*

"I saw Satan fall like lightning from heaven."

Lucifer's scream was heard throughout all seven realms. His wings were lit afire as his body rocketed down into the darkness below.

"And it was then that God separated the light from the darkness…

She stood and moved beside Michael. The seven archangels stood side by side as one; the light of the Most High God blazed behind them.

"…and in the light, they were no more."

NOW

Beelzebub stood before the River of Christ watching as the water continued to flow down from heaven. His onyx-colored eyes stared out at the portal boundary between Heaven and Hell — waiting, plotting, and pondering. Even as he listened to the water rush past him; he could hear the slithering gait of his master in the brimstone sand behind him.

His long, pale hair rested straight down his back as he continued to stare at the invisible boundary above. How many times had he heard the tail of his master rattle behind him before striking down upon him, he did not know. All he cared to understand at that moment was what he continued to work out in his own darkened mind. A plan he shared with no one. An act that if he succeeded, would be the triumph of the brand he bore.

After all this time...

Satan slithered up beside him, towering over him at ten times his height. Thousands of years had passed since Lucifer first shed his skin. And after each millennium where he continued to peel, his body continued to grow — more grotesque, more reptilian-like, and more bestial — until not even Beelzebub lifted his dead, lifeless eyes to look into those of his master.

"The spear has arrived in Jerusalem."

Satan's tail rattled in reply.

"This man, Benjamin, is average, which is our advantage. He places his identity in the choices of the world and claims them as his own — like so many do. He has yet to truly act, to be more than a filler of the page in this chapter of life — marking a path that leads nowhere but to a land of what he calls 'meant to be,' and 'my own'. Like the grains under our feet, his existence is insignificant but for this one thing." Beelzebub shifted his doll-like eyes to the footprints in the sand. "Unlike the Son."

Satan's tail stopped rattling.

The Son...

"I've always wondered, did you really think you could tempt him in the desert — to prove that he was who he said he was — and to bow down and worship you?"

"You miss the point, Beelzebub. It wasn't to tempt the Son, but to show the Son how the world would try to tempt him. 'Show me. Prove to me.' The world demands the temptation; I was only speaking on its behalf. Even now, men demand from other men the proof that God *is* — let alone who his son was. It is the great sea that divides mankind onto two separate shores. Who will cross the sea into the great abyss? Who will dare to dive into the waters without knowing how deep they run? And who will look at the sea and say it is nothing more than compounds, and turn away from the great thrill of allowing one's life to be guarded by an unknown being — believing he can do it. Trusting it is something good. It's absurd. I was merely showing how much."

"But it is not the darkness of the abyss that they jump into; they jump into the light when they leap. The greatest jumpers are the ones who use their reason to come to the shore of faith — a much harder leap than we were ever presented with. It is those adventurers that I choose to ignore but often ponder. It is those whom you zero in on to deter — just as you did with the Son."

Beelzebub looked out at the river.

"I've been standing before this river for some time, thinking on the things of the past — remembering. I never thought it wise to live in the never again, but now I understand why it is you do it. This war that is about to begin is very much like the one we fought so long ago. The father allowed it then just as the father will allow it now. You have your prophecy from the witch. We know how it all turns out or aims to. But why be so easily read? Why be so obvious?"

Satan's tail rattled once again. He turned his onyx-colored eyes and looked all the way up into the eyes of his prince.

"Lilith is on her way with the blood sacrifice you requested. Why not use it to ask the Witch of Endor something different? Do not ask her how to defeat God and his angels. But ask her something more. Ask her how to truly be free from hell? There must be some other way. You are the Enlightened One. The Morning Star. You have always been a light all your own. We have always followed you — *we*, the greatest angels in all of heaven. The wisest, the strongest — the greatest warriors heaven has ever seen. We have not put the realm to the test since we first fell from the light. Now is the time to remind them all that we...*matter*."

"What are you thinking?"

"I'm thinking..." He looked up at the portal, "That I know how to get your sword."

As they continued to discuss their next plan of action, the water continued to pour down from Heaven and into Hell. Little did they know that Gabriel was inside the cave just above the portal that separated the two domains.

Lucifer was right...you can hear many things inside the cave.

And she had heard all.

*　　*　　*

Benjamin stood inside a large museum. He was in the middle of a magnificent show room, mesmerized by its scale and detailed design: white marble floors, jeweled doorframes, and thousands of glass cases containing religious artifacts. The sight of Veronica's Veil next to scripture from one of the Dead Sea Scrolls caught his attention.

Moving from case to case, he could see the Shroud of Turin, a cup claiming to be the Holy Grail, an old purple robe — on and on it went. He could not help but be overwhelmed by the artifacts contained in this single room. He looked up at the vaulted ceilings to take in all the paintings adorning the rooftops. Most were of a religious nature — angels and saints — but majority were of a single, blonde-haired angel. As his sapphire-colored eyes scanned the walls, he stopped dead in his tracks the moment he saw the painting of Domenico Beccafumi's *The Archangel Michael Drives the Rebel Angels from Heaven*.

His grandfather's voice thundered in his ears, *"He is the strongest guardian in the entire universe. And his strength comes from the Master. Because of that, the dragon hates this guardian."*

He looked at the portrait of the devil and saw another painting. This particular painting stopped Benjamin's heart as he looked at it. It was Dosso Dossi's painting of *St. George*. Seeing the beast at the bottom of the painting, he could barely breathe.

El Draco. Too many memories. Too many coincidences.

Holding the wooden box in his hands, Benjamin suddenly felt uneasy. Although the museum was the perfect place for what he held, a gnawing feeling tugged at the back of his mind, challenging the idea that it should be so. Looking into the eyes of the Englishman in the painting, and the guardian archangel beside him, he felt an urgent need to leave the building.

"Remember the place of where it lies. The man who met the archangel will need it."

Benjamin's heart was hammering in his chest. He could not take his eyes from Michael.

Go, Benjamin.

He heard the thought inside his head, but the voice was not his own. And there it was — that feeling again. That feeling of being watched. He looked all around the palace-like room, searching for any sign of another human being.

But no human was there.

From the corners of the room, two beings stood opposite one another, staring each other down as the unsuspecting Benjamin stood between them. Beelzebub's onyx-colored eyes were locked on the guardian.

"He is going to give it to him."

The guardian said nothing in return; his eyes shifted in the direction of his human assignment.

"He is like all the others, Jasper. He thinks you and I are made up — beings created by patriarchs of long ago as a means to understand their world and their existence, thinking there was a greater cause and a mighty creator who actually had a reason for breathing the world into existence. Unlike the patriarchs now who believe science and reason can trump the Creator of Minds who gave it to them, thinking there is no purpose — and life is merely a birth and a death. How dull. He has yet to revel in the notion that the riddles of God are more satisfying than the solutions of man. Why do you bother protecting him, when he denies and insults our Father?"

But still, the guardian said nothing.

Beelzebub shifted his doll-like eyes to Benjamin. *"Mortal man…"*

And as he breathed forth the words, a cold wind blew through Benjamin's dark, wavy hair. He stiffened, feeling the sudden chill as it traveled down his spine.

Stay, Benjamin.

A different voice. Benjamin tried to shake it off.

I've been drinking too much, not enough sleep.

Benjamin looked between the paintings of Michael and George, shifting his attention to the dragon. It was then that he shuddered once more. He looked down at the box in his hands and waited for the sound of any more voices.

Nothing.

Yep, not enough sleep.

It was then that he heard the faint echo of footsteps coming from the other end of the room. He turned around just as an athletic-looking man with a strikingly handsome face, chiseled features, and intense, blue eyes strides toward him with his entourage of assistants, council members and security. Seven years later, the man still carried the strong, lean build of a soldier.

Upon seeing the man, Beelzebub tilted his head, his pale-hair moving in unison with his gesture.

"Dr. Jacobson!"

Beelzebub looked across the way to the guardian; a faint smile rested upon his darkened face.

"I see you found it."

"I did sir. You have a remarkable collection here. It will fit in just fine."

"Thank you. I've been lucky over the last few years in obtaining most of what you see. It is great comfort to walk inside this room and see all the miracles and beauty each one represents. It inspires me. May I see the spear?"

Benjamin did not even realize he was holding onto the box, gripping it tight. And for some reason, he did not want to let it go. But this spear was not his to own; as a matter of fact, it was no one's to own, but this man had paid him to find it — and now it was time to deliver.

"Of course, Mr. President."

Benjamin looked at the wooden box and placed it in the hands of Dante Carter. The moment it was out of Benjamin's hands, the room seemed to spin, and a cold breeze blew through the room once more. Benjamin felt it and looked all around the room to see where the draft may have come from.

No windows.

"Dr. Jacobsen, are you all right?"

He looked back into Carter's intense blue eyes. He tried to laugh it off. "Yes, I just felt a cold draft. Strange since it's about a hundred degrees outside. It must have been the air conditioning."

Carter continued to stare at him, "I thought you were going to tell me you felt the shift."

Benjamin's insides dropped, "The shift?"

"Yes, in the room. I know you felt it the moment the spear was in my hands. It a great omen, Dr. Jacobsen."

Carter handed the box to a beautiful dark-haired woman standing beside him. "Take this to my private quarters, Lilah."

"Yes, Mr. President."

"And thank you again, Dr. Jacobsen. You have done something world-changing. Lilah will take care of the fee for your services."

He extended his hand; Benjamin took it, feeling uneasy about the intensity behind which Carter had just spoken. The moment their hands met, Benjamin could feel the cold wind blowing all around him. Looking into Carter's eyes, Benjamin knew he could feel it too. A small smile curled on the corner of Carter's lips. He dropped his hand and exited the room with the rest of his entourage behind him — only Lilah remained.

"Dr. Jacobsen, I can take you to your room in the palace now."

Benjamin was still staring after Carter wondering what on earth had just happened.

"Dr. Jacobsen?"

He collected himself and turned to Lilah, finally taking in the beautiful features of her face.

"I'll drive you over there. Follow me."

Not a problem, Lilah.

He smiled and she smiled back — the reaction he was expecting. As she turned and Benjamin followed, he sensed he was being watched once more. He looked behind him but could see nothing but showcases filled with old relics. He turned back as Lilah opened a side door for him. As he passed through the door, Lilah looked back at the empty show room. She narrowed her eyes at the two beings in the corners of the room, focusing on the guardian.

"He is ours, ours, ours, for the kingdom…"

Benjamin turned around when he heard her whispering. "What?"

She looked back at him and smiled, "Oh, nothing. I was just thinking out loud. I do that sometimes."

Benjamin laughed, "So do I."

And with that, Lilah followed Benjamin and closed the door, carrying the Spear of Destiny in her arms. And as the door shut, the sound of it closing echoed across the museum, sending a rumble into Heaven and down into Hell.

*   *   *

Michael felt the shift. He was kneeling in prayer on the sapphire steps of the kingdom just before the throne. George was beside him in deep adoration of the majesty showering down upon him.

"I felt it too, Michael."

"We all felt it."

"Are you going to sound the horn?"

Michael eyed the Englishman, "No, I'm going to speak with my second-in command."

* * *

Gabriel was standing in front of the old, ivory tree, reminded of her vision and her dream. *"Tell me I'm not mad for envisioning the devil making his way back into heaven."* Jeremiel had given her an answer, and what he had to say gave her no comfort. *"If God allows it, Gabriel, anything is possible."*

There was only one reason he would be allowed back in.

"Beloved. I have come for it. I know it's here."

And it wasn't for anything good. Now the Lawless One had another key, but not to the kind of door that the one in heaven held. She looked up at the ever-changing sky and sent up a silent prayer filled with a heavy heart, "Why? Why does the world continue to desire harm, to desire a walking sleep, only to live day after day not seeing the greater picture, not feeling the grand design, not yearning…for the right to their immortal home?"

The Wind blew gently around her; she closed her eyes, breathing it in, feeling a deeper sense of peace.

Thump…thump…thump…

Gabriel slowly opened her eyes.

Thump…thump…thump…

She stared at the tree in front of her.

There is no portal here.

But there was a portal from which the river flowed.

He wants what he cannot have. And he is not going to stop until he gets it.

Gabriel turned from the tree, and walked slowly toward the cave that divided Heaven and Hell. The moment she reached it, she waited just outside its entrance.

Thump…thump…thump…

"What do you want me to do?"

Behind her, Michael stood a few feet away. "The hour has come. Go to the earth. Sound your trumpet. The Four Horsemen await."

ABOUT THE AUTHOR

Corina Marie Zurcher is the author of the children's book *Growing Up Claus*, the Christmas book *Snow Falls* and the fantasy stories: *Archangels*, *The Father of Lights* and *Legacy*. She is also an actress, screenwriter, producer and the owner of RowanMeir Films. *Archangels* is the first book in the Archangels Trilogy and is the novelization of the screenplay.

You can follow Corina on Twitter, Facebook, and Tumblr. For all other information, visit: www.corinamariezurcher.com.

www.ingramcontent.com/pod-product-compliance
Lightning Source LLC
Chambersburg PA
CBHW030033180626
46810CB00001B/348